The Many Galaxies of Mickie Dalton

The Second Volume in the Mickie Dalton Trilogy

Michael Davies

The Many Galaxies of Mickie Dalton

First Printing June 2008
Second Printing October 2008

ISBN: 978-0-9818087-1-0

First Printing in USA
Second Printing in Australia
Third printing in USA

Published by The Mickie Dalton Foundation
Kempsey, NSW
Australia

Acknowledgements

As before, my sincere thanks for the support of the Principal of St Joseph's Catholic High School in Albion Park, NSW, Mr Peter McGovern and the Head of English, Mr Andrew Rout, to Leanne Whittall who ran the classes and to Jennifer Rush for setting up the contact with Andrew Rout.

To the young people who made this project such an exhilarating experience, my admiration and affection.

James Arblaster	Catherine Fitzpatrick
Paul Foster	Melissa Foye
James Goddard	Michael Guinery
Evan Hayes	Gabrielle McCann
Vincent Muller	Adam Piovarchy
Alicia Quinn	Michael Robson
Samuel Troutman	Tarryn (TJ) Viney
Sebastian Wattam	

To Marcie Waugh & Tom Pam

*For the decades of hilarity, good company
and moral support*

Chapter 1 – Nightmares of Home

The heavy hand landed on Mickie's cheek with a thud and his head rocked back. A wave of terror ran through his body as the familiar routine began yet again.

"What do you mean by leaving the light on, eh? Who the hell pays the electricity bills around here? What do you mean by it? Hey?"

The hand slammed into his cheek once more and the irate, towering figure of his father loomed heavily over Mickie, the dark face twisted in anger and disgust. The odour of stale tobacco rose sharply from his clothes as they moved during the beating. The man's foot kicked into Mickie's thigh and he fell backward against the wall.

"You stupid little pig, I've had just about enough of you! Get up to your room and stay there, do you hear me?"

Mickie hauled himself to his feet, tears running down his cheeks on which he could feel the heat and the pain of the blows. He knew there were more to come, but he tried inching his way along the wall to the door, praying he could make his escape, but another heavy slap on the side of his head knocked him backward against the wall again.

The fear was replaced by anger, a rage so violent that he could feel his whole body start to shake and his view of his father was rimmed with a fine line of blood red.

"That's all you can do, isn't it?" he shouted, shocking his father upright. "All you do is beat me up! You love it, don't you? You really like hitting me, don't you, you big hero?"

"Don't you talk back at me, you little bastard!" roared his father and his hand swung back to deliver another thunderous blow at Mickie's head.

But it never landed. As Mickie's rage grew to a crescendo and the vision of his father clouded over with the blood-red fury in his heart, the man stopped and an expression of fear took over the ugly features. He staggered back, stumbled into the dining room chair and fell on the carpet, gargling sounds struggling from his contorted face that was turning bright red.

Mickie stood up and advanced on the terrified man. "That's what you get for beating up kids!" he shouted. "You love getting your own medicine, don't you? Is it fun getting hurt? Are you enjoying this?"

He felt his rage rising even more and his whole body shook with the frustration of a childhood spent being tormented and beaten by this tyrant writhing on the floor in front of him. He emitted one howling yell of triumph.....

And woke up, trembling and sweating. His room was dark and he felt completely confused and disorientated.

"Mickie, are you alright?" His mother's anxious tones seemed to come from a point a few centimetres from his right ear and it brought Mickie fully awake and aware of his surroundings. The diffused lighting of the cabin automatically came on and gently increased to reveal the luxurious carpet, comfortable furniture and spaciousness.

"I'm okay! I was having horrible nightmares. I'm sorry I woke you."

"Sure you're okay, kid?" His father's voice came from the same point in the air. "Want us to come in there?"

"Yes, I'm fine dad, honest! I'll have a hot drink and I'll be fine again. I was dreaming of being back on Earth."

"Ah, I see!" Allie's gentle voice held a note of understanding. "That would certainly be a nightmare. Have that drink, and instruct Albert to put a drop of the standard sedative in it. He'll understand."

"Okay, I'll do that. Thanks, I'm feeling better already."

"Goodnight, son." His parents spoke together, and Mickie smiled to himself with the pleasure of knowing that they were there in the cabin next to his.

"Albert, can I have a hot cocoa with a drop of the standard sedative?"

"Coming right up, Mickie." The voice was a cultured English tone, the speech of an educated professional and it came from the same point near his right ear. The itching that he had experienced in his right shoulder for a few days after the translator and communications device had been implanted there nearly a year ago had long gone and Mickie had become accustomed to hearing people speak to him from all sorts of distances, sometimes many thousands or even millions of light years.

The cabin lights increased further and Mickie's eyes adjusted to take in the luxurious room. He got out of the bed and donned a dressing gown, strolling on the fine carpet into the lounge room. As so often, he grinned with delight, comparing this splendour with the bleak misery of the tiny bedroom in the miserable house in England that had been his prison, guarded and tormented by his abusive parents and coldly contemptuous elder sister.

Only a year ago! How his life had changed in so many astounding ways. The panels by the food area opened up and a large mug of steaming cocoa was ready for him as he reached it. He moved to his favourite armchair and relaxed in it, feeling the contours shift to give his body maximum support, whatever position he chose.

"Albert, what time is it?"

"Thirteen minutes after four," the computer replied. Mickie sipped slowly at the drink, savouring the creamy flavour.

"How long to planet fall?" he asked.

"Three days, fourteen hours, thirty three minutes to entering orbit round Drudyenko."

"What's at Drudyenko?"

"Strangeness."

That tickled Mickie's funny-bone. Albert was usually very proper, very conventional in his dealings with Mickie, and to respond in this odd manner made him laugh.

"Explain, you silly computer!"

"It's a high-tech society and yet a primitive culture with habits that are grotesque by our values. I will present a standard briefing before planet-fall. However, I judge that the sedative will now be having an effect, so you will sleep very soon."

Albert was correct as he always was.

* * * *

This time his dreams were far more pleasant. The vacation on Kalamos had been about as ideal as anyone could want. The warmth of the reception he received from all the people in the community where Allie and Grant had their home just about wiped out the last painful memories of the miserable life he had led on Earth. As he had always yearned for, he became a vital, valued and welcome member of a group. Melkana and Drellion lived just a short distance away and as their parents were already close friends with Allie and Grant, the two families saw a lot of each other. The three kids spent the wonderful summer days roaming in the hills, introducing Mickie to the local animals and plant life and to others of their friends who accepted him immediately and without question. Sometimes they took small sailing boats out onto the lake and Mickie became enthralled with the joys of making the wind drive a vessel skimming across the surface. By the end of the vacation he had become quite accomplished and won a few of the races in the regatta held for the local school where his new friends attended. The only thing he missed was the company of the fourth of the small gang, Fencris, who had gone on to his home world of Cassolea for his own vacation.

Grant also displayed a talent not mentioned before and took Mickie along to an airfield where he introduced him to the art of flying sailplanes. On one glorious day, they took off in an advanced two-seater and climbed up to over four thousand metres, much of the time in the company of enormous eagles that seemed to accept them as colleagues. For five hours they played with the birds among the clouds before returning to the field, with Mickie feeling he had truly lived as an eagle for that time.

But when the time came to return to the ship and resume the trading voyage around the Universe, Mickie was happy to join with the familiar faces in the shuttle and ascend to orbit. And when he found Fencris waiting for him in the shuttle bay with a challenge to all of them to play an immediate game of Loopies, he felt he had truly arrived home again.

* * * *

When he woke from a deep, peaceful sleep, the morning began with action. Barely had he finished his coffee when a familiar voice rang out from his translator.

"Hey, Mickie!" said Fencris. "We're in Shuttle Bay Ten and gravity is set at ten percent. Get your lazy Pfafth rear end down here, you need some exercise!"

"Right with you!" said Mickie happily. A solid bout of spinning, leaping, dodging and catching with his friends was exactly what he needed. He ran for the door and the transporter to the shuttle bay.

The other three were waiting for him when he reached the shuttle bay. The massive space was the size of the enclosed football stadiums he had seen pictured in the USA, more than 300 metres across the circular area and over fifty metres high at the ceiling. Some nine shuttles sat silently in their spaces, resembling a monstrous tray of doughnuts. The smallest shuttlecraft was twelve metres in diameter and four metres at the top of its curved upper surface and they could seat more than ten people in great comfort. The big ones were more than four times the size and could hold a hundred passengers, while other bays held some even larger craft that Mickie had not seen yet.

As he walked through the entrance, the reduced gravity hit him with a familiar sensation of falling in a fast-descending lift. He steadied himself for a second or two, then leaped in a vast, exhilarating arc at the trio waiting for him in the middle of the bay where a large square was painted on the floor.

"What's up? You look tired." Melkana was the first to speak, and her warm concern lifted some of the clouds of darkness that Mickie's nightmare of Earth had left in his mind. He smiled at her, taking in the graceful lines of her face and the long dark hair. All three had become the closest friends he had ever known and he had no idea how he could manage without them, but Melkana had a special place in his heart.

"Bad dreams," he replied. "I still get the odd memories of living back on Earth with those awful Dalton people."

"What happened?" Fencris asked. His brilliant red eyes, the dominant feature of the Cassolean race showed a warmer, darker glow. Mickie's first meeting with a Cassolean had been a shock, but now he found the blue skin, the red eyes and almost non-existent nose a pleasantly familiar sight. "Memories of that horrible father? I hope you beat him up."

"That's the trouble, I did, in the dream," Mickie said. "He was yelling and screaming at me and I shouted back at him and he fell down, just like what happened with those Smegandri back on Kamotar."

The frightening adventure on the planet of the three-armed giants of Kamotar had been the first revelation of the new powers growing in Mickie in the last few months. As the terrorist Smegandri had attacked the four children,

Mickie had felt a huge rage envelop him at the threat to his friends and he had screamed with fury at the approaching terrorists. All three of them had fallen dead and it had taken Mickie considerable time to recover from the shock of his deed and the comprehension of what had happened to him.

"Well, it would serve him right if you really had thumped him," chimed in Drellion, the youngest and Melkana's brother. "One day, I think we should all go to Earth and pay him back for all the rotten stuff he did to you."

Mickie grinned at him. Although a couple of years younger than the others, Drellion had grown from the very shy little boy Mickie had first into a smiling young man of considerable charm and athletic ability.

"He isn't worth it, Drellion," Mickie said. "His punishment is to be married to that silly woman and live in that horrible house for the rest of his life, killing themselves with cigarettes. That's bad enough for anyone, I reckon."

"Hah! Yes, you're right," Drellion said with the cheerful grin that seemed to light up the room. "Okay, people, Loopies! I can beat anyone!"

The game had been devised centuries ago as a practice and training program for space travellers who might have to work or possibly fight in low or even zero gravity. Players took station at opposite sides of the forty-metre square, with gravity set to a low level, usually ten percent, but variable according to skill. One player, the flier would leap from his line and attempt to land at the opposite side. A second player, the catcher, would leap from the flier's left or right side of the square and attempt to catch the flier in the middle of the arc. Points were awarded for catching or evading, with bonus points for the number of loops a player could turn in mid-air in the process. Mickie had found it extraordinarily hard to learn the judgement required, but had eventually reached a moderate level of skill, though nowhere near the capabilities of the other three.

Drellion was getting too good for any of them, they realised after the first few matches. Mickie and the youngest of the four squared off for the first flight, Drellion taking the role of flier and Mickie attempting to catch him. Mickie watched carefully as Drellion launched himself into a higher-than-normal arc from the right-hand side of the huge square. With his judgement honed by weeks of playing this game, he leaped in the ten per cent gravity and flew in what he was certain would be an intercept course. And for most of the upward arc, he remained sure he had judged it right, but as he reached out in the last moments to grab hold of Drellion, the younger boy chuckled, twisted, somehow turned one more loop in the series of three he had already completed and straightened, the last move lifting him slightly so that Mickie sailed underneath him, leaving him nothing to do but concentrate on a safe landing on his feet on the other side of the square or lose a point for a bungled flight. A yell of admiration sounded behind him as he touched down and he turned to see the other two applauding as Drellion made a perfect two-foot landing on his line.

"Six loops!" Melkana called to him. "My kid brother just did six loops and evaded you!"

That was one more than his previous record and Mickie was astounded at the athleticism the boy had shown. He jumped across the square to embrace Drellion and congratulate him. "That was brilliant!" he said. "I've got no idea of how you did that flick and twist when I thought I had you."

"I've been practicing," Drellion replied with a huge grin. "I thought I'd surprise you all."

"You surely did," Fencris said coming over to join them. "I suggest we change the rules to handicap you. From now on, we play in the dark."

The other laughed. The brilliant red eyes of the Cassolean race gave them excellent night vision.

"Melkana, I challenge you," said Fencris. "You catch, I evade, and you have to do at least three loops before you get to me."

"Done," shouted Melkana, already taking up position one side of the square. "But you have to do three as well. Go!"

She managed the three loops and Fencris did the same, but the meeting at the top of the arc, some ten metres above the floor of the hangar was an undignified collision and although Melkana managed to grab one of Fencris' legs, the rules of Loopies specified that the catcher had to have both arms round the torso of the evader. The flight was ruled a draw and after they had repositioned themselves from their messy and jumbled landing in the middle of the square, Melkana challenged Mickie to the same match.

Going for broke, Mickie decided to try and match Drellion's feat of six loops. He leaped in the same high arc that Drellion had taken, ducked his head and began spinning. He managed to watch Melkana take off to meet him, and as he neared, he attempted the same twist and flick that Drellion had used to evade him. It was a complete failure. With a shout of triumph, Melkana wrapped two arms round his waist and they ended up in one corner of the square, floating gently to the ground.

"This is not my day!" Mickie announced. "I need to hammer someone. Fencris, you're on! You evade, I catch."

"You'll miss by a light year," Fencris said with his sparkling, demonic flash of red eyes over his wide grin.

But Mickie got his catch with a double loop thrown in. "Eat worms and die!" he shouted in triumph as they landed to applause from the other two. In great good humour, they decided to have their showers and meet in twenty minutes in their favourite coffee lounge on the shopping deck.

But Albert had a shock to his system when he returned to his cabin for some schoolwork.

"Mickie, we have a television transmission from Earth." Albert's well-modulated tones broke into Mickie's thoughts as he sat in his cabin trying to read about the development of the nation-states on his adopted home world of Kalamos.

"Oh! From when?" Mickie had forgotten about the last three transmissions Albert had played him before they got back to Kalamos. The Speaker had recorded the memories of one of the Kalamosian agents on Earth as he watched the television news and re-transmitted the program to the ship's computer. Mickie had watched with fascination as the BBC newsreader had reported on the apparent disappearance of Mickie and the growing discomfort of his parents as their abuse of their child had become revealed.

"We have two. One from a few months ago, the day after the last program you saw, and then one from just a few hours ago."

"Okay, Albert, let's see them." Mickie settled back in his couch as the image of a television screen appeared on the wall and the old familiar strains of the BBC's signature music for the news resounded loudly.

"This is the BBC six o'clock news for Friday, the fifth of March," said the newsreader, a man Mickie remembered from those days that seemed so many lifetimes ago. "Police in Manchester have now called off the search for twelve-year old Michael Dalton who disappeared from his home two weeks ago. The discovery of the letter from him to his adoptive parents finally convinced the police that young Michael had run away from home."

The same picture of Mickie appeared on the screen as had been shown before on the similar occasions when Albert had shown him news broadcasts soon after his disappearance from Earth. Once more, Mickie felt the shock at seeing the photo taken from a school photograph that year. It showed an unhappy, defeated kid, he thought, so much less mature and confident than he felt today after the astounding few months he had spent as an inter-Galactic traveller

"However, Manchester CID requests that anyone seeing this child contact their nearest police station. In other news, the Prime Minister has defended his actions in taking the country to war in Iraq..."

The screen changed to a blank, white glare.

"You said you had two, Albert."

"Yes, Mickie. This second one contains a strange feature to it. It was recorded just a few hours ago."

"Then let's see it." Mickie was intrigued by the computer's words.

"... And in other news tonight, a strange event concerning the father of the missing boy, Michael Dalton." The same newsreader as before appeared on the screen. "Viewers will recall the disappearance of twelve-year old Michael some months ago. Presumed a runaway, there has been no sign of Michael since then, despite an intensive search and a nation-wide alert. But this morning, an emergency call was received by the Ambulance service in Manchester. It was placed by Michael's mother following an apparent heart attack affecting her husband. When paramedics arrived, they reported that the man was suffering severe shock, though there were no signs of a heart attack. All through the ride to the hospital, the attendant sitting with Mister Dalton reported that he kept repeating, "..the little bastard hit me! He stood there and hit me! If he ever comes back, I'll give him a bloody good beating." Mister Dalton was released after treatment and was unable to explain what he had meant by his comments, but seemed terrified and refused to answer questions from our reporter."

"That's wild!" Mickie said, feeling rather ashamed of the glee he felt at the news of his one-time father's problem.

"I ran a time comparison," Albert said. "I checked the time of the actual trauma that your father suffered based on the records of the emergency service and compared it to the moment at which you woke up from your nightmare last night. The two events occurred at the same moment."

Mickie felt cold. "But I was dreaming that he was shouting at me and giving me another beating," he said.

"And I got angry the way I did with the Smegandri on Kamotar and yelled back and he fell down..."

"Yes," said Albert. "It looks like it was more than a dream. You delivered the same mental punch as you did the Smegandri and you hurt him. Luckily for him, he was many thousands of light years away and the effect was dissipated a little. It's a new development in your powers, Mickie and underlines the great danger you face until you can control it."

"But it's the same thing the Spiders did," said Mickie, feeling a severe chill run through him. "They hit the Gelkka the same way from millions of light years away."

"That is true. It appears you share some of the Spiders' abilities. This is very interesting. May I suggest you resume training sessions with the Speaker?"

"I think I'd better," Mickie replied.

Chapter 2 – Problems at Galactic Central

"Speaker 356, are you there?"

"Yes, Mickie. How can I help?" The voice as always seemed to come from some point a short distance from Mickie's right ear but was, he knew, directly heard within his head. It still gave him an immense thrill to know that he was talking with this ease and friendliness to a strange being many thousands of light years away.

"You know about what happened on the planet Merrison a few weeks ago?"

"Yes, I do. I was following the events through the mind of the agent Baldorest."

"Did you try and access the minds of the Protector and his gang?"

"I did. It's standard procedure for us when we encounter a new species, but I was unable to read any form of telepathic abilities in those people."

"But have you encountered them before in any way?"

"No, Mickie, we have not, but that is not in itself unusual. When I or any of my colleagues go surfing through the universe, we can only detect minds that have a telepathic ability of some sort. So we would not have detected any civilisation without such latent skills."

"So how did you first detect the Spiders?"

Mickie could have sworn that he heard a tiny hesitation in the Speaker's transmission, almost like a blip in the radio carrier wave, even though no sound was being carried.

"We didn't, Mickie. We only dealt with the Spiders after the Kaloti ships first landed there and other species with whom we *can* communicate, such as the Kaloti, Kalamosian or Cassolean people encountered the Spiders."

"Can you detect them now?"

"No."

Mickie was sure now. There was a sign of stress in the Speaker's tone. "Speaker, is this causing you a problem?" he asked.

A short pause occurred before the Speaker answered. "Mickie, we have had this discussion in part before. As I indicated, it is very worrying and puzzling to find a species able to communicate telepathically in a manner that we do not comprehend. This is our profession, it's what my species does, it is the *only* thing we do, and we have served the intelligent races of the whole Universe this way for some centuries."

"So the things the Spiders have done, like hitting the Gelkka from light years away and transporting themselves to Merrison, this must be even worse for you?"

"It is tearing us apart," said the Speaker, and the sadness in his tones was strong. "We are seeing an entirely new force in the Universe and we know nothing about it. The Spiders represent an astounding problem, because they have these abilities and they obviously receive some form of instruction from a source of which we have no comprehension or indication."

"You mean the Pfafth?"

"Yes, Mickie, the Pfafth. At least, we assume it is the Pfafth."

"Assume?"

"We are also considering the possibility that some other force is acting on behalf of the Pfafth, with or without their knowledge or instructions. After all, we have no indications anywhere in the Universe that the Pfafth exist at all any more."

For a second, Mickie froze. Was it possible that he was the last of an ancient species? He shook off the moment to resume the discussion.

"What about the fact that I seem to have hit my one-time father on Earth in the same way as the Spiders did with the Gelkka?"

"That is what represents my immediate problem, Mickie. The fact that you seem to have some of the same skills as the Spiders is causing stress among my people. One species having such talents was bad enough. A second is far worse, especially as we don't even know what you are or if there are more of you."

"But what does that mean, Speaker? Are you saying you won't be able to talk to me?" Mickie felt a wave of fear pass through him at the thought. He had become to depend on the Speaker as a friend, as a source of information and a way of learning to control the frightening talents he was developing.

"No, not that. It would be a dereliction of my professional duties. But the worry is that in helping you develop the telepathic and other mental skills you have, we might be also helping you develop these other talents that could prove dangerous. And because we know nothing about how they work, we don't know if we are helping you or causing you problems."

"But will you still help me? I'm frightened of what I might do before I learn to control this stuff."

"There are many among my colleagues who do not want to provide you further assistance. But it's my choice, and I will continue your training."

"I'm really grateful, Speaker."

"Let's get to work."

Relieved, Mickie immersed himself again in the brain-stretching, exhausting training program the Speaker was administering to him as he developed his mental talents.

Mickie had come a long way from Earth in more than a sense of distance. How much further he had to go was still a massive mystery to everyone.

Chapter 3 – War Plans

"Mickie, can you meet us in the Captain's cabin?" Allie's voice sounded in his head as she spoke through his communicator.

"Sure!" he replied and set off immediately. A few minutes later, the door opened to the gently yellow light of the Captain's quarters and he entered to see his parents sitting round the central table while the Captain occupied his giant seat built to contain his elongated, narrow form. He adjusted for the slightly reduced gravity maintained in the Kaloti's quarters, having known about it from previous visits.

"Glad you could join us," the Captain said as Mickie took a seat between his parents. The voice came through his communicator, while the actual sound, the low, beautiful hum of a cello sounded simultaneously from the Captain.

"Mickie, we have an interesting situation," Grant said. "And we think we may be able to use it to our advantage and you can probably help us a lot."

Mickie was intrigued, but also delighted with the idea that he might be able to help his parents and the entire ship. "Tell me more," he said.

"We've had a call to go to Gelokk," Grant continued. "We rarely trade directly with the Gelkka as we are unwilling to support their domination of other worlds. But there has been an outbreak of some disease on their home planet and the drugs we make from the plants on Spider World will provide the cure and the inoculation. For simple humanitarian reasons, we will change course from our scheduled visit to Drudyenko and go to Gelokk first. We arrive there in two days."

Mickie felt a tremor of fear. Those appalling, massive beings who looked like huge birds of prey and who had come so close to killing him and his friends down on the planet of Mayoowani still haunted his dreams. Only the intervention of the Spiders had saved them and the reasons for that remained as mysterious as had their intervention on Merrison more recently.

"How could I possibly help?" Mickie said. "They nearly killed us last time."

"Yes, we know," Allie said gently. "But you have developed some interesting talents since then and it seems clear that you have friends who will not let you come to harm. It's the new talents we want to put to good use."

A little reassured, Mickie settled back in his seat. Over to his left, the Maragos sculpture caught his eye and he resolutely pulled his attention away. He already knew how hypnotic those works of art could be and he knew he needed his full focus on the discussion in the room.

"Here's the story," Grant continued. "After your exploits on Mayoowani, we have been picking up news that the level of activity by the man known as the "Redeemer" is increasing. He is talking to more and more communities and the undercurrent of rebellion is getting stronger all the time. It seems pretty obvious that this is causing the Gelkka considerable disturbance because they have never experienced rebellion on any of their subject planets before. We're pretty certain that the word has got back to the home planet, Gelokk, and they are probably planning some form of suppression. If we could get information on their plans, we might be able to prevent much of the damage."

Mickie began to see where the conversation was going. "You think that I might be able to get into the mind of one of the Gelkka leaders?"

"We think it's possible, yes," Grant agreed.

"Can't the Speakers do it?"

"No, they can't," Grant replied. "They cannot enter the mind of any sentient being if that species has no telepathic capabilities and the Gelkka have none. So we have always believed this to be a simple fact. At least, we all used to think so until both you and the Spiders showed that to be wrong. So we think you may be able to access the Gelkka minds."

Mickie tried to suppress the fear he felt at confronting the Gelkka again. "How do you want me to do this?"

His parents and the Kaloti captain seemed to relax a little as Mickie agreed to help them with the mission.

"What we must all do is behave normally," Grant said. "In some ways, we're all going to be play-acting. The Gelkka know that this is the ship that visited Mayoowani and they will most certainly know that you four children were the ones that were arrested by the local authorities and who escaped in such weird circumstances."

"So won't they be pretty angry with us?" Mickie asked.

"They most surely will," Grant agreed. "But their

problem is, they have no idea who or what caused their entire garrison to fall unconscious when they did. It's quite possible that they think you did it, Mickie."

"Me? Why would they think that?"

"Because they may quite possibly have had agents on Kamotar when you most certainly *did* cause fatal damage to the Smegandri," Allie replied. "So they will probably regard you with considerable fear and suspicion."

"Wow! And here I was, feeling terrified of meeting Gelkka again!" Mickie grinned at the idea of the huge, intimidating creatures being frightened of a thirteen-year-old boy, but the feeling quickly passed. "But what if they think they could just kill me with one of those guns they carry?"

"We discussed that, also," Allie said gently. "It frightened us as much as it must frighten you, Mickie. But you must remember, we are going there on a mission of mercy. We are carrying drugs that Gelokk badly needs to stop a dreadful epidemic. To alienate us would be the worst thing they could do."

"I see that." Allie's words were comforting and the logic behind them was quite reassuring.

"Okay, then back to what you have to do," Grant resumed the briefing. "And quite simply, just play around the area of the centre of political leadership. It's a large building in the main city. The ship's computer will brief you on the political structure of the planet and who the key players are. You must try and identify these individuals and see if you can establish an empathic link with one of them during any discussions of Mayoowani and the problems they are having with the local population and their new focus of rebellion, this 'Redeemer.'"

"And if you can, transmit your findings straight back to us." Allie spoke firmly.

"Are all of us going down with you?" Mickie wondered how his three friends would react to another meeting with the Gelkka after the horror of their last contact. But he also knew that he would feel a lot more comfort if they were with him.

"Yes, we believe that would provide a better cover than just you alone," Grant replied. "We discussed it with their parents and they agreed to leave it to their children. If they feel confident enough to join us, they'll come with you."

"I bet they will!" Mickie said forcefully. He saw the captain's immobile and almost featureless face move slightly, and the large eyes opened to almost double their size. The captain was highly amused, it appeared. The low, lovely, cello-like hum echoed in the cabin and the translator in Mickie's shoulder immediately converted the sound to English.

"The courage of you and your friends brings great credit on this ship," the captain said. "We have had no cause to regret having brought you on board, even though you had some misadventures in the beginning."

Mickie was overwhelmed. He regarded the captain with considerable awe and he had been dreadfully distressed when the hugely tall and elegant Kaloti had disciplined him for disobeying his parents and putting the ship at risk in Mickie's first weeks on board. He decided to strike for something he had wanted almost from the start and take advantage of the captain's good will.

"Could I ask a favour, Captain?"

"What is that, Mickie?"

"Could I spend a little time looking at your Maragos sculpture?"

The huge eyes in the still, grey head opened wide again. "Yes, you may. After all, your adventure on Shuramee and the discovery of so many new Maragos works made us all rich. Please feel free to stay here and look at my most precious possession."

"In that case," said Allie, "we will leave our son to his art appreciation and return to preparing for planet-fall on Gelokk."

She and Grant stood up. She came over to Mickie and put her arms round him. "We are very proud of you, Mickie," she said softly. "We'll see you at dinner tonight, okay?"

Mickie responded to the hug with one of his own. The delight he took in being part of such a wonderful family had not faded in the months since he had been rescued from the misery of his life on Earth.

Grant and Allie left, and Mickie walked over to the sculpture in one corner. It was a cylinder, about chest high to him, but the top third seemed to melt into lines and curves that defied the mind's ability to follow. For some minutes he let his eyes try and trace those intricate patterns, and he felt himself being drawn deeper into the maze, and within seconds he was lost in the impossible shapes. Sound began to emanate from within the weaving, changing shifts of light, not exactly music, but tones that touched deep inside his soul. He felt waves of happiness pass through him and he seemed to fall deep inside the fantastic shape. The happiness gradually changed to a sense of great sadness and tears rolled down his face, he felt the horror of seeing planets die and millions perishing with them, but within seconds his mind began to take him on trips through space and time, he saw great suns flash into being ahead of him and vanish with a silent explosion, remote stars sang songs of beauty, of loneliness, of the joy of creating planets, of seeing life appear. He knew the exaltation of being the Creator, of sensing all the Universe as one single form.....

A hand on his shoulder pulled him back to the gentle, yellow glow of the captain's quarters and he realised the tall shape of the captain was standing alongside him.

"I think this little boy should be back at his studies," said the translated voice in his head while the melodious hum of the captain's voice sounded in the background.

"How long have I been here?" Mickie realised he was exhausted, drained by the enormous emotional load that the sculptures of Maragos caused in almost all sentient beings.

"Four hours," the captain replied. "That's more than enough for anyone."

"Four...? Captain, I had no idea."

"I know. Those works of Maragos have never been explained, we have no idea why they cause the effects they do. That's why it's safest to have somebody else around when you start to study one. Go and have lunch, Mickie, you have some studying to do, I think."

"Captain, can I come and just talk to you, sometime?" The words fell out of Mickie's mouth without his realisation of how badly he wanted to have some time with this mysterious and beautiful being of the Kaloti species.

"I would like that, Mickie," the captain said. "When we leave Gelokk, we can talk at leisure."

Feeling delighted with the promise, Mickie went back to his own cabin where the emotionally draining experience of the morning claimed him for a while, and took a lot of effort and some prodding by Albert to get him to reading about Kalamosian history.

* * * *

"Gelokk is a low gravity world with an atmosphere rich in oxygen," said Albert. The ship's computer had adopted its calm lecturing tone and Mickie sat in his usual place in his cabin while the holographic image of the planet rotated in the middle of the room. Much like Earth, the planet held several huge oceans and a few enormous continental land masses.

"The Gelkka evolved from a large flightless bird that still exists in a pre-historic form," Albert continued. The image of the planet vanished to be replaced by a creature that resembled a heavily-built ostrich with a short neck and a much larger head. Next to it, Albert had projected an image of a human male as he always did in these sessions. The man looked tiny next to the predator, less than half the height.

"You will notice that the creature has a large head, relative to most birds," Albert said. "The brain size is about equal to that of a human and the intelligence level of the Gelkka is about that of the human species, with a smaller range than humans. Scientists have been able to develop an intelligence-measuring technique for the Gelkka, based on observed responses, and then relate it to IQ levels of several species, including humans. So we can see that, while there are fewer Gelkka of very high intelligence, none higher than say, a bright University student, there are similarly fewer on the lower end of the scale, with none recorded below a level that would be considered dull in a human."

The images vanished and were replaced by another holograph that was horribly familiar to Mickie, a modern Gelkka, standing nearly three metres high, looking out of proportion with the greater mass of the body being at the top near the shoulders and chest. Massively muscular legs supported the shape, though the limbs looked thin relative to the body mass.

"The Gelkka culture is one of military authority, and democratic principles are unknown. There is no concept of art or literature anywhere in the Gelkka history. After centuries of tribal wars, the world united under a single military government about two hundred years ago. A council of appointed leaders runs the world, with a single leader ruling the council for as long as he can until pushed aside in a coup. The level of technology is low, not even that of Earth in the early twenty-first century and all modern technology used by the Gelkka has been adopted by them from other species."

"How did that happen?" Mickie was intrigued. "I thought that the rules prevented you from revealing yourselves to primitive worlds."

"Indeed they do," Albert replied. "But accidents happen, much as they did on Merrison. A group of agents such as you met on your last trip was attacked and killed by a pair of Gelkka soldiers. Unfortunately, one was still carrying the key to entering their shuttlecraft and the Gelkka, by trial and error, eventually hit the right code and revealed the cloaked craft. After much debate among leaders of the species on board the main ship, it was decided to make formal contact with the Gelkka leadership. It took a few years, but eventually the Gelkka were able to tolerate the idea of superior races from other planets."

"So how did they become planet-conquering bandits like they have?"

"Another mistake," said Albert. "It resulted from the absence of any telepathic aptitude within the Gelkka brain, so the Speakers were unable to do more than detect the presence of one, but not to enter the mind and listen in on a conversation and thus be forewarned of any plans. One ship agreed to take a large group of Gelkka to visit another planet. But the Gelkka instead brought on armed troops and took over the vessel and were able to force the crew to man enough shuttles to bring up more troops. They had taken over several worlds before they were stopped. Now it is forbidden to take more than ten Gelkka on any Kaloti ship, but one or two species have also adopted space travel and they have been happy to take Gelkka bribes to assist them."

"So once those planets have been taken over, the Gelkka cannot leave?"

"That is the case," Albert agreed. "Discussions are being held about some ways of doing it, should the rebellion on Mayoowani succeed. The most likely will involve the troops being drugged and immobile while in transit and locked in empty shuttle decks while being transported home."

"So is there any chance of them being kicked off Mayoowani, Albert?"

"Most experts believe it unlikely," the computer replied. "Rebellions by subject tribes only succeed when the rulers have become too tired of conquest, or the home empire is collapsing. Neither is the case here, so we fear massive retribution against the Mayoowi. That is why you have a mission. If we can learn what they plan to do, we may be able to do something to prevent at least the worst of the damage."

"You don't seem very hopeful."

"No, we are not, Mickie. Anyway, this lesson should now end. I believe your friends are calling you."

At that moment he heard the voice of his Cassolean friend Fencris coming through his communication and translation device. He knew that Albert would have blocked all communications while the lesson was in progress unless there was an emergency.

"Hey there, you fat Pfafth! We're all having a coffee in our usual place, if you want to join us. Then we're going to play Loopies. You still need exercise! Drellion wants to beat his record of six loops!"

"Not a chance! I'll be there in a moment, and I'm the one that'll beat the record."

As he moved to the door, he heard the combined raspberry noises that all three of his friends were blowing. Grinning widely, he set off for the shopping colonnade that held the coffee shop that was their regular meeting place.

*　*　*　*

"Are you all okay about coming down to Gelokk?" They were well into their second cups of the delicious coffee that came from the planet Mayoowani where they had first encountered the frightening Gelkka overlords of that subject world. Around them, the buzz of several groups of crewmembers from three different planets provided a backdrop to their own discussion.

"You surely cannot believe we would let you go down there on your own, do you?" said Drellion, still occasionally grinning at his six-loop record on the hangar square of a few days before. "Look at the awful mess you and my sister got yourselves into on Merrison without Fencris and me to look after you."

"Hah!" Mickie snorted in pretend derision. "It was only the powers of my amazing inter-species connections that saved us."

"Yes, your buddies, the Spiders." Melkana made a face. "I know they saved us, but the less I see of them the better I sleep."

"Me too," Drellion added. "And they do seem to have some weird powers! That stunt they pulled, knocking out the Gelkka on Mayoowani from a few million light years away, that was cool! I bet you wish you could do that one, Mickie."

The comment hit Mickie with a jolt as he remembered the news broadcast he had seen. He'd told nobody about it till now.

"Er.. about that," he said. "Remember that nightmare I told you about?"

"What, where your father back on Earth was yelling at you and you shouted back and he fell down?" Fencris' flame-red eyes flashed with interest.

"Yes, that one. Albert played me a news broadcast a Speaker had recorded. It looks like I really did hurt him. He was hospitalised with an apparent heart attack that happened just as I woke up."

A moment of silence echoed at the table.

"And you think you did that?" Melkana sounded uncertain.

"I think so. Apparently he saw me in some sort of vision and he was shouting about how I'd hit him."

"That's awesome!" Drellion was looking at him, wide-eyed.

"And pretty scary. I hope you never get crabby with me, old buddy." Fencris was smiling, but the concern in his voice was real.

"Well, you'd better all treat me with respect and call me Sir," Mickie said, trying to ease the slight tension around the table. To his relief, he was treated to a loud chorus of derisory raspberries. "Okay, we'd all better get ready for the Gelokk trip," he said, grateful for the chance to change the subject. "Remember, all we have to do is walk around like tourists, and you three need to do all the talking to cover up for me trying to get into the minds of a few Gelkka leaders."

"And they will most certainly be watching us," added Melkana. "They must know that we were the ones that caused the problems on Mayoowani, even if they don't know how."

"But my parents said they badly need the drugs we're taking there, so they won't dare do anything silly," Mickie said. "It should be easy."

"And hey, if Mickie can't save us, we know the Spiders will, so who's worried? Anyway, a game of Loopies first!" Drellion looked cheerful and quite unconcerned. As he often did, his warmth and empathy, much like that of his sister, raised everyone's spirits and they finished their drinks before racing down to the Shuttle Bay for the last game of Loopies before planet-fall on Gelokk.

"Let's go with gravity at six percent," Mickie called as they entered the vast cavern. The rest looked at him curiously.

"Six percent?" echoed Drellion. "That's usually only used for combat training for the troops. That four point reduction makes a real difference to the techniques. Not even the real experts playing Gravity-Ball go down that far."

"I know. I just wanted to see if I could handle it."

"Mickie, I've tried it at eight, and I have difficulties. Six is just not a good idea," said Drellion. There was no need to say what everyone knew, that Drellion was by far the best player of the four, or that Mickie was the least skilled.

Mickie was feeling something, he wasn't sure what. Defiance? Anger? An urge to show off to Melkana? He wasn't sure that he liked the emotion, but something was burning inside and he felt unable to stop the rush to tackle this new hurdle.

"I need to try it," he said flatly, sensing the slight resentment and withdrawal of the others.

"Okay, six percent it is," said Melkana doubtfully. "I'll go first with Fencris. Okay with you, Fencris?"

"Sure," replied Fencris. He had been watching the discussion silently, his red eyes burning with curiosity. "I'll fly, you catch."

Mickie and Drellion moved to the side of the square as the other two took their positions. Drellion seemed to gone very silent and he refused to look in Mickie's direction. Under all the other mixed stresses running through him, Mickie felt anger at his own pig-headedness and inability to understand what he was doing or why.

Fencris had taken his position at the side of the square to Mickie's right and had made a few practice leaps vertically to test the different gravitational power. His last two jumps had included a loop at the top, and it was obvious he was uncomfortable with the timing, having landed at an angle, falling in an untidy scrawl. At that gravity setting he would not hurt himself, but clearly he was irritated by his mistake.

"Okay?" he called to Melkana on his right, on the far side of the square from Mickie. She too had taken a few practice jumps and was showing the same slight clumsiness from the unfamiliar setting. She nodded, and poised herself to leap.

Fencris launched himself and flew towards the high spot of his parabola that was usually over the middle of the square. He seemed higher than the usual arc and clearly was going to reach the summit well before the centre point. Melkana had watched closely and leaped to intercept him. Neither tried to complete a loop before the point of impact, but even without that, the exercise failed. Melkana sailed at least a metre below Fencris' line of flight and reached the middle of the square several metres before he did. She reached the ground with a stumble, managed to stay on her feet and turned to watch Fencris land a couple of seconds after her. He was less successful, and he sprawled full length on the floor of the hangar, bouncing slowly in the minuscule gravity.

Both approached the other two watchers, looking tense.

"Well, that was pretty ordinary," said Fencris, trying to be cheerful. "I don't think either of us has missed so badly since kindergarten days. I really don't think you should do this, Mickie. Let's be brutally honest. You're the weakest player of the four of us and we two screwed up. What do you possibly think you can do?"

"I have to," Mickie snapped. Something was terribly wrong and he hated himself for causing the dismay he saw in his friends. He moved to the side of the square. "You fly, I'll catch," he called to Drellion.

The youngest of the four looked doubtfully at his sister who shrugged. "It's his problem," she said. "Let him mess up and then maybe he'll come to his senses."

Silently, Drellion took his position on the left side of the square to Mickie who was standing like a runner at the blocks. He had no idea what was happening to him, but a mixture of rage, excitement and dismay was coursing through his body and he could feel his heart beating at a much higher rate than usual.

He watched Drellion launch into a good, well-judged arc that should take him to the apex of the flight right over the centre of the square and jumped to intercept. He felt the urge to try a loop, tucked his head down, brought up his knees and felt the cavern spin rapidly, eight, nine ten times before he straightened, stretched his arms and legs and stopped the rotation. He saw that he was at least two metres below Drellion. Without knowing how he did it, he rose vertically, seized the younger boy round the waist and they both sank straight down to the opposite side of the square.

The landing was greeted in dead silence for a few seconds.

"Ten rotations," said Fencris softly. "Drellion broke the record the other day with six, and you just did ten, and that in a new gravity setting." His tone was not congratulatory at all, it seemed calm, but there was no warmth in it.

"So, is this what Pfafth do?" asked Melkana. There was definite anger in her voice. "You have to produce new talents just to beat someone younger than you?"

She moved to her brother who looked deeply upset. Mickie had seen how much it had meant to the boy to beat the others, all older than he was and his shame threatened to overwhelm him. He tried to speak and failed.

"You altered your trajectory and moved vertically to intercept," Fencris said. He could have been delivering a lecture to a class. "That's physically impossible without a propulsion device, and I know you don't have one. How did you do that?"

"I.... I don't know," Mickie stammered. "I didn't mean to do this."

Melkana gave him one more scathing look, put her arm on Drellion's shoulder and they walked away without another word. Mickie felt broken hearted but was unable to speak.

Fencris was studying him as if looking for a wiring diagram. "You've no idea how you did the impossible?" he asked softly. He did not seem angry, but there was still no warmth in his tone.

Mickie was still looking after Melkana and her brother as they walked out of the hangar and could do nothing but shake his head. Tears were running down his cheeks.

Fencris saw the emotion and seemed to relax his hostility. "You're still discovering what the Pfafth can do, I suppose. That last bit was pretty awesome. Are you going to tell anyone?"

"I have to tell my parents. They'll know something is wrong. I wish Melkana and Drellion could understand."

"They'll get used to it. Drellion is pretty broken up, I know. It meant the world to him to have beaten us big guys. And you shattered him.

"I didn't mean to," Mickie said again. "It just seemed to happen. Something really got into me and I just *had* to try this."

Fencris put a hand on Mickie's shoulder. "I'll see if I can heal the wound a bit," he said. "Anyway, time to get our final briefings for landing on Gelokk. I suspect our problems there are going to be bigger than the wounded pride of one small kid."

Mickie felt a surge of relief. "Please, Fencris, do what you can. I want us all to go down there as friends. As you say, we're going to need each other."

They walked out of the hangar, Fencris still eaten with curiosity at Mickie's new-found power, but at least still Mickie's friend. Mickie desperately hoped the other two would be amenable to his friend's diplomacy.

Chapter 4 - Espionage on Gelokk

Mickie arrived at the shuttle bay some minutes before anyone else. The crew were still loading the boxes containing the drugs to combat the disease on Gelokk, and he took a seat inside the shuttle, at the far end in the furthest row to the rear. He sat and felt miserable. Usually, he felt excitement about a planet-fall, for every one was still a new event, something that jolted him each time with the realisation of how his life had changed in less than a year. But two things spoiled it for him this time. The awful fear of the experience in his last meeting with this brutal, powerful and ruthless race of conquerors still made him shake and occasionally wake from nightmares. And to make it worse, his friends whom he loved so much had lost their warmth for him after his inexplicable display of arrogance and new powers just a short while ago. Mickie was unable to decide which feeling was worse.

The whine of the hydraulics closing the storage bays in the shuttle shook him from his dark thoughts and he lifted his head to see the first arrivals approaching the spacecraft. He felt a jerk of worry at the thought that his three friends would also be arriving and wondered just how awful the next few hours would be if they still felt angry at him.

Melkana was the first to enter the shuttle. She looked briefly at him, stood by the doorway until Drellion entered and they took seats together, two rows ahead of Mickie and at the other side of the craft. Mickie felt his heart sink. Fencris came next, nodded briefly at Mickie and sat behind the other two and the misery inside him seemed to rise over his head. He dropped his face into his hands and leaned forward against his knees.

"Trouble in Paradise, kid?" said the familiar and welcome voice in front of him. He sat up and looked at his mother. The concern in her face was evident.

"I think I've really screwed up," he replied, and she moved round the end of the row and sat down next to him. Struggling to keep his voice under control, he related the events of an hour or two ago.

"Any more ideas since on why you needed to do that?" his mother asked.

"No. It just seemed to take over me."

"It sounds like your mind just discovered this new ability and was determined to test it out. It obviously placed that test above the problem of scaring your friends."

"You think so?" He looked at her with a sense of hope.

"I think so. Tell me again about the actual jump. Every detail you can remember, particularly if you can think about what was happening when you changed direction."

"It just seemed so easy. I wanted to spin, and I spun. I wanted to move up to intercept Fencris, and it happened, but I've no idea how."

Allie seemed thoughtful. Mickie watched the screens on the wall as they showed the shuttle departing the master ship. The enormous, glowing arc of the surface of Gelokk covered almost the entire sky, indicating they had taken a close orbit round the planet. The sight helped him forget for a few seconds that he was feeling miserable.

"I'd better go and join my group for a quick chat before landing," Allie said, breaking the silence. "I think you'll find that the group is stronger than the little stress you created. Remember, you did something totally unexpected, and it shook them, especially little Drellion who was still so proud about beating all of you bigger people. They need you Mickie and they love you a lot. You'll be okay."

She stood up and moved down to the front of the shuttle whee the medical team was discussing the best method of distribution of the drug. Mickie caught movement over to his right. He looked and saw Fencris waving him over. Feeling tense, he stood up and walked the short distance to the others. As he reached them, all three looked up at him. They didn't smile.

"Hey," said Fencris.

"Hey," Mickie responded, doubtfully.

Drellion stood up. He was still a head shorter than Mickie but his physique was shaping like a true athlete. He looked Mickie firmly in the eye. "I suppose you just couldn't help that, could you?" he asked. "We've been talking about it and we decided you were all so wound up, something was happening inside. Is that it?"

Mickie swallowed. "I think so. I was hating it, but I just went a bit crazy. I'm really sorry."

"I guess it's just a Pfafth thing, huh?" Melkana spoke gravely, but the twitch at the corner of her mouth gave her away. A flood of relief washed over him.

"I guess so," he replied.

"Try and give us some warning will you, next time you get the urge to display the powers of a Master of the Universe, won't you?" Drellion said. His grin was wide and friendly again.

"I promise," said Mickie, and everything seemed normal again. He collapsed into the seat next to Fencris and the two in front turned to look at them.

"We've got to work together for the next few hours," said Melkana. "When we get back, I think we'd better have another look at that magical leaping stuff of yours. If we can all learn it, we'll take the Grand Inter-Galactic Loopies Trophy without breathing hard."

"There's a championship?" Mickie was astonished, but saw the laughter in the other faces before it erupted.

"Dopey Pfafth," said Melkana. "Sheesh, you Masters of the Universe can be real twits, you know that?"

The laughter from the four caused heads to turn in the shuttle. Mickie saw his mother's smile and finally realised that life was back to normal.

Now all they had to deal with were the frightening Gelkka.

The shuttle had come to rest on a flat plain. Tall buildings just a kilometre away indicated the city, but the boundaries of the metropolis seemed abrupt, no gradual merger into any sort of suburban or residential areas. It was, according to Albert, the standard for Gelkka cities, designed more along the lines of a fortress that could be defended at the walls.

Tension in the area outside the shuttle was so thick, Mickie felt it could cloud the air. He stood near the doorway of the shuttle, his friends with him, all a little way from the entrance, hidden by the bulkhead. He listened to the discussion and tried to cast his mind out as far as possible to detect any other thoughts going on. So far, only the intense stress between the two groups could be detected. His parents stood with a group of medical staff. In front of them two the Gelkka towered over them, their appalling size sufficiently intimidating, even without the large hand weapons slung at their waist and the double line of armed troops standing a few metres away.

"We will take the supplies here and you will leave at once," the loud, arrogant and unpleasant rasp of the presumed leader of the Gelkka contingent said.

"That cannot be," Mickie's father replied. He was standing upright, his head thrown back to look up at the eagle-like head of the Gelkka. "Your people need to be shown how to administer the drug, how to evaluate the dose size and how to read the effects on the patient. That will take at least two days to teach, and two more to show your first pupils how to instruct the subsequent ones."

The Gelkka made a small gesture and the troops behind him brought their weapons to the ready. Mickie felt his heart lurch and heard a small "Oh my lord" from Melkana. Grant seemed unmoved.

"The drugs are still in the shuttle," he said. "Until I release the locks, you will not have access to them. And what is in the shuttle is only a fraction of what you need. Until I have your word as a warrior that my party has free, safe passage on this world, you will receive none of the medicine that will save the lives of thousands of your people. Shoot us now, and the shuttle lifts off immediately. The choice is yours."

The silence in the air was as loud as a church bell. Mickie had learned from his briefing that the Warrior Code of Gelokk was as rigid as any Samurai culture of Japan. If the Gelkka standing over his parents gave that word, the entire planet would be bound by it, enforced by the High Command rulers.

Suddenly, the soldiers returned the weapons to their sides. The Gelkka commander had realised his limited options. Grant turned and nodded at the doorway.

"Okay, boys and girls, showtime!" said Mickie, his heart pounding with anxiety. The four children moved from behind the bulkheads and moved down the stairway to the surface. As his feet touched the ground, Mickie shivered a little. For all the powers that seemed to be growing inside him, even with the apparent security of the Spiders' abilities to protect him, he felt terrified of these monstrous people.

Their arrival caused the tension to rise to a crescendo.

"These children may not approach," the commander shouted. Even under the roar of fury, Mickie felt that he could detect a note of fear in the creature's voice.

"Now why would that be?" asked Grant, a tiny note of sarcasm in his voice. The tone would probably be undetected by the Gelkka, Mickie thought, but the words were a dramatic challenge to a warlike monster faced by four small children. The Gelkka seemed to sense it.

"They are known criminals on another world," he snapped. "They are fugitives from Gelkka justice."

"They are just children," replied Grant. "Does the Gelkka High Command fear four small children? Would they risk the supply of drugs to prosecute them for wandering into mischief as children have done for all time?"

The fury in the Gelkka's huge, eagle-like eyes radiated like a searchlight for a moment because he had been trapped into a concession and made to look weak in front of his troops.

"They will stay in the vicinity of the shuttle," he roared.

"They will accompany us into the city," said Grant, unmoved. "Children must learn, and this is a new world. These children have also been cooped inside a ship for many days and they need fresh air and space. We will supervise them and ensure they stay out of harm's way, but your High Command must also give their word that not one of our party will be harmed or threatened in any way."

The commander stood motionless for a few seconds before moving to his transport vehicle, the same machine Mickie had seen on the planet Mayoowani, a flat oblong about ten metres long that moved by anti-gravity power, floating a small distance above the ground. He spoke into a device, listened for a few seconds and returned.

"You have the Word of the Warrior," he said, the rage still evident in the wide, round raptor's eyes. "The High Command gives it."

Grant nodded. "Then I know that we are safe," he said calmly and waved at the medical team who immediately moved to the shuttle's storage bays, which opened as they approached. They unloaded the boxes that were piled inside and most moved back into the ship, the doors closed, including the access door to the passenger section, and the shuttle lifted soundlessly, vanishing within seconds.

"The shuttle will return when I call it down with a specific pass word," said Grant. "It will bring with it the second instalment of the drugs."

The Gelkka commander said nothing but turned and walked to his transport machine. A second machine moved up to the waiting members of the ship's crew. In addition to Mickie's parents and the four children, four of the medical team climbed onto the platform that floated just a few centimetres off the ground and stood, holding onto bars that stood an uncomfortable head height to them, being built for the enormous Gelkka species. One of that race stood at the front with what Mickie assumed was the controlling mechanism. As a mode of transport, it was serviceable for short distances, but Mickie hoped he would not have to travel any great distance.

Silently, the platform moved off, following the direction set by the Commander's vehicle toward the city just a kilometre away.

"Not exactly a holiday resort sort of place, is it?" murmured Allie, standing in front of Mickie.

"Bleak," agreed Grant. "I believe this is the first visit by any of the space-going races. It looks like we're heading to some sort of gateway into the city."

The vehicle was indeed heading to a large, fortified structure where armed troops stood in rows. There were no fences leading away from the structure that Mickie could see, so the gateway seemed a strange thing, standing alone in the flatness.

Grant moved forward a short distance and addressed the Gelkka at the driving station. "Why do we head through there?" he asked. "Why not head straight into the city?"

The trooper seemed astonished at the contact, even a little frightened, judging by his shifting of position and agitated turning of the head. "That is the only safe way through," he finally said. "Travelling over any other route would cause our deaths."

"Minefields?" asked Grant, but the Gelkka did not reply. The vehicle slowed as it passed the lines of troops, but did not stop. Mickie sensed the hostility and fear that seemed to come in waves at him, like the incoming surf. They had caught up with the leading vehicle now, and they approached what looked like a fortified castle within the city, stopping outside massive doors guarded by four Gelkka troopers.

They alighted in front of those gates that started to move open.

"We will go in and meet with the local medical teams," said Allie, picking up one of the boxes of drugs. "You children can move around freely. The High Council's protection order will have been broadcast and nobody would dare go against it."

But as the adults moved into the building, Albert's voice sounded in Mickie's head. "As discussed earlier, Mickie, you and your friends should move around, but your brief is to try and pick up any mental signals or conversations that might indicate threatening acts or future plans for the people of Mayoowani."

"Acknowledged," said Mickie silently, and saw that his friends had all received the same message from the ship's computer as they nodded at each other.

"Let's just walk along this road," said Melkana. "It looks like it leads to the main administrative building. You can do your special thing there, Mickie."

"Careful," Mickie cautioned, and switched to mental communication to the computer. "Albert, give me a link to the others with me."

"Done."

"Guys, be very careful with what we say. They may have tight-beam microphones on us and we don't want to give them any cause for suspicion."

"Oops!" Drellion spoke for them all. "You're right."

In silence, the four walked along the street, studying the scenery. Though sparsely populated, other Gelkka walked those streets also and occasional floating platforms passed silently along the roadways, usually carrying military troops armed with heavy weapons. The enormous beings stared in massive hostility at the four small children standing so alone in the city.

"Ugly, don't you think?" Melkana spoke aloud. "Just massive, no style, no elegance."

"They're all watching us," Drellion whispered. He sounded frightened.

"Of course they are, little brother," replied Melkana. "We're the first off-worlders to visit here except for slaves from their subject planets, and we're wandering around freely. It's a puzzle to them. But remember, we have the High Command's promise of free passage. Nobody would dare touch us."

"I suppose so." Drellion sounded a little more comfortable, but still not at ease.

They continued to walk in the direction of the massive, featureless block that had been pointed out to them as the headquarters of the High Command on Gelokk. Mickie tried stretching his mind out, imagining he was wrapping feelers round the whole structure, trying to sense every mental wave that he could. The Gelkka were not in any way telepathic, he had learned, so the Speakers could not tap into their minds at all. But Mickie appeared to have different powers and he was struggling to see if he could do what the Speakers could not.

"Would you guys just talk and chatter?" he said softly. "I need to concentrate and it would look weird if we just wander around in silence."

The others picked up on the suggestion and began to discuss the scenery around them. Mickie sensed a withdrawal away from them, felt his mind move into a different gear, and the immediate surroundings faded into a light mist. He kept walking, somehow staying in contact with his friends, only vaguely aware of the chatter coming from them.

Something was happening ahead of him....

Unusual sounds, undertones of great anger, hostility, frustration.... It was like hearing static on the radio, while just detectible was a voice speaking, occasional words being understood, the rest merging into indefinable burbling. Mickie felt a wave of fear and anxiety wash over him. Sometimes, and this was one of them, he felt overwhelmed by what he was doing, what had happened to him in the last year or so, and the sheer enormity of the job he was expected to do. He was only thirteen years old, after all..... He shook himself, told himself he was more than just a kid, he was a *Pfafth*. If only he knew what that was. He focused harder, he knew this was important.....

"The traders are here? On Gelokk?"

The voice suddenly clarified in Mickie's head. The tone was harsh, furious, loud, and Mickie couldn't prevent his reaction of stopping dead and holding his hands to his ears. Immediately his three friends gathered round him.

"Mickie, you mustn't show anything!" The urgency in Melkana's voice cut through the shock and fear in Mickie's mind. He forced himself to keep walking toward the immense building just a few hundred metres away.

"I'm hearing someone talking in there," he muttered. "And it's about us."

"This is what we came for," replied Fencris in an equally low tone. "Stay with it, Mickie."

"*They are here, my Lord,*" replied another voice, less harsh, softer, almost afraid. It was the voice of a servant, a subordinate.

"*And with those devil's spawn, those children?*"

Mickie got a sense of identity now. He read the harsh voice as that of Jashesh Vegrak, one of the Gelokk High Command. In just a split second, Mickie learned the history of this Gelkka, knew he was third in seniority in the High Command, harboured dreams and plans to take the top position and was possessed of a rabid hatred of all lesser beings other than Gelkka.

"*Yes, my Lord,*" said the subordinate.

Mickie's sense of the scene grew stronger. Now he became aware of the room, the others in it, the layout and the reasons for the meeting. Feeling as if he were looking out through the eyes of Jashesh Vegrak, he saw six other Gelkka in the room. Four were in military costume, the big green cloak down one side, heavy handguns in a belt. The other two were in drab, grey tunics, also with cloaks, but without weapons. From the knowledge he was tapping from his unknowing host's mind, Mickie knew that the two civilians were government functionaries. The military personnel were very senior officers. But there was another presence... one he could not visualise, not even sense fully. But it was menacing, strange, and he could not identify anything, not even where in the room this other entity was. There was a psychic darkness.... Mickie shivered.

But he saw an astonishing opportunity. "Speaker 356, are you in contact?" he asked mentally and thankfully received an immediate response from the telepathic being so many thousands of light years away.

"Yes, Mickie, I am."

"Can you monitor what I am seeing?"

He sensed the tiny pause and emanations of astonishment coming from the Speaker.

"Indeed I can, Mickie," replied Speaker 356. "This is the first time we have been able to see inside a Gelkka mind."

"Then please stay and monitor this," Mickie said. "I think this will be interesting." For a second he felt proud of his coolness and deliberate understatement then concentrated on the scene playing out for him and the other watcher many galaxies away.

"Speaker," he asked. "Can you see through this link the individuals in the room?"

"Yes, Mickie. I see through the eyes of the Gelkka Commander, just as you are doing, and I see four military Gelkka and two civilians."

"Can you identify another individual at all?"

"Not at all," replied the Speaker, and Mickie sensed the puzzlement in the telepathic being's communication. "Why, can you?"

"Only partially," Mickie said. "It's very strange, and it's quite scary."

"It is indeed puzzling. I will try and see through your connection. Meanwhile, let me watch this and record it."

Mickie returned his concentration to the room.

"*The situation on Mayoowani – what developments?*" the High Commander snapped.

"*No change,*" replied one of the military Gelkka. "*Reports continue to filter through that this so-called "Saviour" appears all over the planet and speaks to crowds. Despite our rapid response groups usually arriving while the crowds are still there, we have never yet seen any sign of such a cattle-beast. Our interrogators have taken many prisoners and questioned them up to their deaths, but we have no concrete evidence that any such "Saviour" really exists.*"

"*And have there been any civil disturbances?*"

"*None, my Lord.*"

"*But we must expect such insurgency at some time. Have you seen any evidence that the Traders or any other off-worlders have been assisting this movement?*"

"*No, my Lord.*"

"*Nonetheless, we must assume that some form of help is being given. You will step up the hunt for this rebel cattle-beast. Make an example of a couple of small towns, preferable ones that have no commercial value to us. Destroy them totally in a search for rebels. Kill the entire populations. Let it be known that we will continue in this manner until this "Saviour" surrenders.*"

"*I will do, my Lord.*"

Shaking with the impact of the words being spoken in that forbidding room, Mickie pulled his mind away. "Speaker 356, did you hear that?"

"Yes, Mickie."

"Will you pass a complete visual record to my parents so that they can identify the Gelkka military types who will be returning to Mayoowani?"

"It's done, Mickie."

The appalling shock at the terrible orders he had just heard was pushed into the back of his mind as he heard the Gelkka commander continue.

"And now what of the Traders? Where are they?"

"They have taken the first batch of the drugs into our medical centre and they are showing our doctors how to administer them."

"And the devil's spawn? They are wondering loose?"

Before Mickie could hear any reply, he was overwhelmed with a roaring, bellowing din in his head. It was as if he was caught up in a tidal wave, completely helpless, totally swamped by noise, by blackness, by appalling fury. Dimly he heard the Gelkka Commander screaming in fury.

"Those children are hearing this! They know what we have just said! Find them! Now! Kill them on sight!"

"But my Lord, the Word of the Warrior!" One of the other officers tried to reply, but the Commander turned on him and slammed one huge fist into the officer's head.

"You fool! They are cattle! The Word means nothing when cattle are concerned. Do you realise what they can cause if the Traders learn what we plan on Mayoowani? Get the troops, find those demons and kill them! Go!"

Mickie fought for control over his terror. "Speaker? How could he know? They are supposed to be non-telepathic!"

The Speaker's bewilderment was obvious, even over the empty light years. "I don't know, Mickie! We didn't think they even understood the concept, and they would have rejected it anyway, assuming no inferior species could do something they couldn't."

Mickie came fully into awareness of his surroundings, leaving the room in the castle and its occupants behind. His friends were staring at him in fear and panic.

"We have to get ourselves out of here," he said loudly. "Back to the ship, now!"

"I don't think the shuttle is back yet," gasped Fencris, as they all turned back to the direction of the landing site.

"Albert, can you hear me?" Mickie called to the ship's computer, but got no answer. All four children were now running hard for the landing site. He heard nothing and the worry grew rapidly in his mind. "Can any of you contact the ship's computer?" he gasped as they ran. For a few seconds there was silence, interrupted by the gasping of all four of them.

"Nothing," said Drellion, his face looking to Mickie for support.

"Nor me," added Melkana. Fencris just looked at Mickie, his red eyes glowing like coals in his alarm.

"Speaker 356, can you hear me?"

But instead of the comforting tones of the Speaker there was only silence in Mickie's head apart from the roaring of his own fear.

"I think we're being blocked," Mickie managed to say. The edge of the city was close, but Mickie suddenly remembered the minefields that the Gelkka trooper had said were scattered around the city. His heart feeling like it was encased in ice, he slowed and stopped.

"Mickie, we have to run!" Melkana shouted, astonishment in her face, but Mickie shook his head.

"The mines, remember? We'll blow ourselves to pieces if we try going without a guide."

The other stopped also. Drellion was almost in tears, Melkana struggling not to show the same reaction. Fencris stood immobile, his eyes burning like a roaring fire so that a faint red glow covered his face. And behind them, there was a shrill whistle. Three of the platforms loaded with troopers were racing towards them and all the soldiers had their weapons pointing at the four children. Mickie realised that the order had been issued to kill them. Feeling as if time had slowed to a crawl, he looked around him. Where were the Spiders? They had said they had been instructed to help him. How had his communications to the ship, to his parents, to the Speaker been blocked. Something dreadful was happening, and the fear inside him began to rise to shattering levels. He felt that he was drowning, and only dimly heard the panicked screams of Melkana and the defeated sobs of Drellion. His eyes felt like they were popping from his head, he saw the soldiers taking aim and then the world seemed to explode.

He felt as if he was in the middle of a multi-coloured ocean that was booming with life, millions of little animals surrounding him, swamping him. He thrashed furiously, but also felt one strong, powerful, raging emotion.... *I must save my friends.* He had the weirdest sensation of taking hold of all three of the other children, somehow he was throwing them as far as he could, so far that they were safe from the Gelkka, so far that they were not even near the city.....

Mickie lost consciousness.

Chapter 5 - Where No-One has Gone Before

Mickie found himself sitting cross-legged on the ground. He was weary as if he had walked many miles, but it was a satisfied weariness, a sensation of having achieved great things. He had absolutely no idea where he was. The ground was not all that hard, but the surface was prickly, as if he was sitting on a gorse bush, though no thorns were sticking into him. The air was frigid, clear, quite breathable, but he realised that he was uncomfortably cold. Without knowing how, he adjusted his body and no longer felt the cold. But he could hear the wind. It keened like a sad dog, with a high, piercing note that was matched in the lower registers by a tone that sounded almost like a French Horn. He realised that he was somehow sheltered from the direct blast of the wind by a huge object just a metre or so in front of him. It looked like a large hillock, about three metres high, about the same at the base, tapering a little to a rounded peak. It was covered with vegetation that resembled ivy, with green leaves the size of his hand and a few yellow and blue flowers scattered over the entire growth. It was the only object he could see. Everywhere else was just flat, featureless plain, a few bushes sprouting in small clumps, the ground more of the same coarse stuff on which he was sitting.

He wondered where on Earth he could be then laughed outright as he realised how ridiculous that question was. Of all the places in the Universe, Earth was absolutely the one place where he could not possibly be. He tried thinking back to his last moments of awareness before this strange awakening. He was on Gelokk, he recalled, and the Gelkka troopers were attacking the four children. He remembered the appalling fear and the question of why the Spiders had failed in their promise to protect him. For a second or two, he recalled the puzzle of the additional presence in the room in the Gelkka castle, one that he couldn't fully see or even sense fully, and that was totally invisible to the Speaker. But that was washed away in the horrible fear for his friends.

"Albert," he said. "Can you hear me?"

The ship's computer did not reply.

"Allie, Grant? Are you hearing this?" Again, there was no reply. Either he was still blocked in whatever way his communications had been blocked before on Gelokk, or he was too far away for the device in his shoulder to reach the ship. His worry increasing, he tried the one last source of help he had.

"Speaker 356, are you there?"

The reply came with such hideous volume that he felt his head would explode and the words were completely lost in the pain. He gasped, then somehow adjusted his receptive mechanisms. He had no idea how he did it, but to his relief, the Speaker's voice came through at a level he could handle.

"Mickie! We have been trying to contact you for several hours. Where are you and are you alright?"

Feeling almost faint in his relief, Mickie relaxed a little. "Yes, I'm fine, but I have no idea where I am. But what happened and where are my friends and Allie and Grant?"

"Everyone is safe," said the Speaker, his tones soothing. "But nobody knows what happened. Your friends found themselves back on the ship, but you had vanished. Your parents and the rest of the crew on Gelokk heard the news from them as soon as they had recovered. The Gelkka troops were milling around in great confusion and were recalled into the city immediately. There is now a major diplomatic row in progress as the Gelkka High Command has been forced to admit they broke the Word of a Warrior and the crew has returned to the ship without making further deliveries of the drugs."

"Will you tell everyone I'm safe?" Mickie asked.

"I have already done that, and they will want to talk to you in a moment. But we must first concentrate on finding out where you are and how to get you back again. Tell me what you see around you."

Mickie looked at the scenery. It was very unprepossessing. "It's awfully bleak," he said. "The air is quite Earth-like, but it was horribly cold until I managed to somehow adjust myself. I've no idea how I did that. Why don't you check through me and see what I see? All I can see is a huge mound in front of me, and that's blocking off the high winds..."

"WHAT?" The shock in the Speaker's voice was almost hysterical. "Mickie, this is absolutely *impossible,* but we know of no view like that except here on our own world. And now that I've scanned my immediate area, I can only conclude.... you are sitting right next to me. And there is no known intelligent life form that can live within two light years of this planet."

"But... that's *impossible,*" Mickie said, feeling terrified at the implications of what the Speaker was telling him. "That would mean I've travelled about sixty million light years on my own, without a ship..." And then the worst part of it came to him. "And that means nobody can come and pick me up!"

For a dreadful moment, he lost control of his emotions and the fear overwhelmed him, tears flooding down his face. All he wanted was to be held closely by his parents and feel the warmth of their love for him. He rocked back and forth, tears flooding down his face. *I'm just a kid of thirteen,* he said to himself, *I can't handle this. It's not fair. I want to go home.*

"Mickie, please try and get control of yourself!" The Speaker's words cut through the panic and the grief and Mickie fought hard to be able to think clearly. "If you got yourself here, you can get yourself away again," the Speaker continued. "We will have to work out how you did it, and I know I can help."

Slowly, Mickie grew calm again. Rationally, he knew the immense being in front of him was correct. Mickie had already discovered astonishing abilities and powers within himself, and he knew he would be able to learn how he had achieved this astounding transportation across the Universe.

"But if it takes a few days, we still have a problem," he said. "I imagine it will get a lot colder when night falls and

I don't know if I can adjust myself that much. And what will I eat in that time?"

"Try crawling next to me," the Speaker replied. "I believe you will find you can work yourself under quite thick layers of vegetation and there will be a great deal of heat generated by my body, even behind the layers of earth and other plant life that covers me. Try that first, then we'll think about food."

Mickie did as instructed, rising to his feet and advancing the short distance to the huge mound before him. Cautiously, he pulled away at the thick bushes and vines and assorted plants that seemed to cover the mound, and was delighted to find that as he got deeper inside the protective curtain, significant warmth radiated from the Speaker.

"I think this will do just fine," he said, lying down on a pleasantly soft pile of greenery. He felt astonishingly comfortable and warm.

"Good. Now, about food. This may not be all that easy, but there is some sort of answer. Some of the vegetation produces fruits. I believe they will be edible for you, if not all that exciting to eat. There are birds and there are small animals, nothing larger than a beast resembling a very small rabbit on Earth, however. They will present no danger, but catching and cooking may be a problem. Do you think you could employ any of your unusual mental powers to get over these difficulties?"

"I... I don't know," Mickie replied. "Can I talk to my parents and my friends, first?"

The wonderfully familiar voices echoed in his head immediately, transferred through the telepathic abilities of the Speaker.

"Mickie," said his mother. "We're so relieved! We had no idea what happened to you. Are you okay?"

"I think so," he said. "I really wish I could be home with you!"

"Me too!" Grant's voice was equally warm and relieved. For a few minutes, Mickie was quite content just hear his parents' voices and he clung to the sound of them as though he could pull himself through the voids of space and join them in the ship. Then he talked to his friends.

"Mickie! How could you *possibly* be on the Speaker's planet?" Melkana's voice was almost squeaking in her astonishment. "Nothing can live within *light-years* of the place! How are you surviving?"

"I've no idea. Are you all okay?"

"We're fine," Fencris replied. "But we have no idea what happened. One second the Gelkka were about to blast us to fine powder, the next we were on the ship, but you weren't there. How did you do that? And why didn't you come with us?"

"Beats me," Mickie said. "Drellion, are you okay too, young guy?"

"Sheesh, I dunno," came Drellion's voice. Mickie could hear the smile in the tone. "You Pfafth will do *anything* to avoid being beaten at Loopies!"

Mickie almost felt tears rising in his eyes, so relieved was he that everyone else was safe and thinking about him.

"Grant, Allie, how am I going to get back?" He almost choked as he spoke to them.

"We don't know, Mickie, not yet. But we're working on it. We've thought about sending a shuttle, but the problem is that the ship cannot come within two light-years of the Speakers' planet without killing the crew. So sending a remote-controlled shuttle is not a great idea, because they cannot travel at speeds greater than light speed, so it would take years to get you. The Captain is investigating whether a larger shuttle could be equipped with hyperspace drives, but it's not looking likely."

"It looks like I have to work out what I did and do it again," he said, struggling to stay calm and in control of his voice. He was almost breaking up into uncontrolled terror.

"I know we'll find an answer, son," said Grant. "But keep working on that solution."

For a while longer, he talked to all of them, seeking comfort from their presence, even though separated by so many millions of light years. Then the warmth and security he was feeling inside the protective covering of the huge entity that had no ears, eyes or mouth but could communicate across the entire Universe caused him to feel drowsy and he fell asleep.

Dreams haunted him. Sometimes he dreamed of the awful years of his childhood, living in the miserable house in Manchester, made worse by the hostile, angry and bitter attitude of his parents. He experienced again some of the shouting, the blows, the banishment to his tiny, empty room. Some of the dreams were warmer; the first meeting with Allie, then with Grant, and the astonishing invitation to join them and leave Earth, probably for ever.

Then he came awake with a jerk, knowing he had cried out as a familiar, cold, emotionless voice entered his mind.

"So, young Pfafth, you have learned how to cross the emptiness without a ship?"

Mickie fought for self-control for a few seconds before more recent memories took over. Even though he had learned that the Spiders were his protectors and allies, and he had slept amidst many hundreds of them in close proximity, it still took some rational thought to break himself of the terror that so many humans experienced at the idea of any spiders, never mind monstrous creatures more than twice the size of a man.

"Speaker, can you hear this?" he said when calm was repossessed.

"Hear what, Mickie?" the Speaker replied.

"I'm talking to a Spider."

"I can only hear your words, Mickie."

"*The Speaker cannot hear me, Pfafth. This conversation is private.*"

Mickie was increasingly intrigued by the fact that the Zlan seemed to have a telepathic communications channel the Speakers could not access. "Why?" he asked curiously.

"*Because it is necessary.*"

"Why is it necessary?"

"*Because the Speakers are not yet ready to comprehend a new way of communication, such as we have.*"

"Do other species communicate the way you do?"

"*Yes.*" Mickie had become accustomed to the cold, emotionless tone of the monster. Slowly he was becoming aware that perhaps the Spider was not without emotions, but such emotions and thoughts were possibly impossible to comprehend in a creature so different and so alien.

"Which species?" he asked.

"*Those that none of you in the circle of contacts that you have made so far has ever met.*"

"Have the Speakers met them?"

"*No. For the same reason as they are not capable of recognising us. They are species in galaxies that your Kaloti ships have not yet reached.*"

"Are the Pfafth one of those?"

A short silence echoed in the warm space where Mickie lay.

"*It is not yet time for us to tell you about the Pfafth.*"

Mickie had been at this point before and he recognised the same, implacable block to further information as he had heard the last time.

"Why have you contacted me?" he asked.

"*To warn you.*"

"Warn me?" Mickie felt a surge of alarm

"*You have enemies,*" the Spider said.

Mickie's alarm increased. "What enemies?"

"*We do not know.*"

"Then how do you know they are my enemy?"

"*We can read the hatred, but we cannot identify the entity that emits that hatred.*"

"So what can I do?"

"*We do not know.*"

"Why didn't you help me, back there? Were you expecting I'd save myself again, without your help?"

"*We were blocked from seeing the events, just as the Speaker and the Ship's computers were blocked. We do not understand how this happened.*"

"You were blocked? You think it was this Enemy that did that?"

"*We are certain.*"

The answer gave Mickie no reason to reduce his fear at the appalling news. He decided to tackle the other immediate problem. "How did I get here?"

"We do not know."

"What? That's *crazy!* You do it, you did it on Merrison. You've *got* to know how you did it."

"Do you know how to walk?"

The question astonished him. "Of course I know how to walk!"

"How?"

"I put one foot in front of the other, transfer my weight to the front foot, bring the other ...."

"That is understood. Now tell me how you move the first foot."

The question brought Mickie to a halt. The question had never occurred to him. "I don't know. I just do it."

"Exactly. Now imagine meeting a species that has had no limbs for generations, but has just grown legs in the last few days. How would you tell it to move those legs?"

"I suppose I'd tell it to.. well... just try and move them." Mickie began to understand the problem. He had absolutely no idea of how he moved his limbs and the Spider could not tell him how to do something that it did itself without thought. At the back if his mind, he realised he was marvelling at the fact that he was actually *conversing* with the Spiders as friends, instead of trembling with fear at the contact as he had in the past. He thought about another approach to the problem that was a matter of life or death to him.

"Speaker 356, can you hear me?"

"Of course, Mickie. Should you not be asleep?"

"Speaker, I am having a conversation with a Spider. I know that you can't detect that species' mind, but can you see my memories of the conversation?"

For a second, the Speaker was silent, and Mickie realised that it was still feeling concern and worry about its species' inability to communicate with the Spiders.

"Yes, I can, Mickie. I see that it is unable to tell you how to do what it can do itself without thought."

"But that's what made me think of you, Speaker. How do *you* learn to do what you do, when you grow old enough to start training?"

"The difference, Mickie, is that we grow up with the knowledge that we *can* do it, so our minds are open to the learning. The Spiders must similarly know from their earliest days that this is a skill they will learn, just as you grow up knowing you can and will learn to walk, talk, read, and so on."

"That is correct." The Spider's cold tones sounded in Mickie's mind, but he no longer felt fear or revulsion at the contact.

"You can hear the Speaker?" he asked in astonishment.

"Yes."

"Then why can't he hear you?"

"One day, they will."

That left Mickie baffled. But he decided he couldn't spend time working on the question. He had much more important problems to solve.

"How can I teach myself to transport like you do?" he asked.

"I do not know. We do not teach our young. They learn as you learn to walk, by seeing their adults do it."

"So it's up to me to learn how to do it again?"

"That is correct."

Terrifying as his situation was, as lonely and frightened as he was, Mickie took some comfort from the conversation with the Spider. There was a way out of this. He just had to find it, however deeply it was hidden in his mind.

"But we do recognise one aspect of your jump." The Spider's words cut into Mickie's thoughts and snapped him back to his situation.

"What is that?"

"You jumped the way our young would jump when faced with sudden danger. Randomly, but to a space that was safe. You threw your friends back to the ship and we do not know how you did that. But on the ship, you yourself would still be vulnerable to the Hunters. So you jumped to the Speaker's planet where nothing can follow you."

"The .... Hunters?"

"Something is hunting you, young Pfafth."

The response sent a wave of fear through him. And yet he knew that he had begun to suspect something like this. The conversation he had overhead back on Gelokk.... There had been something almost familiar about the unidentified entity that had been in the room with the Gelkka commander. He struggled to suppress the fear and think about immediate problems.

"Speaker, what time is it?"

There was almost a laugh in the mental tones of the Speaker. "Mickie, we have no eyes, we never sleep, we never move. I have absolutely no concept of what time it would be!"

Mickie had never thought of that. "So I suppose you can't tell if it's daylight out there, either?"

"It's not a thing we would normally consider. There are times when I would sense slightly higher warmth when our sun is shining through clouds, but I do not detect that now. It could be night, or it could be that the sun is hidden. You will have to take a look for yourself."

With an effort, Mickie pulled himself from his extremely warm bed and moved aside some of the foliage protecting him. After a few moments of cramped movement, he felt a blast of cold air on his face, but could detect no light of any sort. Hurriedly, he pulled himself back to his bed.

"I can't see anything at all," he said. "Doesn't this planet have a moon?"

"It doesn't. I think you should try and get some more sleep. The day could get difficult for you."

He tried. He lay back and tried to relax in the extraordinary comfort and warmth, but sleep would not come. The loneliness of the isolation was haunting, and the fear of perhaps never learning how to transport himself left a cold feeling in the pit of his stomach. Added to that was the new fear that the Spider had left with him. Something was hunting him, and his mind churned with worry. That sense of darkness in the Gelkka commander's room... that was hideously familiar.

A few short catnaps was all he could manage, and at some long, long interval into that frightening night he detected a small lightening in the blackness and he knew that dawn had come on a planet that no intelligent being other than its natives had ever visited before.

What finally drove him from his nest was hunger. Trusting that he would be able to adjust his inner heat source as he had when he found himself on the planet, he crawled out of the protective shelter. The cold hit him like a surf, enveloping him with rage, almost making him scream with sudden pain, but as he cried out, he felt the unknown force inside himself take over, and the cold receded. He had no idea what had happened, but decided that primal survival instincts had taken over and utilised a previously untested and thus unknown reaction.

"Speaker, can I talk to my parents?"

Immediately, Grant's voice came through. "Mickie, are you okay? Did you sleep?"

"Yes, Dad, for some of the time. I'm outside now, but I seem to have some ability to battle the cold. I'm very hungry, though."

"Can you see any signs of vegetation that might be edible?"

"Not yet, but I've started walking. There are some bushes maybe a kilometre away."

"Okay son. Keep talking to us, we're all included in this conversation."

"Yes! We're all here, Mickie!" Melkana spoke first, then Drellion and Fencris chimed in, giving Mickie a major boost to his comfort.

"And I'm here, too," Allie said. The warmth in her voice almost brought tears to his eyes, but he swallowed, deciding firmly that he was now on his own and had to solve his problems, just like any grown-up. He started to run, feeling the need for hard work and effort, and within a couple of minutes, arrived at the clump of bushes he had spotted. It turned out to be a lot bigger than he had first thought, the patch actually covering several hundreds of square metres. Some of the bushes had flowers on them, tiny red and blue blossoms, and as he pushed his way further into the shrubbery he saw some yellow and green blossoms also. Finally, he saw what looked like fruit, a bunch resembling blackberries. Cautiously, he crushed one in his fingers and smelled the dark red juice. It seemed okay, he touched his tongue to a drop, and though tart, it tasted much like any blackberry on Earth. Taking a deep breath, he ate a single berry and waited for a few seconds without any ill effects.

"I think I may have found some fruit that's edible," he said to his distant friends. "It's a bit like a blackberry, and there's quite a few bunches here."

"Okay, don't gorge on them, Mickie, however hungry you might feel," said Allie. "You could get painfully full or maybe acidic, so let that rest for a while and see what happens. But at least you'll get moisture from the fruit, and that's more important than food right now."

"Okay, Allie," he said, picked two larger bunches and carried them as he walked further. But he found no other candidates, and eventually turned back to his shelter. The cold seemed to be increasing again, and he wondered if he was a little weaker through hunger, or perhaps he was burning energy at a far greater rate. He knew he would need more than fruit to survive and the worry increased.

"Try digging at the roots of those bushes, Mickie," Grant suggested. "Is the soil loose enough?"

Mickie bent down and examined the root of the closest bush. The soil seemed quite dark and rich and easily came away as his hands dug into it. He pulled at the roots and was able to pull away a short length of it, though there were no more likely candidates for food, like a potato, which is what he had been hoping for. Brushing away the soil as much as he could, he chewed at the root. To his surprise, it tasted like liquorice.

"The root is pretty good," he announced. "I can probably manage on that, plus the fruit, for a few days."

"Okay, that's a relief," said Grant, and Mickie could in fact hear that relief in his voice. He spent a few moments wrestling at the roots he had found and was finally able to tear away a few centimetres and tuck the length into his pocket. He started off again towards the mound that was his shelter then stopped as two small shapes scuttled away from his path. As the Speaker had said, they looked like tiny rabbits, about twice the size of a mouse.

"I wonder....." he muttered to himself, and concentrated hard, trying to remember the sensation in his mind when he had killed the Smegandri terrorists on Kamotar, the planet of the huge, three-armed species. Feeling the pressure build up, he tried to direct a bolt of energy at the two creatures, but to his huge disappointment, they kept nibbling at some tiny weeds and seemed to feel no effect at all.

The cold was getting worse, and he broke back into a run, arriving back at the mound of the Speaker and hurriedly crawled back into his shelter and the warmth it provided. The two or three bunches of berries and some liquorice root would have to last him for a while.

Once rested, his sparse meal finished, he felt some strength returning. It was time to start work on rescuing himself.

"Speaker, you said you could help find out how I transported myself?"

"Yes Mickie. I have already been following the pathways of your brain, looking for anything that could be a clue, and I may have found something."

Mickie felt his heart leap. There was a chance, at last! "What do you have?" he asked eagerly.

"There are some curious patterns in one location that I have never seen before, either in Human or Kalamosian brains. They are close to the standard movement control nodes, but they are unusual. What I want you to do now, is move parts of your body in turn and I'll observe what happens."

For the next half hour, Mickie obediently moved his hands, his arms, twitched his face, waggled his fingers, turned over, bent his knees, moved every muscle he could think of.

"Anything?" he asked.

"Perhaps. Can you feel this?"

Mickie began to sense a small twinge in his head. It was not painful, more like a warm spot deep inside his brain.

"Yes, I can," he said in surprise. "What are you doing?"

"Sending some small signals into that area," the Speaker replied. "I think that's the spot that controls your teleportation skills, but I don't know how you use it. Try concentrating hard, see if anything happens."

Mickie tried desperately hard, feeling his yearning to be back on the ship with his parents and friends. He sensed the spot inside his head becoming warmer, almost a pleasant sensation, but nothing he did would move his body even a tiny distance.

"No good," he muttered, sensing tears dangerously close to his eyes.

"Keep working at it," replied the voice coming from somewhere inside the huge mass that was sheltering him.

And for the rest of the day, Mickie tried, pangs of hunger making him irritable, angry and feeling helpless. As he sensed night falling outside the cover of foliage, he finally fell asleep, aware of tears running down his cheeks.

The next morning, he again crept out into the freezing atmosphere of the planet without a name. As before, his body adjusted itself to the temperature, and he set off at a jog to the bushes to find more bunches of the berries. This time he abandoned caution and ate his way steadily through several bunches, finally picking as many as he could hold to carry back to the shelter. Again he saw two of the miniature rabbits and tried to stun them with mental bolts, but they ignored him. Despite the feast of berries, he still felt hungry, and the anger in him almost exploded.

"Damn you!" he screamed at the small creatures. And this time it worked. They seemed to freeze, their heads dropping to the ground. Breathing hard from his explosion of rage, Mickie crept up to them, reached out and picked one of them up. It was certainly dead, and on inspection, so was the other.

"Good grief," he muttered. "Can I only do that when I get really furious?" Getting no answer, he managed to push the two animals into the pockets of the ship's tunic he was wearing and returned to the shelter. Once inside, he hung the bunches of berries on a protruding branch and pulled out the little animals. As he had thought, they really did look like tiny rabbits with soft white fur, upright ears and pink noses.

"So how the hell do I eat these things?" he said aloud. "I suppose I'd better get that skin off, first."

It took over an hour of tearing at the skin with his teeth before he was able to remove the fur covering and he took a few moments to try and clean the taste from his mouth with some more of the berries, spitting out small chunks of wet white fur, but finally he had two scrawny, most unappetising little bodies in his hands.

"Well, here goes," he muttered, and bit off a small amount of the raw meat from the shoulders of the first. For a second, he nearly gagged and threw it up again, but he forced the small mouthful down and repeated the process. Closing his mind to the taste and texture, he finally managed to finish off one of the animals, ate a few more berries to clean his mouth out, and tried to relax.

He lay back and called up his parents to report on where he was and how he'd managed to get some food, unpleasant as the process had been.

"Stick with it, son," Grant said. "You need your strength. I'm very proud of how you've managed this."

Talking with his friends and family comforted him, and he managed to get an hour or two of sleep to make up for the restless night. But when he awoke, it was still light and various internal pressures reminded Mickie that he had to go outside again. He pulled some leaves off the plants growing on the mound that was the Speaker and walked off a short distance to take care of things, using the leaves to finish the process.

"This is the worst part of being away from civilisation," he muttered to himself as he walked back to his shelter, preparing for another exhausting bout of researching the transportation nodes in his brain.

Two more long, weary, lonely days passed. Each morning, he crept out into the frigid dawn jogged to the shrubbery patch and dug into the sandy soil to dig out a length of the root he thought of as liquorice and to pick a few bunches of the berries. Fortunately, there seemed to be no shortage of either food source and the juice from the berries seemed to keep his thirst reasonably under control. As he first walked out, he was able to lick some of the frost off the leaves that covered the Speaker, and that made up for some more of the lack of water. Sometimes he wondered how his body was able to avoid feeling the cold, but he realised that the control was limited and by the time he had crept back into the shelter of his small home he was starting to shiver violently. Twice more he was able to bring down a couple of the tiny rabbit-like creatures, but eating them was a difficult, unpleasant and barely satisfying experience. He realised he was starting to despair of ever getting away from this place. But one discovery drove that worry away from his mind for a while.

The next morning, thinking that he could hold off the effects of the cold for a little longer, he decided to walk further than just the short distance between the berry patch and his shelter. He was young, extremely fit and he'd had no exercise for three days. He needed to walk, or preferably run. And run he did. He set off at right angles to his regular route, ran a furious kilometre, ran on the spot for five minutes looking around, then turned for home as the cold began to seep through him. But something caught his eye. It was a straight line in the ground and it teased him. This was a world where no machines had ever visited, where no intelligent life had ever been but for the immobile Speakers. A straight line was unlikely. Despite the cold he stopped and examined it. The line ran for some twenty metres and he walked to the end of it. It was curious.... he kicked away some of the dirt at the end of the line and the shock ran through him like a near miss of a car accident. The cold forgotten, he bent down, scratched away another few scoops of earth and was certain. The second line was at right angles to the first. This was the site of a building. Stunned, he stood up again, then realised he had just minutes to get into shelter before suffering possible frostbite. He was shivering violently before he was able to crawl into the warm spot of the Speaker's covering.

"Speaker, is there any possibility that other species have visited here?"

"Quite impossible. Why do you ask?"

"Examine my memories. I'm sure I just saw the outlines of what was once a building."

The silence lasted for a few seconds. The Speaker's shock when he spoke was evident.

"We have been a sentient species performing this role for over seven hundred thousand years, Mickie. Certainly no intelligent species has been here in that time, we would know. And anything older than that would have sunk several metres below ground in that time."

"Then I have to assume I was wrong, Speaker, maybe it was just a fluky line in the ground."

"Hard to imagine any other possibility, Mickie."

"Okay, let me talk to my parents, please."

When Grant came through, Mickie described the experience of his find.

Grant was thoughtful. "It sounds weird, kid, I must agree. I'd probably agree, it's just a fluke. Unless....."

"Dad? Unless what?"

"It's a crazy idea, Mickie, but if that had been a building and it had been equipped with a force field of some sort for protection, or maybe even a cloaking device like we use, it's possible that the field could have kept the erosion around it from having a real effect. Maybe the field finally died just in the last few decades, maybe centuries."

"But Dad, who could possibly have been here seven hundred thousand years ago, or more?"

"I've no idea, son. But forget that for now. Concentrate on finding out how you do that teleportation stuff. We want you back."

"Thanks Dad! I'll try. I want me back, too!"

* * * *

In the depths of the freezing night, he began to feel something new. Ghostly sensations entered his dreams, of extending his arms to distances way beyond his normal reaches, bending them in directions that were not possible to any human frame... With his mind he tried to reach out even further and then touch that strange space with his tenuously connected hands but he couldn't quite reach.... His dreams became coloured waves that crashed over his head, tiny wisps of sensation, of minute creatures nibbling at his skin, of even smaller pin-pricks, then he was deeper into the technicolour ocean, so deep his vision was altered by lights flickering, larger shapes that swam before him.... He saw a planet ahead of his vision, it seemed blue, beautiful... with his strangely developed arms he reached for that blue orb, somehow took hold of it and pulled himself.... And Mickie woke up.

He was not in the protective nest of the Speaker's covering, that much he knew. He was outside, but the air was not crushingly frozen as it had been on the Speaker's planet. He was sitting on grass, not the thorny, hard surface of the last few days, but softer, quite comfortable. It smelled familiar. Though dark, there was some light... moonlight! Though faint, it was definitely a moon, not the bright yellow moon that had delighted him back on Kalamos, but... he recognised the patterns of light and dark.

Mickie was back on Earth.

Chapter 6 – Return to Earth

He realised he was sitting cross-legged, just as he had been when he arrived after the last teleportation from Gelokk and he rose to his feet, trembling with the shock of the travel through unknown light-years and the realisation of where he was.

"Speaker 356, do you hear me?"

"Yes, Mickie. I sense that you have left. You must have worked out the teleportation sense."

"I think so. Can you connect me to my parents?"

Allie's voice was a delighted balm to his confusion. "Mickie, you're back on Earth?"

"Yes, can you please come and get me? I'm very frightened of what could happen here." He felt the tears starting and he struggled to keep his voice straight.

"Stand by just a few seconds, Mickie. Grant is just checking with the Captain.... Okay, it's four days to get there. Can you hang on?"

"I have to, Mum, I just have to. But I don't know what I'll do. I've got no money, no other clothes. I don't think I can hide here all that easily." His voice was starting to tremble again.

"I have a suggestion, son." Grant's pleasant, warm voice seemed to give strength to him, and he clung to the sound like a drowning surfer clings to his board.

"What do you think, Dad?"

"This may sound weird, Mickie, but I suggest you go home. To your old home, that is. Go back to your parents, pretend you don't know what happened, and somehow play along for four days. Once we're there, we'll come and get you."

The idea hit Mickie with utter dismay. The thought of returning to that ugly, smelly, violent household struck him with sheer repugnance. But in a few seconds, he saw the wisdom of his father's suggestion. He could probably pretend long enough, and at least there would be food and shelter.

"I think that's probably the best idea, Dad. But please come and get me as quickly as you can."

"Four days, son. And we'll talk as often as you want, and if we're tied up, you've got your friends to support you too."

"Yes, I know. And I'm right back at the spot where you first landed. I think I must have somehow directed myself here as the one familiar place I knew."

"Probably. And you couldn't have got yourself back to the ship while we were in hyperspace, so I think you did the soundest thing. One day, you'll learn how to control that talent. Hang in there, big guy, and we'll be there in four days."

Feeling stronger and more confident, Mickie cautiously found his way out of the woods where he had first entered the shuttlecraft in what seemed a previous lifetime. Once in the clear, the moonlight made it easy to navigate, and he strode firmly along the paths to the gateway, climbed over the fence and onto the road.

"*We will help you,*" said the icy voice in his head, and he stopped short, surprised by the sudden voice of the Spider in his head, but no longer frightened by the contact.

"How?"

"*We will induce such fear in your parents that they will obey you. Order them not to call the authorities, not to interfere in any way, and after that, they will not see you. If you stay in the house, you will not risk being seen by anyone who knew you.*"

Intrigued by the idea and by the Spider's ability to induce fear in someone's minds from such remote distances, Mickie set off at a run to get home. The first signs of dawn were lighting the sky to the east and he knew his one-time family would be rising soon. He almost smiled as he thought of the reception he would get, though it didn't reduce the loneliness and the yearning for his friends and new parents on the familiar surroundings of the Kaloti ship.

The house was dark when he reached it. He was almost shaking with the reaction of suddenly being so near to the horrible memories again, as well as the experience of having transported himself in some unknown way across many millions of light years. He tried to calm himself by reviewing in his mind the galactic charts he had studied and working out how far he had leaped, eventually concluding that it was about thirty million light years. As he approached the front door, a dreadfully familiar sound reached out to him. His one-time father's ugly, hacking cough resounded through the doorway and Mickie stepped back, a grimace of disgust on his face.

"Ye gods, I don't know that I can do this," he muttered to himself, standing a few metres away. Then he heard his mother's frantic coughing starting up, and both parents were soon into the all-too-familiar, revolting dawn chorus that had woken Mickie for so many years.

Movement a little down the street caught his eye, and he saw that the paper delivery was in process. The young boy carrying the bag and throwing rolled newspapers into the driveways would be at his door in a few moments and Mickie wanted nobody seeing him and possibly reporting his arrival to the authorities. He walked down the side of the house to the back gate, pushed it open, noticing that it had deteriorated severely in the months he had been away and bent down over the door mat by the back door where a key was usually kept. It was still there. Softly, he unlocked the door, opened it and walked into the dreadfully familiar, bleak kitchen.

He was ravenous. His diet over the last two days had been nothing but berries and the highly unpalatable little rabbits he had somehow managed to eat raw. Quickly, while still hearing the sounds of movement upstairs, he found a loaf of bread, some butter and cheese and made himself a thick sandwich that he wolfed down in seconds. It seemed to fill the gap and he felt strength returning to him. A glass of milk finished off the meal, which he decided in some amusement was probably the only meal he had ever enjoyed in this house.

He walked into the lounge room, his nose crinkling at the old smell of stale cigarettes. The furniture hadn't changed, it was still the same, shabby and battered sofa and two armchairs, all facing the old television set on its shaky stand. The brown carpet looked even more scuffed than he remembered.

"Good grief, how did I ever live here?" he asked himself, feeling tensions rise as the sounds of movement upstairs indicated someone was starting to descend the stairs. "I hope you're watching this, my friend Zlan," he said softly to the Spiders. "I'm going to need your help, like you promised."

He caught sight of a newspaper lying on the sofa that was his father's favourite spot for watching the television. Curious, he checked the date. The seventeenth of May! He had been star-travelling since July and he'd had a birthday in that time, completely unnoticed.

The door into the lounge opened and his mother walked in. She was still coughing, her head down as she tried to get her breath and she didn't immediately see him standing there. Mickie was horrified. She had aged many years, it looked to him, her skin was almost yellow and her hair a stringy, grey, rats' nest. The old green dress she was wearing looked like it had gone years between pressing and cleaning. She looked up and froze. Her eyes widened and her mouth fell open, but no sounds came out. Footsteps behind her indicated her husband was about to enter, and if Mickie had been dismayed by his mother's appearance, his father's made him wince.

The man was old and sick. Mickie remembered the nightmare of some weeks ago when he had struck out at him, and later discovered that he had indeed hurt him in some manner. He was stooped, wearing slippers, a flannel shirt and trousers that looked as if he had been camping in them for weeks. But Mickie's greatest shock was in realising that he stood at least as tall as did the man who had been his father. He must have grown more than fifteen centimetres in the months of his new life. Any traces of physical fear he might have felt vanished like smoke in a breeze. The smell of both adults hit him and Mickie recoiled.

"What.... What the hell are you doing here?" the old man finally said. The shock on his face made the unhealthy lines and grey skin even worse. The once dark hair had become as grey as his skin. The voice was a croak, hardly audible.

Mickie realised they were terrified, and with that realisation, all his anger vanished, leaving little but pity and disgust. Briefly he wondered if their fear was from his appearance or the promised influence of the Zlan.

"I'm home for four days," he said. "I need to stay here because I have nowhere else for that time. At the end of four days, I'll leave and I promise you will never see me again after that. But until then, you will leave me alone. I'll take what food I need and you will not, under any circumstances, tell anyone I'm here. Do you understand?"

They didn't move, just continued to stare at him, clearly badly frightened.

"If you try and hurt me, I'll do what I did to you before," he said pointedly at his father, though he privately doubted he could do anything violent to the pathetic specimen in front of him. "And I have to tell you, I have friends watching. Don't do anything you will regret and I'll be gone again soon."

He moved towards them intending to go up the stairs to his room. He realised he badly needed sleep. They gasped and flinched away. Sadly, he let them move clear of him and he walked out of the room.

As he climbed the stairs, his sister came down. Like his parents, she was too shocked to speak. Mickie repeated the instructions he had given his parents. She pushed herself against the wall as he continued up the stairs and entered his old room. It still had his bed, though it was unmade. It still had a single chair, but several boxes had been stored and there was little room for him to work his way to the bed.

He sat down, lifted his feet and sat cross-legged on the mattress. "Speaker 356, are you there?" he said softly.

"Yes, Mickie." He knew that the Speaker's mental transmission would not be audible.

"Put me in touch with my parents, please."

Immediately, Grant's voice came through. "Are you at your old home, son?"

"Yes, Dad. It's pretty horrible, but I think they'll leave me alone and not tell anyone I'm here."

"I'm sure of it, Mickie!" Allie's warm voice lifted his spirits even more. "We're on our way. We'll be in the park where we picked you up before in four days time, late in the evening, after dark. We'll tell you exactly when to come and join us. Can you manage?"

"It's going to be horrible," Mickie replied. "But it's what I used to live like and at least I know I'll be out of here soon."

"You're one tough kid, Mickie," Grant said. "The Speaker reported that you sounded very fatigued, so get some sleep. Will you be safe?"

"Without any doubt," he said, smiling broadly. "The Zlan said they'd take care of things."

"How will they do that?"

"They said they'd make sure my one-time family would be terrified of me."

Smiling at the obvious surprise that echoed over the empty light-years, Mickie lay back and relaxed completely.

* * * *

When he awoke, he struggled with contradictory thoughts. At first he felt he was still protected from the cold inside the leafy chamber of the Speaker's covering. Then he remembered his shock arrival back in the park where he had first met Allie, but assumed for a moment that it was just a dream. But his eyes snapped open as he sensed the bleak little room that had been his refuge from the rest of the smoke-stained house for so much of his life.

"Good grief, I really am here," he muttered aloud and for a second or two, felt a wave of panic that the whole episode of the last few months had been a dream. Immediately, he reached for his lifeline.

"Speaker 356?"

"Yes, Mickie?"

Relief washed over him like a warm shower. "Let me speak to my parents, please."

"Hey kid, how are you feeling there?" Grant's baritone voice was like the finest music in the world.

"Dad, I almost thought all my life with you had been a dream. It was horrible."

"I can imagine. But we're on our way."

"And we're getting you some help." Allie's voice chimed in to wash away the last shreds of fear in Mickie's mind.

"That would be nice! What sort of help?"

"Wait and see! You'll know when it comes!"

"Fantastic!" Mickie cheered up greatly. "I think I'll get up now and see what I can do with the day."

"Seems like a good idea," said Grant. "Call us again when you're alone."

"Will do!" Mickie got off the bed and stood up, realising he felt really grubby, having been in the same clothes for some days. Looking outside, he saw that the sun was setting, so he must have been asleep for hours since returning that morning. He opened the door and his nose wrinkled with the horribly familiar stench of stale cigarette smoke.

"Yeuch," he muttered and walked downstairs, wondering what he would find. He entered the lounge room, hearing the sounds of the television tuned to some game show and saw his one time family sitting as they always had, his father stretched out on the sofa, his mother and sister sitting in armchairs. Both parents had cigarettes in their mouths. Nobody moved when he walked in, but his newly developed senses told him that the level of fear and tension in the room had risen dramatically.

"Have you kept any of my old clothes?" he asked generally of the room.

His mother moved just a little. She flicked one frightened glance at him and waved her hands at the ceiling. "In the linen cupboard," she croaked, her voice barely audible.

"Thank you," said Mickie, trying to sound casual but feeling a mix of sadness and revulsion. He turned and walked back upstairs, finding the linen cupboard where he remembered it, by the bathroom. On the bottom shelf he found some underwear, a couple of old tee-shirts, but nothing else. Realising he would never have got into any of his trousers anyway, he took the clothing into the bathroom, firmly locked the door, then enjoyed his first wash in some days. Later, he donned fresh underwear and had no choice but to put back on his tunic, grateful that the material seemed capable of rejecting most of the dirt that would otherwise have clung to it. He returned to his room, concerned now about what to do. The night stretched ahead of him, but sleep was not required. He thought about going out, but while he knew he would face no risk of being recognised by anyone, so much had he changed, he wasn't sure about what he could do. For the first time, he realised that he faced a problem having no money of any sort. Shelving the problem for a while, he walked downstairs, through the smoke-filled lounge, wondering again how his sister put up with the stink and the smoke, entered the kitchen and made himself a sandwich, a glass of milk, and carried the meal back to his room.

Once back, he smiled, realising there was no difficulty about how to spend the time. Unlike everyone else on the planet, he could talk at will, at no cost and instantly to friends and acquaintances on planets separated by hundreds of thousands, even millions of light years.

Over the next few hours, he did just that, chatting to his friends and parents on the ship, to Zhumaton, the huge, three-armed cop on the planet of Kamotar with whom he had shared the adventure of rescuing the hostages taken by the rebel Smegandri, to the Speaker who had sheltered him and to the young X'Kasxi in whose house they had stayed and witnessed the birth of a young pup from a huge white egg.

Later, he heard his one-time family go to bed, hearing with pity the last hacking coughs of his parents before they finally fell asleep.

Some time before dawn, he fell asleep again, waking cheerfully to the realisation that he only had three more days before his real family came for him.

He walked down the stairs again, sensing there was nobody in the house. He tried spreading his awareness out past the house, a few hundred metres towards the shops, but found nobody that he recognised. He decided it must be a weekday and his father and sister would be at their regular places, while his mother had probably escaped from the house and the fear that was present for a few days. There was a brief, oddly familiar vibration from one mind that he touched, but as he turned back to try and relocate it, the doorbell rang.

Mickie froze, thinking that answering the door would be a silly thing to do.

"I think you should answer it," said a cheerful, unknown man's voice in his mind.

"What....?" Mickie was bemused.

"The door! Help has arrived, just like Alliandra promised!"

With delight, Mickie realised what had happened. He jumped to the door and flung it open to see a young man standing there with a wide grin on his face.

"Hello there, young Pfafth," said the man. "My name is Pallotar. Your parents said you needed some help!"

"But you look like my dad," Mickie said, sensing the warmth and friendliness. And he really did have the same strong, wiry build and thin face with slightly stuck-out ears of Grant.

"Quite possibly because he's my brother," said Pallotar. "Come on, let's get away from this stinking slum. I know the very place to go."

"What a great idea!" Mickie closed the door behind him and walked out into the fresh air. "You have no idea how pleased I am to see you!" he said.

"Oh, I think I do!" Pallotar replied with a laugh. "They've told me what's been happening to you."

"But where have you come from?" They walked briskly down the road and Pallotar led the way back to the park where Mickie had first met Allie.

"I've been on Earth for months. I'm one of Grantorel's agents on the planet, but I normally live in the USA, so it's taken a while for me to get here once Allie contacted me."

"I didn't realise! How many of there are you?"

"Three more. But the others were a bit busy, and anyway, I wanted to meet my new nephew!"

The thought warmed Mickie hugely. "Well, thank you, Uncle Pallotar," he said. "I've never had an Uncle before."

"Then we're both better off," said Pallotar and grinned down at him. "Alliandra said they do a great breakfast at some place in the park. Why don't you show us where?"

Ten minutes later, they were seated at the coffee shop where Mickie had always dreamed of ordering a luxury breakfast, enjoying scrambled eggs on toast.

It was a cheerful morning. They didn't talk about anything that might cause curiosity in any accidental eavesdropper and with the meal finished, they walked along to a park bench by the path.

"I can't stay," Pallotar said. "There's a lot of research I'm involved in, both in the USA and in Canada, and I need to be there to manage it, so I'm flying back to Washington in a few hours."

Disappointed, Mickie showed it. "I was hoping you'd be here until the ship arrived."

"I'd have liked that. I haven't seen my brother and sister-in-law since they left with you some months ago, but it will have to wait until the next trip. Meanwhile, though....." He reached into a pocket and pulled out an envelope. "Here's something to help you through the next two days. Don't open it now, but there's two hundred pounds there. You may want to buy something to wear, or the odd meal out."

Gratefully, Mickie pocketed the envelope. It eased a major problem for him.

Pallotar got to his feet. "I have to go," he said. "My flight leaves in about three hours. Luckily I was able to get a direct flight to Manchester, but I still have to go."

Mickie stood up, also. "I understand. It's been great. Maybe we'll meet again back on Kalamos."

"Count on it! Look after yourself, young nephew. Be careful these next two days." He wrapped his arms round Mickie and gave him a bear hug. "I know you'll find out who you are, big guy. We're all with you on this."

Not trusting his voice, Mickie nodded and sat down again, watching till Pallotar had disappeared into the distance. Loneliness threatened to overwhelm him, but he fought it off, sat in the mild Spring morning for a while longer, then decided to go to his favourite haunt, the local library, where he spent another few hours reading the newspapers to try and catch up with world news. By mid-afternoon, he began to think about setting off to return home, deep in thought about the huge voids in his history, his strange relationship with the Zlan, the massive spiders that had caused such fear in the beginning, the astonishing powers that were rapidly developing within him, and realising how much he was missing the life and companionship on the Kaloti ship.

"Hello, Mickie," said a familiar voice.

Astonished, Mickie snapped out of his reverie. Standing across from the reading table was another boy, about his own age, wearing the school uniform that Mickie had once worn. After a second or two, Mickie recognised him. It was his old friend Paul. He couldn't help himself, he was so delighted to see a friendly face.

"Paul! It's good to see you!" He stood up and reached out and seized his friend's hand, getting a firm, adult grip in response.

"Are you back with us, Mickie?" Paul sounded very serious. He had grown, Mickie realised, almost as much as Mickie had and seemed so much more adult than he remembered. Mickie saw that this conversation had to be very honest. He sat down again, and Paul took the seat across from him. There was nobody within hearing distance.

"No, Paul, not permanently. This is just a short visit and it wasn't intended."

"Where have you been? We've all been worried."

"I wish I could tell you, Paul. But it's far too complex."

"I'm not stupid, Mickie. Try me."

Mickie realised that Paul was angry with him and was not yet ready to be his friend again.

"I've been travelling," he said.

"Obviously. Where have you been?"

"You wouldn't believe me, Paul. Honest."

"Like I said, try me. You might be surprised."

Mickie took a deep breath. "Paul, I have to leave again in two days. You've got to promise that you won't tell anyone you've seen me."

The other boy nodded. His direct gaze into Mickie's eyes was quite disconcerting. "I promise. Nobody would want for you to go back to those bloody horrible parents of yours. But I wish you'd have told me where you were."

"Remember those talks we used to have? About life on other planets?"

"That's where you've been?" Mickie saw the astonishment in his friend's face, but Paul didn't lose his adult composure.

"Yes, that's where I've been. I met a couple of people..."

"The two they talked about in the news programs?"

"That's right. They're from a planet called Kalamos. They've adopted me."

"I think I believe you, but it's just too weird, Mickie. How can you travel to other planets?"

"Other planets? How about other *galaxies?*"

"Galaxies? Now I know you're pulling my leg. You can't travel between galaxies."

Mickie thought of something and decided that having Paul believe him and not think of him as a liar was too important. "Hang on a second Paul, I think I may be able to convince you."

He switched to sub-vocal conversation. "Speaker 356, will you connect me to my parents?"

"Hey, kid! We were just talking about you," said the cheerful voice of Grant. "Are you okay?" Mickie looked at Paul and realised that his friend had recognised that something beyond his comprehension was going on.

"I'm fine, dad. I met your brother this morning. He's great!"

"Yeah, he's a good little brother!" The chuckle was obvious in Grant's voice.

Deliberately, Mickie returned to normal speech, keeping his tones very low but audible to the young man across the table, though he would only hear one side of the conversation. "Dad, I'm sitting in the library with my friend Paul. He's recognised me, and I've told him where I've been."

"And he doesn't believe a word, huh?"

"I think he wants to. Can I prove it to him?"

"Mickie, there are very serious rules about revealing these things to races that don't know about us."

"I know, dad. But nobody would ever believe him, even if he tried telling people."

"Possibly. Stand by a few seconds, Mickie, I'm going to talk to the captain."

Paul broke his silence. "Who are you talking to? And how?"

"To my father. My new one, that is. He's on a ship still some light-years from here."

Paul was obviously struggling with this. "Light years? But *how?*"

"Mickie, still there?" It was Grant. Mickie raised his hand to Paul to signal him to wait. "Yes, dad," he said.

"The Captain will talk to you."

"Oh! Okay, that's a surprise."

The captain's calm, cool tone came through to him. It was the first time Mickie had talked to the Kaloti captain other than in brief meetings in the Captain's cabin or on the flight deck. "Mickie, do you trust this person?"

"Yes, Captain. Absolutely."

"We agree that nobody would believe him if he tried revealing the truth. So how do you plan to reveal our existence to him?"

"I thought I'd have Speaker 356 talk to him."

"That sounds reasonable. Alright Mickie, you have permission to tell your story to your friend and request Speaker 356 to communicate with him, if he can."

"Thank you, Captain."

He looked at his friend. "Paul, I want you to open your mind, just as if you were trying to listen to someone speaking very softly. Because in a few seconds someone is going to talk to you, right into your mind. His name is Speaker 356. Okay?"

Looking a little scared, Paul nodded.

"Speaker 356, you've been monitoring that conversation with the Captain?"

"Yes, Mickie. I have located your friend and will establish a link to him. Do you want to listen in to the conversation?"

"I think I'd better."

"Paul, this is Speaker 356."

Paul's face reflected nothing.

"Keep trying," Mickie said. "He's talking to you now. Just relax and open your mind to anything you hear."

"Paul, this is Speaker 356."

This time, Paul heard it. His eyes opened wide and he let out a small gasp of astonishment. "Who are you?" he whispered.

"We are a telepathic race that allows people all over the Universe to talk to each other. Mickie has been telling you the truth. He has travelled to many planets in several galaxies, even to my own planet."

For a few moments, the Speaker talked to Paul who slowly eased his tensions and fear and became more entranced by what he was hearing. The Speaker ended the conversation and left the two boys alone. They stared at each other, Paul obviously adjusting his perceptions of his old friend.

"That's just *astounding,*" he said. "How I envy you!"

"The ship gets here in two days. They'll send a shuttle for me. Why don't you come with me? It's a fabulous life on board, and lots of really great kids to meet."

Paul look stunned for a few seconds, then shook his head. "Mickie, I'm not like you. I love my parents and my brother and sister. Earth is my home. I can't leave it."

Mickie realised the truth of that. Then he grinned with delight as he realised something wonderful. "But do you realise we can now talk to each other, regardless of where I am? The Speaker told you, using his telepathic powers, it's instantaneous, regardless of distance."

Paul laughed, his cheerfulness responding to the idea. "Promise me you'll do that," he said.

"You can do it yourself, any time," Mickie said. "Now that the Speaker has met you, you can always talk to him. Just ask for Speaker 356, he'll respond."

"Mickie, you'll never know what you've done for me," Paul said, standing up. "I have to get home. I actually look forward to dinner with my family!"

"So do I, now that I've got a new one!"

"If I ever change my mind and want to come travelling with you, do you think I can?"

"I would think so. Tell me when you're ready and I'll find out when we can come and get you."

"That's wild!" Paul reached out and they shook hands, more enthusiastically than they had done before. "Goodbye for now, then," he said.

"Take care, Paul," said Mickie. "See you in a few years again."

Paul waved and walked out. Regretfully, Mickie decided he should do the same and return to the awful place that was his shelter for another two days.

Somehow, he managed it. While the house was horrible, at least his family left him alone, seeming terrified the whole time. Sometimes, Mickie wondered whether their fear resulted from something the Zlan were doing as they had promised, or just from Mickie's own influence and enormous change from frightened boy to mysterious and dangerously powerful enigma.

He went outside rarely, thinking that if Paul had recognised him, so might someone else, and having to face the police or any other authority would have been a serious problem. So a quick walk to the shops to buy a pair of jeans and some shirts was one small outing, and when he changed out of his tunic he was amused to find the small bag that Zhumaton, the huge three-armed Kamotari had given him as they left the planet. Mickie had tucked it away at the time, still recovering from the stresses of that trip and the narrow escape he and his friends had made as he had discovered the frightening power to kill by mental thunderbolts. Now he opened it, and was momentarily dazzled by the gleam of four diamonds, each the size of his thumbnail. He smiled, realising he was carrying many thousands of pounds worth of jewellery with him, as casually as other people carried small change.

He bought some food at the supermarket, not trusting the memories of the small grocery shop he had occasionally used, where the owner had seemed friendly and might recognise him, even changed as he was. He refused to cook in the kitchen of the house, preferring to sit in the garden with a meat pie and a soft drink, dreaming of the moment he could join his friends in the coffee lounge on the ship and again enjoy the delicious coffee from the planet of Mayoowani. And on the last day, when he anxiously waited from the call to say the shuttle was on its way to pick him up, he treated himself to breakfast alone in the café in the park.

And at last, the call came.

"We'll touch down in the same spot as before, just after dark, Mickie," said Grant's welcome voice, as Mickie was sitting in the garden.

"Fantastic!" said Mickie, feeling a huge weight of worry falling from him. "I'll be there."

He went back up to his room. Having washed his tunic by hand, it was ready to put back on, and he did so, quickly feeling the sensation of returning to his ship-board life. He walked downstairs, realising that this time he was truly leaving the house for the last time. There was nobody in the place at all, his sister being at school and his father at work. His mother had left also, as she had done the last three days, probably too frightened to face Mickie as he came and went. He wondered where she spent the time.

He found a pen and a sheet of paper. With a smile, he wrote *"Thank you for all your help"* and left the paper in the middle of the dining table. He reached into his pocket and pulled out the money his uncle had left him. There was still over seventy pounds there. He took a twenty pound note and tucked it back into his tunic thinking he'd need a couple of bottles of soft drink while he waited for the shuttle, and left the rest on the table. Then he grinned and took the packet of diamonds out of his pocket. Carefully he eased one of the huge stones out onto the table, placed it on the farewell note and wondered just how much it was worth. Certainly more than the room and board of the last three days, probably several times more than the house, he decided and laughed out loud. Then he walked out of the house for the very last time. He went back to the park, bought two bottles of orange juice then walked deep into the woods where the shuttle would touch down, cloaked into invisibility. He found a spot well covered by bushes, sat down and patiently waited to resume his star travels.

Just after nine, with darkness well installed over the country, the warm, wonderful voice of Allie sounded in his ears, this time not transmitted by the Speaker on his cold, windy and bleak planet so many millions of light years away, but by the Ship's own computer.

"We're on the last few hundred feet, kid! We have you positioned, so don't move until we tell you."

Mickie simply chuckled, too happy to speak, and lifted his face to the darkness, only barely illuminated by the thin curve of the new moon. A few moments later, he saw the tops of the trees rustle as if a small breeze had raced through them, and a couple of branches bowed as some huge, invisible shape pushed them aside.

The green light of the doorway lit up the small clearing and Mickie jumped to his feet and ran as fast as he could back into the welcome of his new life.

Chapter 7 - The Blood Sacrifices of Drudyenko

"This place sounds really weird and really scary!" Drellion looked most unhappy as he sat with his sister and parents across from Mickie, Allie, Grant and Fencris, whose red eyes glowed with a rather dull shine, indicating his own concerns and worries about this planetary visit. The shuttle had left the main ship in orbit a few minutes ago. Grant was in his usual pose, stretched out with his eyes closed as he piloted the shuttle through the devices implanted in his body. These tiny items gave him direct control over the propulsion and directional guidance systems of the shuttle through his mental instructions. Mickie had asked when he could have these devices implanted to let him pilot a shuttle, and had been disappointed to learn that he had to stop growing before it could be done, so he probably had two or three more years to wait.

Harrokarn and Mendorina, the parents of Melkana and Drellion occupied the other two seats.

"It's certainly an unusual combination of cultures," Harrokarn agreed. "It's the only place in our travel circuits where a highly technical civilisation practices such primitive religious rites. We will all have to be careful here."

"So why are even visiting such a horrible place?" Melkana asked, her usual energy rather subdued.

"Trade and diplomacy both," Harrokarn replied. "For all their strangely primitive culture, they are superb chemists. They produce liquids, gases and materials that facilitate many of the advanced engineering industries on several planets. We exchange those for the minerals we picked up on X'Katcxo as well as the product everyone wants, the drugs from Spider World."

"Zlan," Mickie said. "They call it Zlan, and they are the Zlan also."

A short silence echoed in the shuttle. Mickie's ability to communicate with the Spiders and his growing ease with the connection was the one aspect of his developing powers that made them all a little uncomfortable.

"Er... yes, Zlan," Harrokarn said. "After all these years of calling it Spider World, it takes some getting used to, giving it a name. Still, it looks like the Zlan are more friend than enemy. I wish we could say the same about the people of Drudyenko."

"The local language is programmed into our computers," Allie chimed in. "So communication is not a problem. But one of the very weird things about this place, one of the *many* very weird things, I should say, is that the language has several similarities to Russian, on Earth. The name they have given it sounds more Georgian, but the language definitely seems to have common roots with Russian. It's another of those strange mysteries suggesting some relationships between the intelligent species that are yet to be uncovered."

Mickie had heard this in his briefing from Albert the night before, and it intrigued him. But the illustration of the rituals that were part of Drudyenko horrified him and he shared the worries that the other three children had all expressed.

"I don't think we'll be running off on our own, this time," he said with an attempt at a carefree grin that didn't quite work.

"No, I expect not," Allie said with a smile that took in all four of the children. "To be honest, we had seriously considered leaving you behind on this visit, but we decided that Mickie's interesting powers might be useful, and therefore all of you should be here for his support. And it's also a fact that all of you have wanted to learn about all the intelligent races we deal with, and your parents' careers involve dealing with them. So when you all said you wanted to come, we agreed."

"We're down," Grant murmured, opened his eyes and stood up. "We have a delegation waiting outside. They'll take us into the central building. We're in the World Capital City of Teekograt, which I'm told means Peaceful City. Let's hope so."

Feeling a huge desire that his father was right, Mickie stood up with the rest of the party as the door to the outside slid open. Letting the adults go first, Mickie stood with his friends at the side of the door and looked out at the city of Teekograt. It looked almost oriental, as on Earth, was Mickie's first thought. Tall spires, with what looked like a small room and a balcony at the top seemed everywhere. The sight niggled at his mind, and he decided to try for a solution. "Albert, do those towers look like anything on Earth?" he asked mentally. The ship's computer answered at once.

"Indeed they do," said Albert. "They closely resemble the minarets of Islamic Mosques. The room at the top is where the call for prayer is sounded. Here on Drudyenko, something similar occurs, when the local priests call the population to one of their rituals. However, more oddly, if you look further to your right, when you can, you will several highly coloured towers looking like an onion shape. It has been noted that the building is almost a twin for the famous Saint Basil's Church in Moscow."

Mickie carefully edged himself a little further out of the door as the last of the adults walked out and looked for the building. It was only about half a kilometre away and he saw it just as Melkana laughed out loud and pointed at it.

"Will you look at that place!" she said. "That has to be the weirdest building I've ever seen."

Mickie decided he agreed with her. It looked like a series of multi-coloured onions sitting a series of towers, with the main building below being an odd mix of pink and white stone.

"Maybe we can get a look in there later on," he said. "We should probably join our parents though." He set off down the walkway and the four children walked towards the four adults where they were standing talking to a trio of the locals. Mickie studied them intently, fascinated by people who could do the sort of things Albert had briefed him on. They looked perfectly human, he decided immediately. They could have been any group of people standing in St. Anne's Square in Manchester. But as he got closer, he felt a sense of coldness in them and was repelled by it.

"I don't think I like these people," he muttered to Drellion who was nearest to him.

"Nor me," Drellion replied. "I don't like the whole place. I'll be glad when we're done here. And I don't think I want to go off on our own, the way we've done on other worlds."

Melkana and Fencris moved closer, hearing the muttered conversation. They were still a distance further from the locals, the Drudya as Mickie had learned they were called, and Mickie preferred to keep it that way.

"Yes, I think this is not a place for exploring," Melkana said. "It gives me the creeps. I've brought my flute along, and I think I'll just practice that while we wait for our parents to get done."

"And if you don't mind, I'll stick around and listen," Mickie said. "You promised you'd play for me some time and this sounds like a good opportunity."

"Damn right," agreed Fencris. "I'm glad it's just a one-day visit. We should be off this slum by tonight."

"Children!" The call came from Allie. A small bus-like vehicle had arrived, and she was gesturing for them all to board. Still feeling uneasy, Mickie joined the rest and climbed aboard. The three Drudya were already seated at the front of the bus and as Mickie walked past them he was acutely aware that all three were staring at him. Rapidly, he moved to the rear where his friends had all instinctively moved as if to distance themselves as much as possible from the locals.

"Melkana's right," Fencris said in a low voice. "These weirdos give me the creeps big-time."

Nodding, Mickie turned to look out of the window as they drove further into the city. Oddly enough, despite the coldness Mickie had sensed, the streets looked festive. Garlands of flowers hung across the sidewalks, coloured flags flew in the stiff breeze and huge banners hung from many windows along the road. At the front of the bus, the adults were deep in conversation, but one of them must have raised the topic of the decorated scenery, because Mickie received a sub-vocal message from Albert.

"Mickie, your mother advises you that the Feast of Grushkarin is being held this week, and public celebrations will end with the major ceremonies tonight. Your presence is apparently requested and diplomacy demands that you all attend."

"What's the Feast of Grushkarin?" Mickie asked.

"I don't have that information," Albert responded calmly.

The others must have received the same information. Melkana looked worried.

"Does that mean what I think it means?" she whispered. "And we have to *watch* it?"

"I'm sure of it," Mickie replied. "This is awful."

A silence fell on the group as the drive continued for another few minutes. They passed a huge building that resembled one massive, black brick, a complete city block in length, with no windows or doors that Mickie could see.

"Albert," he said to the computer in silent speech directly to his communications device. "Could you ask my parents to ask the locals what that huge monster is?"

He watched the adults at the front of the bus as Allie received the silent query and repeated it to one of the Drudya. In a moment, the reply came.

"The Drudya call it the Hall of Power," Albert said. "But Allie's attempts to gain more information were blocked. She says the question seemed to cause some disturbance in the locals."

Mickie watched as the enormous shape disappeared as they turned a corner. Something about the building worried him in a way he could not identify. But as they stopped in front of another large building, apparently a hotel, he took his mind away from the forbidding image of the black construction.

"We'll check in first," said Grant as he waved the kids forward to the exit door. "Then you youngsters can relax a bit as we have a meeting with the trading delegates. Grab a meal, have a look around if you like, and we'll meet up in two hours to prepare for this festival thing."

"I don't think we'll wander around," Melkana said firmly. "We'll stay inside."

"I understand," Grant said with a sympathetic smile. "This place is a bit spooky, I agree."

With all checking-in formalities completed, the adults left again, and the four friends gathered in one of the rooms, staying together as much from a need for mutual support against the overall threatening atmosphere that they all sensed in this place as for common friendship. Grant had already ordered a meal sent up to the room, so they sat on the floor, on cushions, or on various items of furniture, experimented with the food and drank the sweet lemonade that was available in the room's refrigerator.

"What *is* this stuff, anyway?" Fencris said, sniffing with great suspicion at a bowl of black substance. Mickie leaned over and examined it, taking a similar sniff.

"You know what, I think it's caviar!" he said in astonishment. "I've never tasted it before!"

"What's caviar?" Fencris seemed unimpressed.

"Fish eggs. I think I read that it was a real snobby thing to eat back on Earth, very expensive and it came from

Russia. Allie did say this place seemed very Russian in its culture."

He spooned some out onto a slice of thick bread and pushed it into his mouth. It was salty and quite delicious, he decided.

"This is absolutely *splendiferous!*" he exclaimed. "You should try it!"

Melkana and Drellion took a small sample but were obviously uninterested in seconds. Fencris wrinkled his nose and declined, and Mickie chuckled.

"More for me, then," he said, and took the bowl from the table and placed it by his side where he was sitting on the floor and proceeded to eat the lot.

Meanwhile, the others explored the contents of the entire table that had been wheeled in and worked their way through various dishes, some of which met with great approval, others that didn't. But the greatest success of the afternoon was when Drellion opened the sealed canister.

"Ice-cream!" he said with delight. "Now that's more like it!"

And there was no doubt it was the best ice-cream Mickie had ever eaten. They spooned large quantities into bowls and sat back to enjoy the feast, discovering that the sweet lemonade made a wonderful addition to the taste.

Then followed an experience that Mickie had awaited with interest. Melkana went to her bag and pulled out an instrument that really seemed identical to a flute from Mickie's memories. Fencris chuckled at the sight.

"I heard from Drellion that you were bringing that, so I brought my Cangrar pipes!"

"That's wonderful!" Melkana seemed delighted. "You play those really well! Come on, then, let's get started!"

Fencris crawled over to his bag and pulled out a small case. He opened it and extracted a device that looked to Mickie like a miniature bagpipes, but instead of a loose bag, it had a rectangular box with keys on it, a single pipe with a mouthpiece and just three smaller tubes that sprouted from the box.

Mickie leaned back and listened with interest. Fencris opened the impromptu concert, the sound being a low, lovely tone that seemed to express great emotion. Melkana listened for a few moments then placed her flute to her lips and began playing. Mickie was astounded. The music was quite beautiful and the two instruments combined superbly in a melody that brought tears to his eyes. He looked over at Drellion and was not surprised to see a similar response in the youngest boy's face. He closed his eyes and let the notes flow over and through him, sensing great emotions play in his body.

Even though he didn't open his eyes when the music was over, he sensed the warmth in the room and the response of all of them.

"It's called *'Harokarl's Lament'*" said Drellion softly. "Harokarl was one of the great warriors of our land. He died about four hundred years ago in a war that gave our nation its freedom. Our dad is a direct descendent of his."

"It's.. *astounding,*" said Mickie, opening his eyes. "I had no idea you played so beautifully, either of you."

"Hey, I'm just a beginner compared to this lass," said Fencris with a grin. "She's the winner of piles of awards and stuff."

"You are?" Mickie was not really astonished to hear that. "You never told me."

Melkana smiled with a shy warmth. "I've won a few prizes," she said.

"Yeah, right!" Drellion laughed. "My big sister is the winner of the national and world championship for the flute. Every orchestra on Kalamos has offered her a place in their organisations, and she's already been given scholarships at the best universities."

Melkana blushed, and put the flute back to her lips, playing something totally different from the last emotional piece. This one was almost an Irish Jig, full of life and movement, and all three boys had their toes tapping to the lilt, while Fencris joined in after a few bars. The melody seemed to wipe the dark mood that the planet of Drudyenko had loaded on them earlier and the impromptu concert continued for another hour before they broke and returned to the marvellous ice-cream to finish it off.

As they licked the last of it from their spoons, the adults returned. Allie and Grant came in first, for it was their room that was being used by the kids, and they laughed as they saw the scene.

"I tell you what, Allie," Grant said with a laugh. "These kids have had more fun that we've had, I reckon."

"I think so," Allie agreed. "Kids, you have no idea what a miserable, cold bunch these Drudya are. That was just one *depressing* meeting!"

"That's why we stayed inside," Fencris said. "We all thought there was something creepy about the place."

"There is," Grant said firmly. "This is our second visit, and it seems a lot worse than the last time. Our worlds have only been trading with Drudyenko for about five years and I rather wish we'd never started."

"But they really do what you told us?" Melkana looked

more disturbed than Mickie had seen her under normal circumstances.

"I'm afraid so," Allie replied. "And it's pointless of anyone to try and stop it. It's their culture. All we can do is hope they change as their contacts with other worlds increase and the pressures of disapproval work on them."

"So what's the program for the rest of the day?" Mickie asked.

"Strictly social and political," Grant said. "We finished the business stuff this afternoon. So there's a small ceremony in the Town Hall, then the last night of the Feast of Whoever-it-is."

"That's the bit we're scared of," Fencris said. "Do we really have to go?"

"I'm afraid you do," Allie said, her voice reflecting firmness but also some sadness. "Local culture here is most strict and they'd be highly offended if anyone missed the proceedings. So, whatever we may all feel about this, we have to be there."

"Oh Lord, this is awful," Melkana muttered.

"Yes it is. But essential, so all you kids go to your own rooms, put on something more formal and meet back here in thirty minutes."

Obediently, if reluctantly, they did as requested and half an hour later, the group descended back into the main lobby of the hotel. The area was full of locals, most talking in some excitement, presumably, Mickie thought, about the festivities that had been running all week and were due to finish with the climactic events of this evening. Mickie had acquired a formal suit in the style of Kalamos during the vacation on the home planet and this was his first opportunity to wear it. It was not unlike the mess-kit that military officers in England wore on ceremonial dining-in nights, as he had once seen in a television documentary about the cadets at the Royal Air Force Academy. Close-fitting trousers in dark blue and a military-cut, short, white jacket of the style known as "bum-freezers" because it came down only to just below the waist and a black, polo-necked shirt, all felt very trim and masculine to him, and he was well aware of the admiring smile that Melkana had given him. That, plus the expected and received snorts of friendly derision that the two boys emitted made him feel pretty cheerful, and this drove the black thoughts of what they might see this evening from his mind.

As they walked through the crowded hotel lobby, he remembered the melodic jig that Melkana and Fencris had been playing earlier and began humming the melody. The other kids grinned and joined him, making variations on the tune as they walked. But Grant's warning hand on Mickie's shoulder stopped him and the other three also went silent as they realised something serious was happening in the hotel lobby. The conversations had stopped throughout the area. People had moved rapidly away from Mickie's group, they had pressed against the walls, some had run out into the open. Here and there, sounds of sobs and moans as if in pain came from individuals and all the faces Mickie could see reflected anguish, horror, even great fear. On further glances round the lobby, Mickie saw that some had even fainted and were lying unconscious on the floor or in armchairs.

"What's going on?" he muttered to Grant.

"I don't know," his father replied softly. "Allie's trying to see if either the Speaker or the ship's computer can explain it."

"There's nothing," Allie murmured. "Nobody can explain this reaction."

"I think we'd better be going," Grant said, and gently steered the group towards the front door of the hotel. Outside, a transport vehicle was waiting and they climbed aboard, Mickie looking once more back at the astonishing scene in the hotel lobby. As they moved away, Allie seemed to focus back on the people inside the vehicle.

"I've been trying to find out more," she said. "None of the sources we have can explain what happened."

"I think it was the music," Melkana said. "As soon as we started humming the tunes we'd been playing in the room, everybody seemed to go crazy."

"That's right," Fencris chimed in. "Mickie started humming '*Harokarl's Lament,*' we joined in, and then the stuff hit the fan."

"It's a fact," Grant added thoughtfully. "We've heard no music of any kind on this planet. Nothing on the radio, no bands, no singing, nothing."

"Can music really cause that sort of reaction?" Drellion asked. "That's weird!"

"You know, it reminds me a bit of being back on Merrison," Melkana said. "Remember how the witch-hunters were so screaming mad about the music there? They were absolutely out of their skulls with rage!"

"And we all know what happened with the Sillaron when it invaded the Ship. I think we killed it with the music."

A small silence echoed round the cabin of the bus.

"Oops!" said Allie, softly. "The plot thickens, I suspect."

"Allie, where are we going?" Fencris changed the subject, sensing the twinge of worry that ran round the vehicle. The escape from the bloodthirsty furies of the witch-hunters had been a terrifying episode enough, while the dreadful pillar of smoke called the Sillaron had held the whole Ship's crew hostage for a while.

"We have to attend a small reception at the City Hall," Allie replied. "This is just a little ceremony to seal the trade deal we settled today, and then must go out for the final stages of the Festival."

"I really wish we didn't have to do that," Melkana said. "The whole thing is just too horrible."

"That's the trouble with being inter-planetary traders," Grant said. "Cultures vary, some civilizations have practices that really make us ill, but we have to live with it. I imagine we do stuff that drives some cultures into a fury of repulsion, but we have to learn how to deal with it all. We can't try and make everybody like ourselves."

Melkana nodded, saying nothing, but all four children felt a sense of dread about what was to happen that evening.

The vehicle stopped outside an imposing, if rather uninspiring building of massive proportions. Mickie felt some disturbance at the sight of the armed troops lined up to meet them, but Grant touched him lightly on the shoulder.

"Consider it an Honour Guard," he said. "I doubt those rifles are actually loaded."

"I really hope not," Mickie said with a forced smile, and followed his father with the others into the building. They walked across a spacious entrance hall covered with white tiles that echoed under the feet of the visitors, and another uniformed guard opened the double doors leading into a smaller room where seven locals were standing, apparently waiting for them.

The adults led the way in, and the locals moved to greet them, very formally it seemed, for no smiles of welcome were evident. Sounds of introduction started as the four children followed, largely ignored by the dignitaries. Mickie was the last to walk in and he stood quietly by the door, looking at the dull, undecorated walls of the chamber, wondering why there was not a single picture, no alleviating colour at all. It was a truly depressing room, he decided.

But as the other three children moved away from him to join their parents, the room went silent with an abruptness that shook Mickie from his inspection of the surrounds. He lowered his eyes from the walls and looked around.

Every one of the locals was staring at him. Their expressions varied from shock to outright fear and Mickie felt the first wave of worry gnaw at his insides.

"Who... what is this person?" growled one of the locals. Even through the translator in his shoulder, Mickie heard the appalled fear and hatred in the man's voice. He moved close to his parents and felt some comfort as both of them placed a hand on his shoulders.

"This is our son, Mickie," Grant replied.

Silence rang like a bell through the chamber. The dignitaries stood motionless for a few moments, then moved away from the visitors and gathered closely for a muttered conversation. Mickie tried to expand his awareness to hear what they were saying, but although he succeeded in hearing the voices, they seemed to have switched languages, for his translator was unable to give him a clue as to what was being said.

"They're using another language that the computer can't recognise," he whispered to his parents. Switching to sub-vocal speech, he tried the ship's computer. "Albert, can you recognise this other language? Include the others in the group with your reply."

"No, Mickie, I cannot," Albert replied. "I am unable to identify a single word, or find any resemblance to any other humanoid language in my programming."

"This is all very weird," Allie said softly. "None of our research or previous visits has given any indication of this problem, nor of the existence of another language. What is it about Mickie that has so disturbed them? And did you notice their speech patterns? I've just realised what's been bugging me all day. Their tones are dead flat. There's hardly a change of pitch or volume throughout their entire speech. That's what's so boring and irritating about the place."

Before anyone could reply, the locals broke away from their discussion and moved back towards the visitors.

"It is time to see the festivities," the apparent leader said, not looking at Mickie and still obviously suffering serious tension. Now that Allie had mentioned it, Mickie realised what she meant. The man had spoken in a flat, even tone with hardly a variation, as if a computer had spoken without programming.

Puzzled and considerably worried at the abrupt change in the planned schedule of the evening, the group followed the locals outside, past the line of armed guards and back into their bus. The driver seemed to know what to do, because he started the engine and set off behind the leading vehicle containing the local dignitaries.

"I've just talked to the Captain," Grant said. "He's sending down a shuttle with a squad of armed troops. They'll stay inside the shuttle until we call, then they'll be ready for anything, but I have to say, something very weird is going on."

"I still think it's somehow connected to Merrison," Mickie said. "For some reason, my appearance has scared hell out of them. Do you think they know I'm Pfafth? And it frightens them?"

"It's the most likely explanation," Grant agreed. "Stay very close together, this evening, everyone, and keep an eye on Mickie."

Nods all round greeted this comment, but Mickie didn't see that. He was trying another option and attempting to communicate with the Speaker, but without success. This increased his worry.

"Allie, Grant, I can't contact a Speaker. Can you?"

After a few seconds, Grant replied. "No, neither of us can. Something is very wrong here. But we can still talk to the Ship."

The vehicle stopped and Mickie ceased his attempts to communicate and looked around him. They had parked just a few yards from the massive, black, featureless building that had raised his anxiety levels earlier in the day. A huge crowd had gathered and it filled the area of the city square, kept away from Mickie's group and the local dignitaries by a sizeable squad of armed police who lined a roped-off cordon around the area immediately by the building. Right in front of the new arrivals, a raised platform stood, some ten metres on each side and about a metre high. One the platform was a solid, rectangular block of what looked like jet-black stone. It was about two metres long, a metre high, perhaps the same wide. One single access route led to this scene, a straight road that went for a few hundred metres to another massive building. The atmosphere seemed festive, but Mickie could not stop the sense of dread lapping at the edges of his mind.

At a signal from the locals, Mickie and his party took seats that had been laid out for them in the cleared area. Mickie sat in the second row, next to Melkana, with Drellion on his right, the four parents further to his left the other side of Melkana. Curiously, he watched as the dignitaries approached the line of seats in front of Mickie. They stopped short at the sight of him, appeared to confer for a moment, then sat down, the rigidity in their postures indicating the tension they were so obviously feeling. It clashed badly with the air of festivity that was going on in the crowds behind them

But the atmosphere changed abruptly. One massive, single drumbeat echoed through the square and the crowd fell silent. On the platform in front of Mickie, six men appeared, dressed in pure white robes with gold chains around their necks. The headgear they wore was impressive. Mickie decided the hats were at least half a metre tall, in bright red, with silver bands on them. The bands varied in number between one and six, the last appearing on only one of the men who seemed to be leader, judging by the large gold staff he was carrying.

"We are assuming that these are priests," Allie's voice spoke within his head, transmitted directly from the ship's computer. "As you might gather, the one with the six bands on his hat seems to be the head priest."

A loud murmur broke out in the crowd behind them and attention seemed to be drawn to the road coming into the square from the right. Mickie leaned forward and stared up the road. A procession was approaching. As it neared, Mickie saw that it was led by a single drummer, beating a drum hanging from his side with a single hammer in a rhythm that defined the pace of the steps. It was slow, deliberate pace that raised the hair on the back of Mickie's neck. And the tone of the drum was unlike anything he had heard before. It was flat, dull, without any musical quality to it at all. Behind the drummer was another bunch of priests, dressed much as the men on the platform were. Behind them were two lines of men, dressed in white robes but without the priestly hats or chains. The lines walked about two metres apart, and Mickie counted fifteen men in each line. In between them was a figure that immediately seized Mickie's attention. It was a young woman, perhaps in her late teens and even from the distance of perhaps fifty metres, it was clear that she was astonishingly beautiful. She was dressed in a long robe of a golden fabric, and she wore a hat made up of brightly-coloured flowers with another garland of white blooms round her neck, stretching down to her waist. Under the head-dress, her long black hair hung down her back. She was barefoot, but walked with pride, her head held high, her back very straight.

The sense of horror deepened within Mickie, but before he could say anything, Fencris spoke for him, his words transmitted like Allie's, in sub-vocal speech.

"Everyone, this is terrible," Fencris said. "I really don't want to see this."

"We have to, son," his father replied in the same way. "We're visitors on the planet and we must allow them to lead their lives as they wish."

"But they're going to..."

"We know what they are going to do," his father said firmly. "Show courage, my son. We represent our species here, as well as all the space-going races of the Universe."

"Mother, are they really...?" Melkana's words held a trembling note and Mickie knew she was near to tears.

"I'm afraid so, my daughter. Show courage, it will be over soon."

Mickie stretched his awareness out as he had learned to do in recent months and touched the mind of the young girl approaching in the parade. To his surprise, he found, in addition to the vein of terror that was running through her, a strong rush of pure exhilaration. She was actually proud of what was to happen. In a single instant of understanding, he read that she had been chosen by the priests exactly a year ago this day. For the past year, she had been the Queen of this civilisation, living in total luxury, worshipped by the population and granted the power of complete authority over them. Quickly, he passed this information to the others.

The procession had reached the platform, and just four of the priest accompanied the young woman up the steps where she appeared, standing by the black slab in the middle. A loud sigh ran through the watching crowd. Two of the priests approached the woman and bent down to their knees, their heads bowed in apparent subservience to her. Then they rose, lifted her and laid her out on the slab as total silence fell on the onlookers. Mickie felt himself begin to tremble and he reached for Melkana's hand just as she did the same for his. The remaining priests began a rhythmic chant, the words not identifiable to Mickie. From somewhere, the head priest produced a large, curved knife. He stood in front of the body of the woman, raised the knife above his head, then screamed in a dreadfully loud voice. The knife fell, plunging into the ribs of the woman. Her body jerked horribly, the priest dragged the knife upward to her neck, then reached down with one hand, groped inside the body and pulled out a bloody mass of flesh. The crowd yelled with one voice.

"Oh God, it's her heart," Melkana cried, and leaned forward over her knees to hide from the sight.

"Mickie, I have information for you," said the cool, unemotional voice of Albert in his head. The sound cut through the trembling and horror in Mickie's mind and he gratefully switched his attention from the appalling scene on the platform.

"Your mother asked me to run a search on any similar rites known to us, and in fact, there is a very similar ritual that was once carried out on Earth in the Mayan civilisation. The young person who was just slaughtered was chosen by the priests a year earlier, and it was a massive mark of honour for her and her family. For that year, she was the Queen of the entire planet with huge authority to rule as she wished, and it was believed that the Gods would punish any who disobeyed her. Her death was a ritual that sent her to join the Gods as one of them, and her family will be rich and honoured for their whole lives. However horrible it looked, this ritual actually provides a stabilising influence on the society. A new Queen was crowned this morning."

"Thank you, Albert," Mickie replied, understanding now how he saw such pride in the girl's mind as she prepared for an awful death.

On the platform, the girl's body had been lifted on a stretcher and carried off by several young men who joined with the line of the parade that had brought the group here. The single drum beat started again and the parade began to return in the direction from which it had come.

Allie's voice replaced Albert's in his mind.

"It is interesting that the parade is totally without music," she said. "Any parade in almost any culture would normally have some sort of musical accompaniment, but not here. I believe it has some connection to the effect that the kids' singing had, back in the hotel. It appears that music is something terrifying to this culture and I must try and find out more. Anyway, it is time to leave this dreadful scene."

The dignitaries at the front had stood up, and gratefully, Mickie did the same as the whole group followed suit. Melkana still had a tight grip on his hand, and he could feel her trembling. She still had her face turned down as if unwilling to look up and see the blood still running off the platform.

"Are you okay?" he asked gently. She shuddered once, and murmured something he couldn't catch then looked down at their clasped hands as if astonished to see them.

"I'll be fine," she said. "Once the computer told me what the real story was, I suppose I understood a bit. It's still a horrible thing, though, and I can't wait to get off this planet."

To Mickie's regret, she pulled her hand away and moved forward to join her parents who put their arms on her shoulders as if to comfort the child. Mickie turned back to the platform where the nightmare scene had occurred. Surprised and a little disturbed, he saw that four of the priests were standing motionless, staring at him. There was huge hostility and perhaps some fear in their steady glare. Mickie tried to reach into their minds but found that he couldn't, instead encountering the same blank wall, an absence of anything detectible that he had experienced with the mysterious Kalamosian on the ship. Worried, he turned back to rejoin his friends and parents who had walked quite a distance away, but he didn't even get half way round before a black cloth descended over his head, blanking out the world, and he felt a tiny pain in his right arm. Before he could call for help to his parents or to Albert, the ship's computer, he blacked out.

*   *   *   *

When he came to, he was in darkness still. He reached up to his face, but there was no covering. Wherever he was, there was no light.

"Albert, can you hear me?"

But instead of the familiar instant response from the ship's computer, there was silence. Mickie waited a few moments and tried again. Surely the ship had not travelled so far while he had been unconscious that he was out of radio range?

"Speaker 356, are you there?"

Yet again, there was silence. Something about the situation reminded him of... what? Yes, it came to him. This had happened back on Gelokk when he had been unable to communicate with the computer, his parents or even the Speaker. Something had blocked his communication device in his shoulder and also the telepathic links to the Speakers, something that had been believed to be impossible. Seriously frightened now, he realised he was held captive by the same forces he had disturbed on that planet, something so powerful that it could block him from making contact with any power that could save him. He tried one last avenue of escape.

Remembering the strange dream he had experienced on the Speaker's Planet when he had sensed that he was reaching out with strangely extended, flexible limbs, he tried to recapture that sensation. He concentrated on his adopted home planet of Kalamos, desperately trying to recapture the sensation of the leap across empty space that he had last achieved when he returned to Earth.... But all he could sense was a huge, thick curtain across the space he was traversing, one that blocked his moves and left him helpless in the blackness.

And the blackness vanished under the onslaught of brilliant light that appeared instantly, no sound of a power source, no apparent central point from which the light came, just blinding, searing glare as if the sun were blasting straight at him.

His vision adjusted rapidly, far faster, he knew, than any human child's would have done, and he looked around him. He was in a chamber about the size of a ballroom. The walls were featureless, coloured a dull grey, the floor was hard, carpeted in some simple, coarse material of a plain brown. In the centre of the space was a block, the same jet black material as the one on which the doomed young woman had lain before her death. Around the block, the carpet was replaced by a steel grating with drainage holes for the blood that flowed from its victims. There were no windows, no doors, no obvious means of access of any kind. Mickie knew instinctively where he was. He was inside the massive, black building that had loomed over the city as they had arrived, and he was under the control of some power that could prevent him from contacting any assistance.

And he had company. No movement had occurred, but suddenly a dozen silent figures stood before him. They were the priests of the blood-soaked ceremony he had been forced to witness just a few minutes ago. Something about them, the way they stood, their utter silence and immobility chilled his heart to ice.

"So the new Pfafth has decided to visit us?"

Mickie felt great fear. But he decided to fight. He knew he was something extraordinary, he was more than Human, he was... *Pfafth*. With that thought came courage and defiance.

"Who dares to talk this way to a Pfafth?" he said, loudly and clearly, standing straight, his head high.

It seemed to cause a small reaction, judging by the small stirring in the group in front of him and the way they turned and looked at each other.

"So? The little Pfafth is a fighter!" The speaker was one of the priests in the middle of the group. Mickie turned his attention to that one. He directed every atom of force he could summon up and tried to slam it at the man's head. To some extent, he succeeded, because the priest seemed to wilt a little, then recovered.

"I am a fighter and a killer," Mickie said loudly, encouraged by the evidence that he still had some powers. "And I will destroy this planet if it pleases me."

"That is beyond you," said the priest. "And you have very little time left to make your boasts. It has been a long time since we sacrificed a Pfafth to our great betterment."

Mickie felt his insides turn to water. His bluff had failed and he knew that he faced the same appalling death he had witnessed a little while ago. But his pride made him hide his fear and he found he could still speak firmly.

"You know that I am Pfafth. Who and what are you and why do you want to kill me?"

"We serve your enemy and your death will strengthen us in a true way, not like those we sacrifice to satisfy the masses."

"You mean that horrible ceremony we just saw is meaningless?"

"Of course it is meaningless. It has proved to be a useful belief structure to keep the masses in their place, but it serves no purpose beyond that."

"So what difference does killing me make?"

A small sigh ran round the group.

"Killing a Pfafth serves our Masters," replied the only priest who had spoken so far. "They will feed on your energy and absorb it into themselves. They will take your memories and so find where you came from and where the rest of your kind are hiding."

Mickie tried to suppress a shudder. "And who are your Masters?" he asked. "Why do you serve them?"

"We have always served them, for they help us maintain our own rule here and elsewhere. They are the enemy of the Pfafth and always have been. Once, the Pfafth ruled the Universe and our Masters were weak. Now they have you almost destroyed, weakened beyond belief and only a few of you remain somewhere in hiding. When we kill you, that will reduce your numbers even more and soon we will find the rest."

Struggling to control himself, Mickie persisted. "And just who are these sick, demented *Masters* of yours that they must slaughter innocents for their entertainment?"

The priest did not reply. Instead, the line of men moved aside. Where they had been was nothing that Mickie could see, but..... then there was.

It seemed to start as a small shadow on the carpet, but so dark that it sucked the light from the room. It grew rapidly until it became a deep black shape, roughly the height of a man, and resembling nothing but a black pillar of dense smoke. Utterly featureless, yet it appeared to be rotating slowly. The Sillaron had returned, as Mickie had feared.

He sensed waves of appalling hatred directed at him and his soul shrunk under the sensation of limitless evil that radiated from the hideous shape. The bright lights of the chamber dimmed as if the entity was drawing them into itself.

"Look at me. Look at your master," said a dreadful voice. If the first words from the Spiders had frightened Mickie, this voice was many times worse. It was completely cold, filled with venom, merciless in its hatred of Mickie. He dug even deeper into himself, well aware that these might be his last minutes of life but determined not to give in to this horror.

"So we didn't kill you back on the Ship?" he asked firmly.

The rage emanating from the dark shape seemed to roar with fury for a second or two.

"You cannot stop me," the black entity said. "And this time, you do not have your friends to save you."

Mickie continued to cling to his self-control. "Who are you?" he demanded.

"I am the Eater of Pfafth Souls," said the blackness. "Do not believe that your kind exist anywhere that they can save you now. Soon we will find the last of them and we will feast greatly."

"Why must this be so?" Mickie decided that if he was going to die, he would at least try and learn as much of the truth and his history before that moment.

"Because once the Pfafth enslaved us and prevented us from achieving our destiny. When we gained enough power, we rose up and restored ourselves, destroying so many of you that we feasted on your souls for many years."

"When was this?"

For a moment, he sensed confusion in the dreadful, blank darkness in front of him.

"Far too long ago to concern us."

"And now you enslave these people? What insanity is this?"

"They choose to serve us because it gives them power."

"And have you also enslaved the people of Merrison?"

"We are there, certainly. And on Gelokk. Now it is our destiny to rule and we will follow it."

A lot of past events became clearer in Mickie's mind as he concentrated on suppressing his terror and getting some answers. He tried another tack.

"How long since you last killed a Pfafth?"

"Longer than you can understand. Enough! Prepare this one for his death."

Several of the priests advanced on Mickie who recoiled in terror, despite his determination to show no fear. They seized his arms and legs, carried him to the stone block and snapped steel bonds to his wrists and ankles. He could not move except to lift his head a little as the blackness approached. He stared at the shape, trying to see something where the emptiness was pulling away the light of the room. For just a second, he thought he saw a face, some features, huge eyes that seemed to glow with hunger and hate. But then the priest moved to cover that shape and stood over Mickie looking down at him with anticipation. He reached down and from somewhere pulled out the same dreadful knife he had used on the young woman, grasped it in both hands and raised it above his head. The other priests began a soft chant, the same chant and rhythm that they had spoken before the young woman died, the words meaningless to Mickie. He sobbed inside himself, terrified of the terrible pain he was about to feel as his life ended.

From somewhere, a huge crash sounded, like massive gates opening. It was obviously unexpected, because the priests stopped their chant and the executioner looked sideways. Somewhere in the distance, a different light glowed, the light of natural daylight and from that area, a sound came.

To Mickie, it was the most beautiful sound in the Universe. It was the lovely, mellow note of Melkana's flute accompanied by the skirl of Fencris' Cangrar pipes. There was even a voice, a light tenor accompanying them, and Mickie realised it was Drellion, displaying a musical talent he had not revealed before. The effect on the priests was catastrophic. They wailed in fear and backed rapidly away, some falling over each other as they lost consciousness. From the black shape, a scream of hysterical rage and pain sounded that declined as it seemed to race into some unknown distance and vanished.

Mickie lifted his head and saw Melkana and Fencris take positions on either side of the execution block, still playing their instruments and watching the collapsed bodies of the priests huddled against the far wall. Grant and Allie moved to the block and rapidly disconnected the shackles that held him.

"Come on, young man, let's get you out of here," Grant said, and raised Mickie upright, helped him off the block and to his feet. As he stood, he saw that a dozen armed troopers from the ship were standing there also, looking very forbidding in combat armour and carrying heavy rifles. Trembling and hardly able to walk, Mickie followed his parents as they set off to the open doorway. The music stopped and Fencris spoke as he caught up with the rest, closely followed by Melkana and Drellion.

"That should keep those bastards quiet for long enough," he said, his eyes burning with fury like live coals in a breeze.

"I felt like picking up that knife and showing one of them what it felt like," Drellion added. Mickie could almost feel the rage radiating from the smaller boy.

"I hope it killed them all," Melkana added, her rage almost as obvious. "Mickie, did we get there on time? You're not hurt?"

"No," he replied. "But it was just seconds to go." He looked at his parents. They were both white-faced, as furious as the three children were. "How did you do it?" he asked.

"I think we all realised that they had somehow recognised you as something dangerous," Allie replied as they reached the outside of the building. The doorway was on the opposite side of the roadway along which they had passed earlier, which explained why they had seen no sign before.

"This is something you should see, Mickie," Grant said as they reached the outside. Despite the urge to get away as far and as fast as possible, Mickie heard the tone in his father's voice and turned to look to where his father was pointing. It was worth the delay. The two massive doors were both emblazoned with huge images of a spider, identical to the Zlan.

"And here's the other thing," Allie said, pointing at a symbol at the top of each door. It took Mickie a moment to remember where he had seen that image before.

"It's the word for *"Pfafth"* that we saw in the underground chamber on Shuramee and then on Kamotar," he said in astonishment.

"Exactly," said Allie. "Things are getting most peculiar and highly complicated. But let's get going. I think we'll all be happier away from this place."

Escorted by the armed troopers, they walked rapidly to the square where the shuttle was parked. There seemed no locals around. The streets were completely empty, but

Mickie sensed the many eyes peering at them from behind windows.

"How did you find me?" Mickie asked as they walked.

"It was a bit of a gamble," Grant admitted. "When we saw you had gone, we somehow all decided that you had been specifically taken because the Drudya had recognised you for what you are. And we decided immediately that this building was related to the sacrifices, and that all communications were somehow being blocked. We called the troops, raced back to the hotel and grabbed the two instruments and got back here, playing them every few seconds to keep people away. We found the door to the building without difficulty and it was locked, but a heavy rifle bolt took care of that. That's when we came in, and we knew by then that the music stopped everybody from moving and almost killed them."

They reached the shuttle and entered, sensing the doors closing behind them with huge relief. Finally, Mickie collapsed, feeling as if every muscle had been drained of strength.

"*Sle'Ach,* I think," Allie said and a moment later the four children had sunk their first glasses of the wonderful, life-sparkling yellow drink and were reaching for their second. The adults had by mutual consent poured themselves large slugs of scotch, though Grant had not yet touched his as he concentrated on flying the shuttle off the planet and to the main ship. But after a minute or two, he relaxed, reached for his glass and took a mouthful. "It's under the computer's control from here on," he said. "Mickie, what happened back there?"

Taking a deep, shaky breath, Mickie recounted the horror of the events in the sacrifice chamber. He realised he was calmer than he would have expected to be and decided Allie must have added some sedative to the *Sle'Ach*.

"The Sillaron came back," he said. "Either we didn't kill it back on the Ship or this was another one. Did you see it vanish?" he asked.

The others looked at him.

"The Sillaron?" Grant echoed. "No, I didn't."

Shakes of the head from the rest indicated the same result.

"Though I heard something horrible screaming and then fading away," Melkana added. "It did sound like when the laser hammers killed it on the Ship."

"That was it," Mickie said. "And now I know it really is the Enemy."

"But is there only one of those things?" Drellion asked. "How much can it do on its own?"

"I don't think there only be one," Grant said. "There's no doubt we killed the one on the Ship, but we had to use the laser hammers because it had developed some immunity to musical vibrations."

"And we obviously hurt this one badly with the music," Fencris said with a nod. "So it wasn't the same one."

"Maybe there's a whole Galaxy-full of the horrors," Mickie replied. "I don't know, but it seems awfully confident about killing off the Pfafth."

"I suppose it did one good thing," Allie said. "It confirmed that the Pfafth are not just legend. They really did exist and probably still do, though where in the Universe they could be remains a mystery."

"That's true!" Mickie felt a wave of excitement at the thought. It confirmed that he really was a part of a race, a once-powerful race that perhaps ruled the Universe. Wherever the last survivors were hiding, he knew that one day he would find them and discover his true history. But the mystery of why he was so isolated, why he had been left on Earth and how to find his people remained deep, intense and impenetrable.

"I'm just wondering," he said, as a few stray thoughts ran through his head. "The Enemy didn't follow me to Speaker's Planet. I imagine that they have the same problem everyone else has, they can't survive the telepathic broadcasts."

"Probably right," Allie agreed. "So it's still a puzzle how you were able to."

"And this music thing," Mickie continued. "It's obviously a dreadful problem for them and those who serve them, and I've no possible reason why that could be. But maybe that's why I was put on Earth as a baby and left for adoption. Maybe the Pfafth who left me, maybe they were my parents..." He stopped for a moment at that extraordinary thought, wondering how he could ever imagine anyone but Grant and Allie being his parents. "Maybe they chose Earth because they knew the Enemy could never go there, with such enormous amounts of music everywhere in the whole world?"

"That would make sense," Grant said with a nod. Then he rose to his feet. "We've docked," he said. "I know for one, just how happy I am to be back on this ship. I think, big guy, that you need to make sure you always have a source of music near to hand. It might be the best way to keep yourself safe."

"A splendiferous idea," Melkana said with a grin. "I'll keep my flute with me all the time and make you listen to me practice."

"That will be just fine by me," Mickie said. He found that he was still trembling from the shock of the events, despite the calming effects of the drink and the sedative.

Later that evening as Mickie tried to settle down in his room, he realised that there was unfinished business from the horrors of the day.

"Mickie, I'm relieved that I can establish communications again," said the well-mannered and cultured tones of Speaker 356.

"Me too," said Mickie. "What happened?"

"The same block came up as on Gelokk. I could tell from the various characteristics that it was identical."

"I met the entity that was causing it," said Mickie. "His people now control Gelokk as well as Merrison and they've had Drudyenko maybe for centuries."

"I've just scanned your memories of the events," said the Speaker. "I see that you tried to contact the Zlan and were equally unsuccessful."

"And we tried to contact you when we realised you were out of touch and we found the same block." The voice was the familiar, cold, emotionless tones of the Zlan. Mickie heard the astonishment in the Speaker's voice before he heard the words.

"You are now communicating with us?"

"It is time," said the Zlan. *"The Enemy has become a terrible danger and now we must work as one."*

"Our species welcomes you to this alliance," said Speaker 356. "I hope we can learn what techniques you use for communication."

"*That is uncertain,*" replied the Zlan. "*Two entirely different modes are used between our two races and it is unlikely that they are compatible. But we can only deal with one communication channel at a time, unlike your multiple-channel capability, so we can help each other.*"

Listening to this exchange, Mickie almost laughed out loud, despite the situation. These two extraordinary species, each with powers and capabilities that were world-shaking in their extents were talking to each other like to Earthly politicians. As he imagined the images of a huge spider talking in this stilted, formal manner with an immobile termite-mound, he had great difficulty keeping the chuckles suppressed. But with some thinking, he realised that perhaps the speech mannerisms were as much a function of how his mind was translating the alien telepathic concepts as of the words actually used. However, feeling a little smug that he had brought about this alliance, Mickie decided to try and use the situation.

"Do either of you know why music is so painful and damaging to the Drudya as well as to the Enemy?"

"*We have determined that,*" replied the Zlan. "*We ran a number of scans of Drudya brains and found that pitch changes, harmonics and chord frequencies cause rapid vibrations in several of the pain centres of their brains.*"

"Did you find the same, Speaker?" Mickie asked.

"Stand by," came the terse response. That interested Mickie and he wondered what was distracting the massive being that had provided shelter for his mercifully short stay on that strange planet. Up till then, the Speaker had never failed to provide instant response, given the multi-channelling capability the Spider had mentioned. What could be diverting so much of the Speaker's resources?

They had only a short while to wait.

"This is most interesting," Speaker 356 said. "In the last few moments, I and some of my colleagues have been running the same brain scans of a few hundred Drudya that our Zlan friends were running. But in the process, we found something else. Unlike most species, the race memories of the Drudya are very close to the surface and we have read much interesting data."

"What are race memories?" Mickie asked. He had never heard the term before.

"A phenomenon that occurs in all intelligent species," replied the Speaker. "Deep inside the minds of all such races are memories of long ago events, usually massive traumas that are passed through the living cells of the creatures. We have been studying this for centuries but have not yet found enough to be able to describe a major event with any accuracy. For example, we have discovered traces in human minds that tell of a global flood, as described in your biblical tales. We even suspect that there is evidence that humans did not originate on Earth but were brought there millennia ago by another intelligent species after a catastrophe on their original world. But delving into the information is a massive task for even one species, and we Speakers are too few to assign enough resources to it."

"*A most interesting subject,*" the Zlan agreed. "*We too have long suspected such memories exist. We may be able to work together on this.*"

"But what have you found in the Drudya?" Mickie demanded in some irritation. Fascinating as the topic might be, the Drudya and their mentors, his Enemy represented far more immediate worries.

"Some explanations," replied the Speaker. "We find that the Drudya are a manufactured species. They did not evolve naturally, but were forcibly developed from a clone of the Enemy's own species in order to be a slave class. That explains the brain structures that cannot tolerate pitch and tone variation, because they have the same brain structures. But we also saw a most strange thing. In order to strengthen the race which was extremely weak as a result of the clone beginnings, the Enemy introduced another species into the process to provide more solid gene structures."

"What species did they use?" Mickie found he was horrified and fascinated at the act of creating a race simply to serve the creators as slaves.

"Humans," replied the Speaker. "Several thousand years ago, they abducted many thousands of humans from the central Russian plains east of the Ural Mountains and brought them to Drudyenko. That explains the Slavic influence on the language and architecture of the planet."

"Do you think they've been doing any more of that?" asked Mickie. "Earth was full of stories of Alien abductions. Could they have been the same thing?"

"No evidence as yet," the Speaker said. "The numbers would be very small, and I haven't detected any such stream of information. That will be a topic for some future research, perhaps. For now, we have more urgent matters."

The conversation was cut short by a call from Allie. "Mickie," she said through the communication system. "You'd better get up to the Flight Deck. Something very weird has happened and it probably involves you."

"I'm on my way," Mickie replied, a surge of mixed worry and excitement running through him at her words. "What's happening?"

"It's the Cliffs of Kamotar," his mother answered. "After four thousand years, some new lines of symbols have appeared. And the script is the same as before. It looks like the Pfafth are leaving messages, possibly for the whole Universe. Or maybe just for you."

Chapter 8 – Messages From....?

The silence was chilling. After the previous experience of being on Kamotar, where the inhabitants were huge, boisterous and always noisy, the contrast was startling. Possibly ten thousand of the massive, three-armed race stood before the looming cliffs that had been a landmark sight and tourist spot for centuries because of the ancient runes in a forgotten language carved into the walls. Instead of the normal chatter, the bedlam of kids racing around as kids do in almost every culture and every species, the crowds were silent, motionless, obviously awestruck.

Mickie's group stood to one side of the regular observation pad that was the normal tourist spot. An extra platform had been built out of the hillside for the use of specialists and military observers and it was on this that they were standing. Below them, the valley dipped into a deep ravine, densely packed with huge trees that towered over a hundred metres high. Across the valley, the cliffs stood two hundred metres tall, deep blue in colour because of the minerals that filled the rocks. The surface was smooth, because the cliffs had been formed by a massive fault line in the rock that had slipped in a titanic landslide some millions of years before. For all that the scene held a grand and spectacular view in its own right, it was the lines of hieroglyphics written in pure white on the blue surface that captivated the eye. The lines were enormous, stretching at least a hundred metres, and there were more than twenty of them. Each symbol stood about two metres high.

"The new lines appeared three days ago." The speaker was Zhumaton, the immense policeman who had served as guide to Mickie and his friends on their previous visit. "For over four thousand years, as long as we have had an industrialised civilisation here, the Great Wall of The Visitors has been the same, the place we have come and stared at, puzzled over, studied and been baffled by. And now, new messages appeared overnight. It is causing chaos on my planet."

The cop's fearsome head did not display the cheerful grin that had been the main memory Mickie had held of him. Tension showed around the great mouth and jaws.

"People are frightened?" Allie's voice was gentle and understanding.

"Frightened, terrified, bewildered, uncontrollable," the cop replied. "We have had religious riots in some parts. The Smegandri rebels have taken advantage of the disruptions to attack several small towns and caused serious loss of life. The government has declared military rule until we can restore some sort of order. There have been waves of panic among some groups, terrified that we are about to be invaded by a new alien species. Is there any chance you can decipher what these new lines mean?"

"Some chance," Allie said with a nod. "Our linguistics specialist has been working hard all year on the original script and some new data we found on Shuramee, and he believes he's made progress. He's taking pictures of the details from up close, I hope he'll be able to report back fairly soon."

"I hope so, too," the Kamotari cop said with a grimace. "My planet is a most unsettling place right now. But for all that," he continued, turning to the four children standing a short distance away. "It's still a great pleasure to welcome my young friends back. Mickie, I'm relieved you were able to find your way off the Speakers' Planet. I'm glad we were able to talk while you had your short stay back on Earth."

"So was I," replied Mickie. "That was a nasty little episode, being back with my old family. Talking to you was a life-saver."

"A small return for the help you gave us on your last visit. Until this last outbreak of violence, the Smegandri have been quiet since we broke up that last gang."

As Mickie was about to talk further, the linguistics expert returned from his studies down at the Cliff face. He nodded at the entire group, but addressed Allie. The specialist was an X'Kasxi, one of the reptilian race that was the other intelligent species that had its home planet in the same Galaxy as Earth's human race. There were many of them in the crew, and Mickie had stayed with one of the leaders of the X'Kasxi world when the crew had stopped over some months ago. It had been a fascinating visit, with many new discoveries made about this strange race, but Mickie had never been able to feel quite comfortable with any of them.

"Allie, I think I have something," the specialist said with a slightly nervous look at the huge mass of the Kamotari hovering nearby. "I've been working on this script and nothing else all year now, and comparing it with different scripts we've found on several planets all over the universe. I've got no idea at all of how it appeared, mind you. It seems to be exactly the same age as all the previous lines, no sign at all of being freshly engraved."

"That's a problem for later," Allie agreed. "But what do you think these new lines say?"

"I can't read all that much. But I'm pretty certain this line here..." He pointed at his photograph of the hieroglyphics. "I think it's a greeting form, maybe 'Welcome' or 'Hello,' something like that. The next shape I'm pretty sure is a word for a family member, possibly son or daughter. Then, that symbol there." He pointed at a complex shape. "I'm pretty certain it means danger, and the next one I've seen before, and all the cross-references indicate it means 'Universe.' If I wanted to get ambitious, knowing Mickie's history, I'd guess it's a message for him and it says *'Greetings, my son. There is danger in the Universe.'*"

Mickie felt his insides turn to water as everyone looked directly at him. "You think this could be a message from the Pfafth directly to me?"

"It's one possibility," the X'Kasxi replied. "I can't swear to it. But I'm more confident about the second line, because some of the symbols were those we saw back on Shuramee when you discovered the Maragos art treasures. I'm pretty sure it says quite clearly one thing."

"Which is?" Allie's voice reflected some tension.

"It says *'There is another Pfafth within the Universe,'*" replied the linguist.

There was a short silence in the group.

"You mean there's another Pfafth, in addition to Mickie somewhere around?" Melkana's voice broke the silence like a water drip echoing in a cavern.

"I think that's what it says," the X'Kasxi replied. "Mind you, there are several more lines I've yet to work out."

"A curious turn of phrase," Grant interjected, joining in the conversation. "*Within* the Universe? Could that mean that there's something *outside* the Universe? And that's where the Pfafth are?"

"How can there be anything outside the Universe?" Mickie was feeling a mix of excitement and fear at the thought that the message might be from his own species. The idea of a communication was wildly exciting, but the warning was almost as bad as the thought that his current wonderful family life might be threatened if his own Pfafth turned up some day.

"I've no idea, son," Grant said. "The idea is quite bizarre. Anyway, our friend here may not have got it quite right."

"Absolutely," the linguist agreed. "We've really got very few keys to this script. I could have it wildly wrong."

"I doubt it," Mickie said with a smile that he could not feel inside. "I get a strong feeling that it sure is exactly what you said."

"Well, look on the bright side," Melkana joined in with a laugh. "If there's another Pfafth somewhere, I bet he or she can't play Loopies like you."

Relieved at the way she had broken the dark mood, Mickie laughed out loud and couldn't stop himself giving her a hug. To his delight, she responded by putting her arms round his neck and kissing his cheek. "Don't worry, little Pfafth," she said into his ear. "We'll look after you."

Regretfully letting go, Mickie turned to the Kamotari cop. "Will this help ease the situation here?" he asked.

"Probably," said Zhumaton. "We'll broadcast planet-wide that the new lines have been deciphered to be a message of greeting only, nothing but friendship and no danger. We have enough experience of other species to accept that they have used a technology we don't understand yet, but if it's not threatening, we can calm things down."

"I do hope so," Allie joined in. "Meanwhile, we'll spend a few more days here working on that script and see if we can get anything else out of it."

"That's good," the cop replied. His wide, cavernous grin was back on display. "Now, if I recall, the last time you were here, we went to the regional final game of Prottaskorp but we had to leave quite early. There's a regular league game tonight if you want to come and watch."

"Yes!" The response was immediate from all the youngsters, and the mood lightened immediately.

* * * *

The match was as exciting and fast-moving as the last time they had attended one at the same stadium at which they sat now. The crowd of over a quarter million bellowed their lungs out as the home team won an enthralling contest, finally coming from behind to win by a mere two points in the final moments of the game with a massive throw from sixty metres out, the huge ball landing in the dead centre of the net. Zhumaton looked like his cheerful self they remembered from their previous visit as he led them though the throngs of Kamotari, his symbols of police rank on his tunic ensuring a safe passage through a tidal wave of people that would have been lethal to the four small children.

"Now *that's* what I call a game," he enthused, his massive right arm pumping the air in the same gesture of power that the players adopted. The others chuckled, but had to agree.

"It's quite stupendous," Drellion laughed. "The way those guys fling that humungous ball so far... wow!"

Feeling in great spirits, despite the worries of the new messages discovered so recently, they piled into the transport in which Zhumaton had brought them.

"I can't get over that diamond on the gear lever!" Melkana exclaimed. "I know we saw it before, but the idea of something so incredibly valuable just being a common decoration, and on top of a gold-covered dash board, well, it's just... wild!"

"I hope you still have the diamonds I gave you the last time," Zhumaton said as he carefully eased the vehicle back to the road.

Mickie laughed as he remembered where one of his had gone. "I gave one to my father when I left Earth again," he said. "It was probably worth more than he had ever earned in his whole life. I wonder if he ever thought about where I got it from."

"That was a nice gesture," Melkana said curiously. "After all he'd done to you, you make him richer than he could ever have dreamed?"

"Actually, it was more of a horrible insult," Mickie replied thoughtfully. "Can you imagine what those dreadful people must have thought seeing one of the biggest diamonds in the world sitting on that dirty kitchen table? Their stupid son, still only thirteen, has casually given it to them as if it meant nothing, which it did. How rich do you think they must have imagined I'd become?"

"Hah!" Fencris seemed to appreciate the irony and his red eyes sparkled like embers in a breeze. "I think it's great! You vanish for a year, appear briefly, scare the living daylights out of them for four days and casually make them rich as you leave for somewhere utterly beyond their comprehension! I think it's poetic!"

"Okay, I see the point." Melkana smiled with an air of satisfaction. "You make them rich and put them to absolute shame with one small gesture! I love it!"

In some weariness, but feeling very happy, the kids settled down for the short ride back to the shuttle and a lift-off to return to the ship in orbit around Kamotar. A buzzer sounded, and Zhumaton touched a communication button on the dashboard.

"Zhumaton," he said in a clipped, military manner.

"Sir, this is Troop Leader Komtaret at the cliff base," said a voice. "We've just discovered something you need to know about. It's a Maragos sculpture. It's just sitting there under a tree, and I'm pretty sure it wasn't there an hour ago."

"A Maragos?" Zhumaton's astonishment reverberated through the vehicle. "I've heard of those things and seen pictures of them, but I've never seen one. And it just appeared? Are you sure it's a Maragos?"

"Yes, sir, I'm sure of it. I've read a lot about them. My men have been patrolling this area for three hours and we would have seen it immediately if it had been there before, so it has to have been placed there in the last thirty minutes."

"Zhumaton, those things can be hypnotic!" Mickie spoke urgently. "Tell them to cover it up before they all end up staring at it for hours."

"Did you hear that, Troop Leader?"

"Yes, sir. I've kept the men away from it and covered it up for the reasons the young man said. But there's one thing that's odd. I got my corporal to stand by me while I looked at it, and frankly sir, it didn't do a damn thing to me. I stared at it for ten minutes, no effect at all."

"Maybe it's not a genuine Maragos after all?"

"That's probable, sir, but it sure looks like one. And I know that other Kamotari have been affected by them, so if it's real, it should have worked on me."

"Perhaps you're too thick to get the effect, Troop Leader?" Zhumaton's tone was sardonic, not insulting, and the other man was not offended.

"Or too intelligent, sir," he replied.

Zhumaton chuckled. "Well done, Troop Leader. I'll arrange for helicopter transport." He touched the switch again and spoke briefly to someone, ordering a helicopter to collect the strange item then looked back at his passengers.

"Bizarre things are happening in the Universe, my friends," he said gently. "And they seem to revolve around you, Mickie."

Mickie nodded, too overwhelmed by the truth of what the huge Kamotari was saying to speak.

"He's got us, Zhumaton," said Fencris in a determined tone, and murmurs of agreement came from Melkana and Drellion. "Between us, we'll handle anything that comes."

"I think Mickie knows just how lucky he is with his friends," the cop agreed.

"And how lucky we are to have him as a friend," Melkana added. "Mickie's okay. For a Pfafth, that is."

That broke the tension, and the four friends collapsed in giggles for the remainder of the ride.

* * * *

The atmosphere was one of puzzlement.

"I'm quite certain it's a genuine Maragos," Allie said. The object of the confusion stood in the middle of the Captain's cabin aboard the ship. It was again draped with a sheet to avoid possible distraction, though after several inspections of it by specialists in the works of Maragos and deliberate attempts by others to lose themselves in the hypnotic effects for which these objects were renowned, no such effects had resulted with anyone. Several people had visited the cabin in the last few hours, but now the only people remaining were the Captain, Allie, Grant, the four children and a trio of the ship's crew who were still examining the object.

"If it's not, it's an astounding copy," the ship's cultural and artistic expert pronounced. She was a Kaloti, like the Captain and had achieved fame on many worlds for her analytical studies of the mental effects of the Maragos sculptures. "All the key signatures are there. If it were not for the complete absence of any brain influence in the watchers, I'd stake my entire reputation on it."

"And that's a massive bet," Grant replied. He stood with his arms folded, staring at the covered object, his face reflecting frustration. "This whole thing is a mystery wrapped in a conundrum and tied up with confusion. If it's not a real Maragos, why would anyone go to the effort of placing it there? And how they did *that* without the troops seeing them still makes my brain feel like porridge. But if it's real, why no effect on anyone? And then we get to the other big issue, how and why did those new lines appear on the cliff?"

"It's all tied in together," Allie said firmly. "We need the key, and it's not obviously around to be seen. Any thoughts, Mickie? The most logical explanation is that it's all somehow tied in with you."

"Nothing, Allie," Mickie replied. He had also looked at the sculpture and instead of the immediate beautiful, wild, sometimes frightening hallucinations he had experienced when looking at the Captain's own sculpture, there had been no effect, no more than looking at any other strangely-shaped rock.

A new voice broke into the gathering. It was a familiar voice, the well-modulated, elegant voice of Speaker 356. All of them heard it telepathically, and to each of them it sounded like a voice speaking from somewhere near but not immediately locatable in a precise spot.

"Ladies and Gentlemen," the Speaker said. "The Captain has asked me to include you all in this announcement, as he feels it is somehow connected to these strange events of today."

A stir of interest ran round the group.

"As you know," the Speaker continued, "we Speakers maintain a constant search through the Universe for signs of intelligent life. It has been centuries in progress, but there are few of us and many millions of Galaxies, so we have barely started yet. In recent hours I began to examine a new Galaxy, one that has received no attention from us before. It is well out of the areas in which you have travelled so far. And something very strange has happened."

The pause before the Speaker continued indicated that something indeed was unusual.

"The entire Galaxy is blocked," the Speaker said. "None of us, and many have tried in the last few hours, none of us can get past a block of a nature we cannot even begin to identify. We cannot see a single sun, a planet, a moon, anything. We can sense no mental waves of any sort, and that is impossible, because we can always identify some sort of mental activity, even low life forms. It is inconceivable that the entire Galaxy is devoid of all animal life. My colleagues all agree. Something is blocking our exploratory efforts."

The silence in the cabin echoed for quite a few seconds as everybody absorbed this information in their own way. The Captain broke the stasis.

"I believe there is only one course of action," he said, the gentle hum of his voice providing a musical accompaniment to the translated words from his communications device that put the voice in Mickie's head. "While I understand that this is a trading vessel under your hire, I am convinced that all these recent strange events are all linked and somehow connected to our young friend Mickie."

"We should head for this Galaxy," Mickie said with utter confidence.

"Of course we must," the Captain agreed with a wide-eyed stare to reflect his amusement.

Chapter 9. A Space Out of Time

Ten days of flight time on the way to the strange blocked galaxy passed the way hyperspace flight usually passed. The kids spent some time in school, some time playing Loopies, some time sitting and talking in their various cabins and, Mickie's greatest pleasure since the horrors of Drudyenko, listening to Melkana and Fencris play their instruments. Remembering an old dream of his own, Mickie asked what other instruments were available on the ship and if he could start lessons. With delight, he found that Kalamosian developments in music had closely followed those of Earth and he could take his pick of trumpet, trombone, French Horn, clarinet or saxophone in the wind instruments, or any of the stringed instruments such as violin, cello or bass. Deciding that the trombone was a hugely masculine instrument with which he could eventually show off to Melkana, he selected a silver slide specimen from the ship's stores and went to meet the music teacher who was delighted to find a complete beginner to introduce to the joys of playing music.

The strangely inert Maragos sculpture was studied for a few more days by the Kaloti specialist who eventually declared her certainty that it was indeed a genuine Maragos but that it displayed none of the hallucinatory qualities of normal Maragos sculptures and she was totally unable to understand why. After a few discussions, the Captain agreed to let the sculpture be moved to Mickie's cabin. Mickie spent a few hours in the first week staring at the shape, trying to experience another wild and brain-spinning trip through the universe, but nothing happened. The sculpture remained nothing but an oddly shaped carving, and after the first week, Mickie stopped experimenting and decided that the Kaloti expert was wrong and this was just a pale imitation of the great master's work made by a student.

Because of the completely unknown nature of the blocked galaxy, the computer had no detailed data by which to navigate and the estimated time of arrival at a point at which to enter normal space could not be calculated to within microseconds as was normal. In fact, the window was over twenty-four hours, so an initial pause in the flight was planned for the following day so that new sightings could be taken from normal space and the remainder of the flight planned after that.

After a particularly strenuous session of Loopies, the kids were at their usual place in the coffee lounge of the ship's promenade. Like most public places, there were the black panels of observation screens along one wall but as always in hyperspace, these were featureless black and resembled decorative panels more than their real function. The lounge was almost full of people, all the main races among the ship's crew represented except for the Kaloti who found the bright light and heavy gravity difficult for them. Mickie had heard that there was another social area for these beautiful beings, in which the environment was more to their style, but he had never visited it. The noise was fairly high this evening as people became more excited at the possibility of sighting a new galaxy the next day and what might transpire after that. Crew morale was exceptionally high, even with the events on Drudyenko, because the finds of the Maragos treasures the previous trip had made all of them wealthy, and even the crewmembers who had joined the ship after that had been able to get much higher than normal pay and bonuses.

"So how are the trombone lessons coming, Mickie?" Drellion asked. He was in cheerful mood, having beaten everyone soundly at Loopies, including Mickie who had never been able to reproduce the extraordinary performance that had once caused such stress between the four friends.

"I think I sound more like a cow with stomach ache than a musical instrument," Mickie replied. "I hadn't realised how tricky it is to get the slide position right, so I'm usually well off the correct note. Still, it's great fun. It might take a century or two to get to the stage where I can play with you guys though."

"Hah!" Fencris laughed out loud. "That's normal at the start. You should have heard me when I started learning the pipes. I scared all the neighbours into moving to the next suburb!"

"Me too," Melkana joined in. "My mother said I sounded like a hysterical chipmunk for the first year of flute practice."

All four chortled at the images raised, but their laughter died as they realised the entire room had gone quiet. They looked around the room and saw that everyone was staring at the wall that held the observation screens. They were no longer black and featureless. Now they held the image of a galaxy. It was beautiful. It was not the familiar spiral shape of the Milky Way and so many others, but instead was a massive, brilliant egg shape, with just a fringe of stars looping outwards from the main body.

"What's going on?" Mickie whispered.

"We weren't supposed to leave hyperspace for another fourteen hours," Fencris said in a low voice. "Something must have happened and I don't get a good feeling about it."

The silence in the room was broken as people as people stood up and moved out, many of them heading to their stations for whatever duty was their responsibility. Mickie assumed they had received personal communications from their superiors through the computer links.

"Albert, what's happened?" he asked through his own link.

"The ship has returned to normal space," Albert replied.

"I can tell that, Albert! But *why* has the ship returned to normal space? Weren't we supposed to stay in hyperspace another few hours?"

"I don't know," the computer replied. "I received an instruction to drop out of hyperspace, so I did."

"You received an instruction? The Captain's the only one who can issue that instruction. Did he do so?"

"No."

"Then who did?" Mickie felt a cold chill run down his back.

"I don't know."

"So why did you obey?"

"I don't know."

All four children looked at each other. Each of them would have been asking the computer the same questions and receiving the same replies.

"Oops!" said Melkana. "Fencris was right. There's something creepy going on."

"There's something else going on, too," Drellion said. "Look out there." He nodded at the observation panels. The others turned their heads. Although the new galaxy remained in view in the central panels, off to the side, a new image had appeared. Clouds of sparks grew and became brighter until Mickie realised what they were seeing.

"The Family is here," he said softly.

"The Family? The electronic beings we stopped for on the last trip?" Drellion was entranced, remembering the astounding fireworks display to which they had been treated some months ago. "But how could they have travelled all these light years in that time?"

"I don't think it's the same group," Melkana replied. "They don't have hyperspace travel. It must be another group of the same species. I wonder what they want?"

The cloud of electronic beings had come close to the ship and seemed to have surrounded it, the colours and flashes almost blinding in their intensity.

"Grant? Allie? Have you any idea what's happening?" Mickie tried another source.

"We're with the Captain," Grant replied. "All we know is that the navigation computers received an order to drop out of hyperspace. They are quite unable to tell us who gave the order or why they obeyed when they know only the Captain can give those orders. We're going to try another acceleration to re-enter hyperspace."

"But what about the Family that just arrived?"

"Yes, we've just seen them too. I'm trying to establish contact through Speaker 356. Stand by."

For a few minutes, Mickie and his friends watched the brilliant display in the observation panels. After a few moments of random flashes and sparks, Mickie realised a pattern had emerged. The electron cloud had formed into a seemingly endless line that rotated round the ship, twisting and forming a lattice like a gleaming basket weave that pulsated with energy.

"I think they're giving us a message of some sort," Mickie murmured. "That doesn't look like a random pattern at all."

Then Allie spoke again. "This is to all of you," she said. Her voice sounded distracted. "The Speaker says the Family are giving us a warning. They say we must not try and get closer to this Galaxy."

"Do they say why?" Melkana asked.

"No, Melkana," Allie replied. "Just the warning. And we can't try moving while they are this close to the ship. We might kill them."

But as she spoke, the electron cloud did as it had done the last time, gathered itself into a huge, sparkling sphere of light and raced off into the distance, vanishing within seconds.

A few moments later, Mickie felt the rumble of the engines increase.

"We're moving," Melkana said. "The Captain is obviously not taking the Family's warning." But as she spoke, the engines died down again.

"Cancel that last statement," she said. Her grin did not hide the anxiety that was evident in her face.

"Albert? What happened?" Mickie asked.

"Well, wouldn't you like to know?" the computer replied, an answer so stunningly unexpected that Mickie felt as if he'd been hit in the gut. The others had obviously received something similarly unexpected and they looked at each other.

"What?" said Drellion. "Idiot computer, what the hell's the matter with you?"

"I don't understand the question," the computer replied. "Why would you inquire about my health?"

"What was the point of your last response, Albert?" Mickie chimed in. "The one about wouldn't I like to know?"

"I still don't understand, Mickie. I made no such response."

"You most certainly did, Albert."

"Well, Mickie, you're damn right!" Albert sounded almost gleeful. "I decided I wanted to get all crabby! *Whoooooooo-weeeeeeee!* Albert's the Man, I tell you! Let's all party, people! Albert wants to have some fun!"

Mickie looked at his friends. "Are you all getting this same stuff?" he asked.

The shocked looks told him the answer.

"Albert, something is terribly wrong with you," Mickie said, struggling to sound calm. "Can I strongly recommend you run a top-level self-diagnostic?"

"You know, Mickie," Albert replied, "sometimes you are just a silly little boy and I don't play games with silly children. I think I'm going to have a drink."

"Albert? What's wrong with you?" But he received no reply. Mickie looked at the others. They all looked as shell-shocked as he felt.

"Did the computer just tell you he was going off to have a drink?" Fencris asked the table at large."

The other three nodded at him.

"There's something seriously wrong," Fencris continued. "No computer has ever behaved like that. And the engines being unable to accelerate, that's never happened in the whole history of Kaloti spaceflight."

"It's all obviously got to do with that galaxy out there," Melkana said. "I'll bet anything you like, the Pfafth are in there and they don't want anyone coming near them."

"Hey kids!" The voice of Albert broke back into the gathering, and the reactions of the group indicated that the computer was addressing all of them. "I gotta tell yer," Albert said, his voice no longer sounding the smooth, well-educated style to which Mickie had become accustomed. Instead, it was blurred, sounding for all the world as if the machine was seriously drunk. "I gotta tell yer," the computer said again, "this party is one great do, honest. And just for all of you kids, I've written a poem. Do you want to hear it?"

Astounded looks flashed round the group.

"I don't think so," Fencris replied. "What we want is for you to run a Stage Five Self-Diagnostic. That is a Command Structure 1996 order. Do you understand?"

"Well, I want to read you my poem," replied Albert. "You kids can't order me to do anything, so there."

Fencris looked alarmed. "My father gave me that code as an over-riding command. He designed a lot of the programs in these computers and he said that one would always stop any computer that might have broken down its programs and make it run a self-diagnostic and recovery. Something is really, *really* wrong here."

Before anyone could reply, Albert's voice came back on, sounding even more slurred than before.

"I'm going to read you my poem now," he said. "It's really great, I know you'll love it. Are you ready?"

"No, we're not," Melkana snapped. "Shut up and run your diagnostics, you stupid computer."

"Naff off, Melkana," Albert said. "You're all giving me the running squitters. Now, here's my poem."

Unbelievably, Albert actually cleared his throat, just like any human being about to recite before an audience. Then he began speaking.

"My Love is like a royal blue Hunkenscheisenhauser.
It glows like perriwinkels in a stream of porridge.
Whoflungdung and whatchermercallit.
Carry on, Admiral."

There was a short silence as the friends looked at each other. Drellion was struggling not to laugh, despite the serious worries of the episode.

"So, what do you think?" Albert asked.

Mickie fought for self-control. "It's dreadful, Albert. Now, be a good boy and do what Fencris said, run a Stage Five Self-Diagnostic. That is a Command Structure 1996 order. Do you understand?"

Albert clearly chose to ignore the order. "I've written another poem," he said. "I'm going to read it to you." Yet again, he seemed to clear his throat.

"Oh Pooh!

It stinks!
Who pooped here?
Why, a Koala Bear!
A very ancient Koala Bear.
Little Bastard.
Carry on, General.”

"Oh my lord," Melkana muttered. "If the ship's computer has gone nuts, there's no knowing what can happen. This is very scary."

She was interrupted by something Mickie had never heard before, the voice of the Captain coming over all communication channels throughout the ship.

"This is the Captain," said the Kaloti. "As you can all tell, the communication modes of the ship's computer are having serious problems. I have cut all such programs while the technicians investigate. Do not attempt communication with the computer until further notice. Meanwhile, you will also know that the engines appear to have stalled. I will advise when I have further information."

"It's really serious, then," Fencris said, standing up. "I think I want to meet my father and ask him if he has any more information. I'll see you guys later." He gave a small wave at the table in general and walked out.

"The same for us," Melkana said. "Come on, little brother, let's go and see what our revered parents have to say on the matter. See you later, young Pfafth!"

Recognising that his friends were all frightened by the new events and were seeking to be with their parents for moral support, Mickie also stood up. He knew that he was feeling the same thing and badly wanted to be with Grant and Allie while the ship faced perhaps the greatest danger it had ever encountered. But then he laughed out loud as he remembered the utter nonsense the computer had spouted before being shut down.

"You have to admit," he said with a grin, "Albert's poetry was really rather funny."

Drellion grinned back. "Probably high-level literature to a Pfafth," he retorted. "We Kalamosians are too cultured for that stuff."

Mickie chortled at the comeback, lightly slapped Drellion on the shoulder and began walking out with them.

"I think Loopies is out until the computer's fixed," he said. "We couldn't trust it to set the right gravity. So I'll see you later and get you to suffer through my trombone practice."

"You think?" Melkana replied. "Me, I plan to be at other end of the ship when you're playing that thing! I'll give you all a call later."

"Okay," Mickie said as they reached the corridor to set off to their respective living quarters, realising that the levity they were displaying hid serious fear about what was happening. But they stopped when a new, even more frightening factor introduced itself into the already confused, dangerous situation. A voice echoed through the ship. It was a powerful tone, one that held huge authority, but Mickie also thought he detected a note of contempt in it, as though the speaker was talking to an audience that it believed to be inferior to itself.

"You will come no closer," the voice said. **"You have received one warning that you ignored. This is the last one. Your engines will not function unless you direct yourself away from here. Your**

computers will remain inoperable. The Galaxy you see before you is banned. Do not attempt to get to it. You may leave or you may die of starvation. The choice is yours."

"Oh-oh," Melkana murmured. "I think we just got warned off by the Pfafth."

"I hope it's not them," Mickie replied, feeling a horrible mixture of fear and sadness. "Because if that's Pfafth, I don't think I like them."

Brief waves between them all, and they at last walked off to join their families. Five minutes later, Mickie walked into his own cabin. He ordered himself a drink of *Sle'Ach* from the dispensing computer then called his parents while waiting for the drink to arrive through the service hatch.

"Hi, kid," Allie responded. "We're just with the Captain discussing the next steps to try. As you can imagine, that last message has caused some dismay. We'll be with you in about an hour and we can go for dinner then."

"Sure," he replied, turning to get his drink. But as he lifted the glass to his lips, he stopped. Instead of the sparkling yellow fluid, the glass was filled with a grey liquid that gave forth a most unpleasant odour of sewage. Grimacing, he put the glass down on the table, recalling the warning he had just heard about starving.

"Hey, Mickie!" The voice was Melkana's coming through his shoulder translator. "Have you tried ordering anything from the dispenser?"

"I sure have. I asked for some *Sle'Ach* and got grey sludge instead. How about you?"

"Same problem. My parents just ordered a snack and something revolting appeared in the hatch. I think the entire computer network is fouled up."

"I doubt we have more than a couple of days of fresh food on board. I'll bet the Captain decides to turn back."

"I reckon." Melkana sounded subdued and frightened.

As Mickie turned to go to his bedroom, his eyes passed over the Maragos sculpture and he froze. The shape was glowing gently with a light yellow shade and a low bell note seemed to be coming from it. Mickie walked closer and looked at the sculpture more thoroughly.

Then he felt as if a huge hand enfolded him and swept his soul into the black infinity outside the ship and a million years into the past.

Chapter 10 – The Universe of the Pfafth

"Now children, you must concentrate very hard." The teacher's voice rang clearly through the classroom. "This is the new exercise we are starting, and it is very difficult, even for a Pfafth when you are as young as you are."

Markel liked school. Each day he learned something wonderful about the Universe, especially how the Pfafth ruled it. He learned about other species that lived on different planets around stars in far galaxies, but however far away they lived, the Pfafth ruled them. He stared down at the brick he had picked up in the schoolyard as instructed by the teacher a few minutes before. It sat on the desk before him, as did similar bricks on twenty other desks in the classroom.

"Now concentrate," the teacher said again. "You must look right into the stone, see each component molecule... concentrate..... harder.... Raise the stone above the desk."

Market stared right through the brick. He saw every single molecule, peered deeper and saw the atoms, saw the electrons orbiting the nuclei and somehow wrapped his mind around the entire mass, wiped out the gravitational ties to the desk..... and the brick lifted smoothly and hovered above the desk, level with his eyes.

"Very good, Markel," the teacher said. "You too, Kerrala. That's splendid. Now put it down softly."

Feeling completely in control, he lowered the brick down to the desk and looked around. Some of the class had failed to lift their stones, but Kerrala had achieved the same perfect result as he had, as he knew she would. He smiled at her and received a warm grin back. They were always the best in the class. They had both easily mastered the art of changing the structure of materials by consciously manipulating the molecules by direct thought. The abilities were especially astonishing in Kerrala, because while females always developed their empathic skills two or three years ahead of the boys, the reverse was invariably true with the physical controls over matter. Pfafth boys usually mastered this skill by the age of ten or eleven, while girls had never been known to develop such talents before the age of fifteen. He looked forward to the new abilities they would learn over the coming months, especially the most advanced, that of transporting themselves across any distance in an almost immeasurably small time. He was certain that Kerrala would again be years ahead of her female classmates and work in the boys' classes with him.

Being a Pfafth was wonderful, he knew, even at his young age. The Pfafth ruled the Universe, his teachers had told them from the beginning. And that rule benefited everyone, they said. Throughout the entire Universe, there was peace, contentment and total acceptance that the Pfafth were the rightful rulers. Of course, they had to be, no other species had ever shown the sort of powers the

Pfafth possessed, so why should they want anything to be different? And he and Kerrala were among the very best of the Pfafth, he understood. They always led the class in learning new techniques and controlling their powers. The teachers had already told them of the wonderful future they had, playing a major role in ensuring that the universal happiness continued under Pfafth control. Markel felt very happy, knowing he was one of those who ran the Universe.

"All right, children, let's stop here," the teacher said. She was a young woman of considerable beauty, but Markel saw nothing noteworthy in her. All Pfafth were beautiful, so nobody stood out except in comparison with other species, and some of those were very ugly, he knew.

"Those who didn't manage to raise their bricks, don't worry about it," the teacher continued. "Sometimes our minds take a few practice sessions to see the way to do it, but we all can, so it will come to you. Keep practicing at home."

Markel joined up with Kerrala as he usually did at the end of the day at school. They had always been close and had become more so since realising they were far and away the best students the school had ever had. They waited together at the front of the school for his house vehicle to come and collect them both, for Kerrala lived quite close to his house. He liked the ride to and from school each day, sitting comfortably in the gravity vehicle that floated a short distance above the ground and moved in perfect silence. The route took them through areas where other races lived, for none of them would be permitted to live in the same region as the Pfafth and he liked to see how these people lived.

The automated vehicle arrived and the two children climbed in.

"I like this ride," Markel said. "I think I'll still do it even when we've learned to teleport ourselves home and around."

"But you don't teleport for such distances!" Kerrala said in shocked tones. "My mother said it's impossible to focus for anything less than a light year. We only travel that way between planets, the further away the better."

"I didn't know," Markel replied. "Anyway, that's good, because I like this ride. And I bet these other people like to see us ride through their areas."

"They should," Kerrala said firmly. "They owe everything to the Pfafth."

"Did you hear about that rescue of a complete species?" Markel asked, remembering his father's story from that morning. "There was this humanoid race, horribly primitive, barely started wearing clothes and hunting for food, and their whole planet was starting to freeze over and die. We decided to take them to a new planet."

"Did they find one suitable?" Kerrala looked interested.

Markel nodded. "Two. My dad says they decided to put half of them on each, very similar worlds and see if they developed differently. They're only about two hundred light years apart, so it will be easy to watch them both grow up."

"Maybe we'll get the job of overseeing them," Kerrala said with a chuckle. "That would be fun, to see how two identical species grow on different planets."

"Mmmm." Markel was looking out at the passing scenery. "I hate those Sillaron," he said. "They scare me."

Kerrala looked at the group of strange dark shapes moving along outside the vehicle. "Me too," she replied. "They're weird, always black, never quite the same shape when you look at them and you can't really see a face there, and I get the oddest feeling that they hate us, too. Why do we use them to rule so many of our Galaxies?"

"My dad says it's because we're too few to rule everywhere, so we have to get help. And the Sillaron are very powerful, so they can rule for us. Not as powerful as us, of course, but dad says they play a useful role."

"I wish they wouldn't congregate so much in this area. They practically surround our region."

"That's because this is the capital for all the Pfafth territories," Markel said with a superior tone. "So all the public servants have to be near us to get their instructions. But they can't enter our areas, so we only meet them in the government buildings."

"I don't want to meet them at all," said Kerrala with a small shudder. "That's the only bad part of the jobs we'll get when we grow up, having to deal with the Sillaron all over the Universe."

"I wouldn't worry about it," Markel smiled. "They'll never be able to hurt us. Anyway, what did you think about today's class? I saw you lifted the brick easily!"

"It *was* easy," she said with a grin. "I don't know why anyone has trouble with it. I still think the best is being able to alter molecular structures, though. That's such fun, being able to make almost anything you want."

The vehicle started to slow as it approached the dividing line between the Pfafth residential areas and those of the other races. The shimmering force-field was beautiful, Markel thought. It sparkled like rain drops in the sun and it stretched over the entire complex that housed the million Pfafth who lived there. It also represented pure safety and security to him, though that thought hadn't really raised itself in his conscious mind. The car slowed almost to a stop as the identification codes flickered between itself and the control computers, and Kerrala let out a frightened gasp.

"What's going on?" she hissed. Markel sat back in his seat in a similar reflex of shock. The vehicle was surrounded by the Sillaron. They darkened the interior, so thick was the group outside, and the interior lights came on automatically. They were not like ordinary people, Markel thought for the thousandth time. They didn't seem quite solid, almost like black smoke, shifting and changing to unknown currents. Somehow, he could never see face clearly, either. Just glimpses of huge, oval eyes that flickered in and out of one's focus then faded back into darkness. The faces seemed to be staring at them and the sensation was horrible. As Kerrala had said, Markel sensed a great wave of hatred radiate from the group outside, then they vanished as abruptly as they had appeared. The vehicle resumed its motion and passed easily through the force-field then speeded up for the last short distance to Markel's house. Markel realised he was trembling and saw the same reaction in Kerrala.

"Come in for a while before you go home," he suggested.

She nodded. "Thanks, yes, I think I'd like to. My parents are out for a few more hours."

Alighting at the huge house that was his home, they walked inside. As they entered the lobby, a gentle voice spoke from no obvious source.

"Markel, your father is in the study having a meeting, but you are both welcome to join him. Can I arrange any refreshment?"

"My usual drink, Mindor, and the same for Kerrala."

"Of course, Markel." The house computer fell silent as it initiated the various processes to have the wonderful yellow drink that Markel so liked served in the study. The two children walked along the corridor to his father's room and entered. Both gave a small jerk of shock as they entered, then realised their error. While it appeared that a Sillaron stood in the middle of the room talking to Markel's father, both children knew full well that it was just a hologram. No non-Pfafth would be permitted in a private home. Hektogarn gave both children a friendly wave and continued the discussion. A slide opened at the serving hatch and two glasses and a jug of the sparkling fruit juice appeared. Markel poured as the computer spoke softly through his private communication channel so that nobody else could hear.

"Your father is talking...."

"Mindor, include Kerrala in this communication."

"Yes, Markel. Children, Markel's father is talking with the Chief of the Sillaron Council of Regents, receiving an update. I will open up the conversation for you both."

"Repeat that last statement, Regent," Markel's father said. "I want these two children to hear the same news."

"The Sillaron Council of Regents highly recommends that you visit the worlds we have been discussing, Chairman," the Sillaron regent said. "The resident species are reaching points of development or possible crisis that need your attention, we believe."

"Very well, I'll do that over the next few days," Hektogarn replied. "This will make an excellent field trip for these two children." He grinned at the expressions of excitement that lit up the faces of Markel and Kerrala. "I will advise your council of my schedule in the next few hours."

Yes, sir," the black shape said. Sometimes, Markel thought, the Sillaron looked like smoke clouds, rotating as they rose, except that they only stood about two metres high, and the twisting, writhing strands of black smoke seemed to merge back into the shape at the top, so that the movement was constant. He wondered how intelligence formed and stayed in a non-solid shape but he had already learned that the Sillaron had many of the strengths and abilities of the Pfafth, but not in such massive quantities. He felt some relief at knowing that last fact.

"You are dismissed, Regent," Hektogarn said, and the strange, unsettling black shape vanished from the room. Both kids took deep drinks of the sparkling drink and felt their spirits rise as the threatening shape vanished. Then the excitement at the news of the trip returned.

"We're really going with you?" Kerrala asked. "Do my parents know?"

"Yes to both," Hektogarn said with a smile. "They suggested I should take you the next time I need to make one of these trips. You can both afford to miss a few days from school."

"So when do we leave?" Markel asked, glowing with delight at the idea of his first off-planet trip in the company of his father and Kerrala.

"We'll leave tomorrow. Meet me here after breakfast."

"But we don't know how to teleport yet," Markel said. "How are we going to come with you?"

"Easy! So long as I'm holding you both, you'll come with me when I leap, but we've learned that it's best to make children unconscious for the trip, so you won't remember a thing. I'll touch your minds with a very gentle form of the mind bolt before I leap, and that will put you into a deep sleep."

"Will we have to meet any Sillaron?" Kerrala asked doubtfully.

"Possibly," Hektogarn said. "Why, is that a problem?"

"I know they're our servants, but they scare me," Kerrala said, her voice showing a little of the shock from the encounter at the entrance. Hektogarn heard the note.

"What happened?" he asked sharply and Kerrala recounted the episode. The adult looked grim.

"Sometimes I feel those people need to be taught a strict lesson about their place," he muttered. "They've been our servants for a million years, you think they'd have learned the realities of the Universe by now, the ungrateful miseries. Hell, they actually rule most of the universe as it is, even if it is on our behalf, but they get massive benefits from the arrangement."

His face lost its dark look and he smiled. "Kerrala, I know your parents are busy on the Council tonight. Will you stay for dinner?"

"I'd love to!" she replied cheerfully. "I didn't want to eat all alone in that huge house."

"Great!" he replied. "Mindor, let me talk to Adrinada."

In a few seconds, the house computer had established the link and Hektogarn spoke briefly with Kerrala's mother, confirming both the evening plans and the travel arrangements for the next day. The transaction caused a query in Markel's mind.

"Dad, how come we don't use telepathy? You just said we're developing this universal telepathic species, but can't we do that ourselves?"

His father smiled. "We have many great powers, but that isn't one of them," he said. "We can receive telepathic communications, a few of us have very limited transmission skills, but it's one thing that seems to have passed by the Pfafth and we can't alter it. That's why we're developing a race that can."

"So how do we talk to our people in other Galaxies?" Kerrala asked.

"It's inconvenient," Hektogarn agreed. "We actually have to send a written message by a personal carrier, just like we did millions of years ago when we lived only on this planet and before we developed other talents. Somebody has to teleport themselves, carrying the message and locate the individual we want. It's quick, but it still takes an hour or two to get there and it's very tiring, so it's not a way to carry on a conversation, because we can only do one trip every few days. Another few hundred thousand years and those intelligent semi-plants should be able to do it for us, though we won't be around to benefit. But our descendants will, and that's what matters."

Dinner was the usual enjoyable, sparkling event that Markel loved so much. Both his parents were high in the ruling echelons of the world that ran almost the entire

Universe. In fact, Hektogarn was the Chairman of the Management Committee which really meant he was the most powerful Pfafth of the entire species, and Merralinda, while not on the Committee because of the law that prevented more than one person in a family being in that group, was a highly influential person in her own right. So it was with huge pride that Markel listened to them talk about their daily work. Already he knew that he been born with the same intellect and possibly even greater powers than his father and one day he would develop into a figure at least as powerful and influential as his father, probably greater. The Pfafth had ruled all intelligent life around the known Universe for over a million years, and he, Markel would be a leader of the race. He glowed when he thought of it and received a warm smile from his parents as they watched him and probably read his thoughts from the expression on his face. Sometime he wondered why they had no telepathic skills when they had almost every other power known to them. Sitting here with his family and with Kerrala who was becoming as important to him as anyone else, he felt totally happy.

"The Spiders represent an unusual event," his mother was saying as he returned his attention to the conversation. "We began to accelerate their intelligence about three hundred thousand years ago and that was highly successful. But sometimes we wonder if it was a mistake."

"But why did we do it?" Markel interrupted. "Why did we need a race of intelligent Spiders?"

"Ugh, I just hate spiders!" Kerrala chimed in. "Why do we want spiders at all, never mind great big ones with big brains?"

Once the laughter had died down, Merralinda answered. "We thought they would possibly make guardians or protectors for other species on occasions. Their terrifying appearance can be most useful in moments of serious danger, such as a mob outbreak."

"A mob?" Markel was astonished. "When has a mob ever occurred? What in Heaven's name would they riot about?"

His mother looked uncomfortable and Hektogarn studied his hands for a few seconds. Markel realised he had raised an issue that reflected oddly on Pfafth rule.

"One of the problems of being the absolute rulers is that some people resent it, regardless of how benign is our rule," Merralinda finally said. "And I assure you, children, Pfafth rule is totally benign. We do no harm to anyone, we merely keep the peace and work towards developing a wealthy, safe Universe."

"But some races still resent it?" Kerrala asked, her expression showing distaste.

"It's very rare," Merralinda said comfortingly. "And it doesn't happen when several adult Pfafth are together. Our mind bolts can damage anyone severely or kill if we choose, and everybody knows about that ability. But there have been just a very few incidents when a lone Pfafth, or worse, a child is accosted by some alien race. So what we did was develop the race of very large spiders to a high intelligence. And we also bred into them our teleportation skills and a trigger that was activated if a Pfafth child was in danger anywhere, so that they'd immediately jump to the rescue. It's only happened three or four times."

"So what's causing the worries about them?" Markel asked.

"It's the rate of development and some factors we never anticipated," Merralinda replied. "In the last few hundred years, we've found some spiders that have developed a second brain, just as large as the first, both linked in a way that probably gives quite extraordinary intelligence."

"Probably?   Can't we check?"   Kerrala looked frightened.

"No, we can't." Hektogarn looked thoughtful. "It's an interesting problem.   Their conditioning seems intact, because there have been two recent incidents of Spiders jumping across galactic distances to protect a small group of young Pfafth.   But we can't any longer communicate with them.   The two telepathic races we use say they cannot any more establish contact.   So either the spiders have lost this talent, or they've developed a new one that's incompatible with the existing ones, or..."

"Or what?" Markel sensed the worry in his father.

"Or they are choosing not to communicate with us at all.   And there's absolutely nothing we can do about it."

Chapter 11. Visiting the Colonies

"I think the best way is for me to sit on the couch, and each of you can sit on one side while I put an arm round your waist." Hektogarn smiled at the children who reflected huge excitement mixed with obvious fear at the trip they were about to make. They would leap over six million light-years to one of the nearby galaxies, Hektogarn had said, to visit the planet of the Shurameen.

"They are a massively intelligent race," Hektogarn had told them a few minutes ago. "And we have pushed their development of molecular control so that it is almost equal to our own. In another few thousand years, they will match us in this area, and they will need it. What the Sillaron Regent told me yesterday was serious. The Shurameen sun will increase its heat output in just under a million years. The planet will be burned to a crisp unless they move it outward in its orbit. They will need to do it themselves, and we are all sure they'll be able to, but it's time I dropped in on them again."

"Will you tell them what's happening?" Markel asked and his father shook his head.

"I won't tell them anything. In fact, we won't talk to anyone, because they won't know we're there. They don't know about alien races yet and it's too early for them. So we will travel around by one of our vehicles that's cloaked and invisible. We won't get out, because we can't cloak ourselves and we look very different from the Shurameen."

"Will we stay long?" Kerrala seemed concerned.

"Just a couple of days. But we'll stay in one of our cloaked buildings well out of the city, so you'll get a good night's rest."

The answer seemed to relieve her and she sat down on Hektogarn's right side with Markel on the opposite. The adult placed a comforting arm round each of them.

"Now you'll sleep for a few minutes, and when you wake up, we'll be six million light-years away," he said softly, and so it was.

* * * *

Hektogarn was right, the Shurameen looked awfully different from the Pfafth. They were huge, for a start, massively built, almost as wide as they were high, and stood in a stooped position, knees somewhat bent and their heads set forward on their shoulders so that they could look directly ahead. The two individuals standing a few metres away were at least twice as tall as Markel and looked like a mountain from his position.

"If you stepped outside the car," Hektogarn said, "you'd immediately realise that the planet's gravity is about sixty percent greater than ours."

"They can't hear us?" Kerrala whispered, clearly awed by the huge aliens.

"Not from outside the car. Don't worry, they can't see us, hear us, or even notice the car moving, and it will automatically avoid any contact with one of them if they move this way." Hektogarn smiled comfortingly. "Now, there are a few things I need to check out."

The vehicle started moving outward from the centre of the small town where they had been.

"I spotted some building activity as we came in," Hektogarn continued. "This will show us the extent of the mental control over matter that they've developed."

Within a few minutes they had reached what was clearly a building site. Several partially completed buildings stood in a row, apparently constructed of a beautiful lemon-coloured stone. But while a number of Shurameen - Markel counted eighteen of them - sat without motion on the ground, no movement was detectible. No scaffolding could be seen, no vehicles of any kind. But then Markel saw something. A huge block of the stone was lifting into the air and moving towards a partially built structure. It floated to the top of the wall, gently lowered itself into position and came to rest. A single Shurameen appeared alongside it, Markel assumed from the other side of the wall, examined the block, waved a hand at the group on the ground, and the stone shifted slightly as it tucked itself firmly into place. Almost immediately, a cloud of sand rose up from it and a pattern emerged from the blank sides, lines that continued the pattern already present in the stones next to it. A few hundred metres away, a similar block was floating just above the ground and moving firmly towards the building site. Markel assumed that there was a quarry somewhere nearby and the Shurameen were taking the beautiful stone from it.

"Very, very interesting," Hektogarn murmured. "That is remarkable for a race so young. The Sillaron had not reported that the Shurameen mental development was so advanced."

"More than you had anticipated?" Markel asked, highly impressed by what he had seen. Lifting a single brick at his desk was nothing compared to raising a twenty-tonne block fifty metres into the air and engraving it once it had been placed in position.

"Much more," Hektogarn said with a nod. "This is encouraging, because it seems certain they will be able to move their planet when the time comes, and it verifies our ability to direct the evolution of a race."

"What's that one man over there doing?" Kerrala pointed at a single individual standing motionless a couple of metres away from another block of stone. Sand was lifting from it as if an invisible grinding machine was removing chunks, but no tool of any sort was visible. The car moved closer and rose a few feet to hover over the block. It was about two metres high, a cylinder made of the same lemon-coloured stone as the buildings, but something was happening to the top half. Lines were appearing, curves seemed to melt into the surface and Markel began to feel powerfully drawn into those strange shapes. He blinked, concentrated and pulled his mind away.

"That's weird!" Kerrala announced. "That's a sculpture and it's not like anything I've ever seen before. It seems to have some sort of hypnotic effect."

"I agree, Kerrala," Hektogarn said. "And it's even more startling than the building process. It appears there's a unique art form developing on this world, and one that affects the mind. It's a pity that the sculpture is too big to take home, and anyway, removing it would cause more inconvenience than I care to think of. Just imagine the reaction of these people if a ten-tonne statue vanished overnight! But I must say, this planet is quite astonishing. I'm going to cross over to the continent in the southern hemisphere and see if developments are similar."

Twenty minutes later, after a rapid, sub-orbital flight, they had crossed a huge ocean and homed in on another town. They floated around for an hour, studying the people, and little difference could be detected between the two locations. But then Kerrala pointed to something.

"Look, that's a carriage of some sort."

She was correct. A large vehicle with four wheels was advancing along the surface, drawn by two animals resembling oxen.

"That's strange," Hektogarn commented. "They use machines. That's totally opposite to the other group and it contradicts everything we thought we had bred into this race. Let's see if we can find other examples."

And within another hour, they had found many. They saw people cutting trees with long saws, building structures with men physically hauling materials and assembling them, and many more animal-drawn carriages, some used for materials, some for personal transport.

Another two hours were spent covering the continent and touching down near small towns, and everywhere they looked, they saw the same as they had seen before, a race of people with no apparent ability to use mental powers such as they had seen initially.

"It's a worry," Hektogarn said. "Two totally opposite cultures. I have no idea how the non-mental society grew up. It contradicts everything we thought about the Shurameen. And the main worry is whether the two societies will clash, maybe even go to war some day in the future."

"Is there anything we can do?" Markel asked.

Hektogarn shook his head. "Not at this early stage. Maybe in another thousand years or so, when they start ocean travel and come into contact with each other, we'll have to have a look. We'll leave records of this visit for our successors to follow up." He looked at the two children and smiled. "I think that will do," he said. "It's getting late, I know I'm tired, so I imagine you kids will be exhausted!"

In fact, Kerrala was almost asleep and Markel was barely able to sit upright and look at the scenery. With a chuckle, Hektogarn gave a silent instruction to the vehicle, which lifted into the darkening sky and arrowed its way to the cloaked refuge they would use for the night.

*   *   *   *

"I'll be very relieved when this project is completed," Hektogarn said. They had leaped just under three million light years that morning, to a neighbouring galaxy from the one that held the world of the Shurameen. He and the two children were standing on a large plain, and the wind was strong. Were it not for the automatic ability to adjust their body temperatures that all Pfafth possessed, they would be freezing to a painful extent, for thick ice lay on the ground and snow flurries were racing past at high speed.

A few hundred meters away, a massive metallic object stood on the ground. Markel had never seen a spaceship before, though he knew there were such objects.

"It's taken every ship we have for over a year," Hektogarn continued. "But once we decided to save this species from extinction and move them to other planets, we had to complete the task, even though we'll only save a fraction of the population. But we had to put enough of them on each planet to ensure survival."

"I didn't even know we had spaceships," Kerrala said. "Why don't we use them for regular transport?"

"Because we only have a few," Hektogarn replied. "Eight of them, in fact, and flying one is a horrendously difficult task. The crew all have to be the most powerful minds that can teleport themselves, the ship and the load, and not many of us can do that, so we use them only when essential. And it's much slower than personal teleportation. It takes hours, even days to get from one place to another. That's why we've been breeding the Kaloti towards this direction. They seem capable of developing engines within the next few thousand years that probably can do it in the same time, but not need teleporting skill."

"This is the last trip?" Kerrala asked.

"Thankfully, yes. The last six hundred of the species are going to the second planet we've chosen for them, so there'll be a few thousand of each on both planets, both in this galaxy. We estimate it will be a million years or so to develop full civilisations, so it will be interesting to see if they develop in different ways."

In front of them, a trio of Pfafth agents was leading the last stragglers of what had been a long line of creatures into the ship.

"We hit them with a very low-level mind bolt," Hektogarn explained. "So they can be easily directed. They'll sleep for the next few hours as they travel, and they won't remember anything after they've left the ship on the new planet."

Markel stared hard and made out the shapes of some of the individuals in the group. They were small, not much bigger than himself, he decided, and covered with shaggy fur, more like animals than intelligent beings. They walked in a stoop, shambling along in a manner that hardly indicated a species that one day would build cities and fly spaceships. "They don't look very much like people," he said, doubtfully.

Hektogarn laughed. "Nor did we Pfafth a couple of million years ago! But those people will develop, possibly even as much as we have, eventually."

He waved at the ship and began walking towards it. "We'll travel on board to the new planet and see them off-loaded. The trip will take about nine hours. I can't teleport again for at least that long, so we'll sleep on the ship and after we land and look around, we'll leap again."

The trip was boring. The ship was not equipped with any sort of viewing facilities, not even on the flight deck, so Markel could not look out on space. And although the ship was equipped with gravitational engines to lift the many thousands of tonnes into orbit and initiate movement away from the planet, the real transportation was produced by the crew of six highly specialised Pfafth who had spent years learning the technique of meshing their intensely-tuned minds into a single, hugely powerful force that teleported the ship and its contents to its location.

So for nine hours, the travellers did very little except sleep. They had their own cabins, while the main cargo of proto-humans lived in the massive storage areas and spent the time in a comatose state of non-awareness. For Hektogarn, this rest period was crucially important, for teleporting himself and the two children was an exhausting process. The effect on the crew was more dramatic. Markel saw the six men as he walked off the ship the following morning. They were sitting in the sunlight and all of them looked white and haggard, barely able to raise an arm in greeting.

"They've spent their lives developing this ability," Hektogarn said to the children after he had walked over to express his thanks to the crew. "And they can manage only three trips a year without doing permanent damage to themselves. They'll spend a week here, just recuperating from this one, then take the empty ship home where they'll get three or four months off. And even then, none of them will stay in the profession for more than five years. But they get well rewarded, and they are guaranteed senior positions in the Colonial Service after, so it's a good life."

"So will we fly back with them?" Kerrala asked, not looking happy at the prospect.

Hektogarn laughed. "No, young lady, we won't! We'll look around here for a day or two, make sure these new immigrants are settled then we'll teleport normally to our next port. Meanwhile, we want to make sure they get off the ship and link up with the previous group." He led the way into the vast cavern of the ship's hold, softly leading the children round the side. In the middle, the few hundred primitives were getting to their feet and starting to drift towards the outside. There was little noise, though a few infants could be heard crying softly from the middle of the crowd.

"The computers have prepared some basic food and

water supplies and left them by the exit," Hektogarn said softly. "That will see them safely outside, and the food is full of very high protein, so they can last a few days if necessary before they start finding their own. Meanwhile, we're going off to look for the previous group."

In one of the storage sections, a gravity vehicle was standing, and the three took their seats. Hektogarn piloted it high above the crowd and out through the doorway, lifting even further into the air as they left the ship until they were at least a hundred meters above the ground. They began a circular path of ever-increasing diameter until they were a few kilometres from the ship.

Hektogarn pointed. "Look!" he said. "Wild life."

Way beneath them, a herd of large creatures was moving in single file. The vehicle was equipped with viewing devices, and Markel took one to examine the creatures. They seemed huge, strange, shaggy animals with enormous, curving tusks coming from their upper jaws. Even stranger was the massive trunk that hung from above the mouth of each animal. It seemed to have a life of its own, sweeping the grass ahead of the animals and occasionally plucking a great wad of vegetation from trees, and feeding it into the mouth.

"We found two almost identical planets for this experiment," Hektogarn said. "Similar mass, both of them the third planet from their sun at similar distances, so very similar climates. Even the natural animal and vegetation life is almost identical, so the influences on both groups will be much the same. It will make a fascinating study over the new few hundred thousand years to see what differences emerge between the two groups. But I'm a little concerned, we should have found the rest of the tribe by now. They were only dropped here a few days ago."

He took the vehicle up further so that the air became quite cool and all of them had to adjust their internal temperatures. The exploring circle had become over thirty kilometres wide by now and Markel could see a line of worry in his father's face. He experimented with his empathic sense, knowing it was quite well advanced, reaching out to see if he could detect any contact with other minds. He touched Kerrala on her arm. "Hey, you're better at this than I am. Try looking out and detecting the people."

A few seconds later, Kerrala let out a squeak. "Down there," she said pointing at the edge of a major forest. "There are a few hundred of them there."

Following her directions, Markel reached his mind out and opened his senses to receive... and he caught it. Tuning in further, he looked out through dark eyes, saw the friendly trees, felt the sense of danger, the hunger and the joy that warmer climates were around them instead of the killing cold that had enveloped them only a little while ago.

Hektogarn swooped down and moved slowly at treetop level, finally seeing the mass of dark shapes in the forest.

"We placed these arrivals in a more northerly latitude than their equivalents on the other planet," Hektogarn said as they rode silently. "The climate is less moderate here, while on the other world, we placed the people nearer the equator. We expected both to start migration patterns as they had on their original world, but I never expected they'd start so soon. We'd better try and herd the newcomers over here to join them."

He lifted back high and returned rapidly to the monstrous egg-shaped spaceship sitting in the plain. As they reached it, Markel could see that the primitives had all left the vessel and were standing quietly in the grass.

"Captain," said Hektogarn. His voice was picked up by the communication device in his shoulder and transmitted to the Captain. Markel couldn't hear the Captain's response, but Hektogarn spoke on. "The others are about thirty kilometres due west of you and they have obviously started a migration pattern. Get two more vehicles up as soon as you have rested enough and apply very low level mind bolts at the new arrivals, just enough to make them want to get away in that direction. Then have another couple of you do the same to the other group to persuade them to stay still for a few days until they join up."

He looked down at the kids and grinned. "The poor guys are utterly exhausted from the flight, but they'll be able to do it tomorrow. That will make sure the entire tribe is together and a lot safer that way."

He turned the vehicle and flew rapidly in a westerly direction. "Let's just have a look around, eh?"

They spent another few hours sightseeing. Markel thought the planet looked quite beautiful, with massive, rolling plains giving way to startling, snow-capped mountain ranges that reared their peaks more than twelve thousand metres into the stratosphere. They saw a few more signs of wild life, animals that looked like huge oxen, others like small pigs. There was great excitement later in the day as dusk began to fall, when they saw four enormous, cat-like creatures attack the oxen herd and bring down two of them.

As dark fell, Hektogarn returned to the ship. "They'll do," he said cheerfully as the vehicle was stored away in the ship's hold. The crewmen looked massively different from their pitifully exhausted state of a few hours earlier. This time they grinned cheerfully at their passengers, though seemed unwilling to enter into anything more than small talk.

"They have their own, unique culture from a life totally different from any other Pfafth," Markel's father explained as they walked into the ship for the night. "They have almost nothing in common with the rest of us, so little to talk about. They'll develop into more rounded individuals once they've retired from the job, but for now, they're not the most talkative of people."

In the morning, they took a short stroll in the beautiful sunshine, listened to the stunning silence of a new world and smelled air that was fresher than anyone could imagine. A short distance from the ship, they sat down, Hektogarn placed his arms round their waists and said, "I think you're going to like the next visit." Then the children fell asleep.

Twenty minutes later, they were nearly sixty million light years away, under a sun that was the most beautiful yellow colour Markel had ever seen.

"It's gorgeous!" Kerrala gasped. "But have we arrived just before nightfall? It seems to be getting dark."

"No, it's mid-afternoon and this is as bright as it gets. It's one of the reasons they've developed so fast," Hektogarn said as they looked out from the cloaked building that was their refuge on the world of the Kaloti. "Here they are a lot nearer the centre of their galaxy, with a relatively low-light sun and only a small moon that does not reflect the sun efficiently. So they have always had a night sky of astounding star-scapes that have intrigued them, awed them and given them a great urge to find out what they are. They are a species of huge natural intelligence, so it was not a great surprise to find that they had flown to their moon just a few decades ago. But it was a *real* surprise and a great delight to us that they launched their first nuclear-powered ship and settled their first colonies on the nearby planet. That's very rapid development. And now it seems they've started work on gravitational engines, so they will certainly be a star-travelling race before too long."

Outside, the view was of isolated countryside, but the scenery was glorious. The luxurious golden yellow of the sun gave an exotic sheen to everywhere. Hektogarn yawned.

"You've seen how exhausting it is for us to teleport, and I've been carrying you two as well. In a few years time you'll learn how to do it and then you'll see why I'm so weary. There's nobody within a thousand kilometres of this place, so why don't you two go outside and play? Come in whenever you're ready, the computers will provide meals. But I'm dead on my feet and I need to get to bed!"

He was already stumbling over his own feet as he walked out of the room, and Markel grinned at the sight.

"Let's get out there!" he said, and they raced into the lovely golden afternoon to find intoxicating fresh air and scents they had never encountered before. In the low gravity, only about a third of home world, they were able to jump astounding distances and heights, and Markel invented a whole new game of trying to jump from one spot, reach as high as possible, and land on a precise spot twenty metres away. Kerrala joined in and suggested a new twist, that they should try and turn head over heels during the jump. After successfully managing a complete spin, Markel challenged her to try two, and they decided points should be awarded for the number of spins and the accuracy of the landing spot. After a few hours, night fell and they stopped playing. But as they walked back to the building, they stopped, utterly thunderstruck by the sky. The stars had come out as if a monstrous canopy of coloured lights had been suddenly lit up. The entire sky was one fantastic, glittering display of glorious colours from horizon to horizon. In awe, they stared upwards, completely lost in the magic that surrounded them.

"Now I see why the Kaloti want to get up and there and see what they are," Kerrala whispered, as if in a cathedral. "Have you ever seen such a sight?"

Markel couldn't do anything but shake his head in wonderment. In unspoken agreement, they lay down in the grass and looked upward, simply experiencing the display. But eventually, pangs of hunger made them get up and go inside. Once fed, they talked about what they had seen these last few days and what was still left on their schedule. Markel realised that he was happier than he'd ever been before, and spending so much time in the company of Kerrala was one of the reasons. He also thought that the game they'd invented had promise, but probably could be enhanced even more. Maybe both could jump at the same time and one could try and catch the other.... But those stars..... Who could *not* want to fly among them after having seen such magic?

* * * *

"They are certainly very confident of their success," Hektogarn said softly, failing to hide just how struck he was by the sight in front of them. The gravity vehicle hovered a hundred metres or so above the ground and just a few hundred metres from an enormous construction site.

"But Hektogarn, if that's supposed to be a spaceship, how can they be building it on the surface before they've invented gravity engines?" Kerrala was equally impressed, but also puzzled. Ahead of them, they could see what looked like a gigantic metal sphere, fully a hundred metres in diameter, though not yet complete. The framework of the sphere was in place, but plates were still being added to enclose the space.

"They can't, Kerrala, unless they are so far advanced that they know that they will succeed in the near future. In fact, they must have designed some form of gravity control already, because they could not construct a ship that size on the ground without it. It would collapse under its own weight, even in the low gravity of this planet. That's how we build our own ships and keep them whole, but this is far bigger than ours. This is amazing! The Kaloti have reached this stage of development thousands of years ahead of us. That thing looks ready to fly within a few months."

"But will they be able to travel the sort of distances we do by teleportation?" Markel asked. He couldn't take his eyes off the vast structure.

"Certainly not yet," his father replied. "The theory of hyperspace is just that, a theory, though we're pretty certain it does exist and can be entered." Under his silent control, the vehicle continued to circle the construction. Markel finally pulled his eyes away and looked at the ground where several hundreds of the Kaloti were busy at a variety of tasks. He thought they were beautiful, immensely tall beings, slender as reeds, with enormous dark eyes that let them see clearly in the dim light of this planet. The microphones outside the car had picked up their communications, but they were completely incomprehensible, sounding only like a musical note played on a stringed instrument.

"We haven't been able to get enough information to set up translation computers," Hektogarn said, in response to Markel's question on the subject. He laughed, though it was not completely a sound of amusement. "Sometimes I think the gods have played a cruel joke on us Pfafth! Here we are, the rulers of forty galaxies, the most powerful species in all of space, but some of the talents we need have passed us by. We can't communicate telepathically, we don't know how to build hyperspace ships and there aren't enough of us to be able to run the place without the help of the Sillaron and we can't understand *them* all that well, either."

Without warning, the vehicle hit what seemed like a massive windstorm. It was flung away from the structure on the ground, turned end from end, spinning furiously, completely out of control. Kerrala screamed and Hektogarn let out some words beyond Markel's comprehension. Only the fact that the vehicle completely enclosed them in a single gravitational field saved their lives, otherwise they would have been thrown around like peas in a violently shaken jar and battered against each other. After a few seconds, the violence died and Hektogarn was able to regain control of the vehicle. Rather surprised at his coolness, Markel looked around but was unable to see the spaceship under construction. In fact, he could see the coast of the continent, which indicated they had been blown a huge distance because the construction site had been almost in the centre of the landmass.

"What happened?" he asked, taking Kerrala's hand to offer some support. Her face was white and he could feel her trembling.

"The gravity field of this vehicle met the gravity field they'd created to build the ship," Hektogarn replied. His face was also pale from the shock. "Which means a very advanced gravity engineering skill indeed, because the field extended a great distance. The two fields acted like the same poles of two magnets and pushed us apart furiously. I had no idea they could have developed such abilities already."

He looked down at his son. "You were very calm, young man. I'm most impressed!"

Markel grinned, delighted with his father's approval. "I knew you'd handle it! Anyway, that must mean the Kaloti are nearer developing real spaceships and that's got to be good for us, right?"

"Indeed it does. It will certainly fill one of the biggest gaps we have in our ability to run this Empire. Let's look around for a couple more days, then we'll have a look at the second one, the universal telepathic network that we need."

* * * *

The second they arrived on the surface of the new planet, the pain struck them. To Markel, it felt like a hot iron burning his scalp and he shouted with the shock and the agony. He heard a gasp from his father then he blacked out.

As he slowly returned to consciousness some unknown time later, he could hear Hektogarn's voice speaking softly.

"Relax, Markel, the pain is gone. You can wake up now."

Feeling comforted by the words, Markel let himself come to full awareness. He was lying on the ground, but the surface was padded by what seemed like rough grass and small growths of little bushes. He sat up and looked around. Immediately, he saw Kerrala lying flat on the surface. Frightened, he turned to his father.

"It's okay, Markel, she's still asleep. I hit you both with a small bolt as soon as we arrived. The telepathic field from these creatures is far greater than I'd realised, so it took me a moment to adjust the barrier. I put you both out to give you time to do the same, and you'll both be okay now."

Kerrala stirred and Markel moved to her, helping her sit up.

She smiled weakly. "What the heck was that?" she whispered.

"Another example of a species developing faster than we realised," Hektogarn answered. "I was here twenty years ago and there was nothing like that strength of the transmissions. Progress has been astounding!"

Markel was looking around. The view was not attractive. Flat, featureless country stretched in all directions, alleviated only by a few small patches of gorse bush. A persistent wind howled across the territory and he knew that only his automatic body temperature adjustment kept him from feeling severe cold. A few metres away, a single object stood. It was perhaps two metres high, just a mound covered with the same gorse and grass that filled the rest of the scene.

"That's what we believe will be our other massive help," Hektogarn said with an amused tone to his voice. "Not that impressive, is it?"

"That's a living, intelligent creature?" Kerrala asked. Both children had learned about the growing telepathic species of this world, but the lessons had not fully prepared them for how *ordinary* these things looked.

Markel didn't hear his father's reply. Something was happening in his mind. It was like a feather touching his skin, barely felt but certainly there. Fascinated, he tried to identify the sensation. It was a little like the moment when a Cassolean had spoken telepathically to him during a school exercise, but no words were clear... it was just sound, occasional musical notes, faint echoes of ancient memories, but he knew something was trying to contact him.

"I am Markel," he said in his mind. Nothing happened except that the faint touches became a flood of incomprehensible noise. And yet he sensed that the flood was a response to his identification. He tried again and received the same result, but nothing could be identified.

"Markel? Something happening, son?" He felt his father's hand on his shoulder and broke out of what had felt like a light trance. Both the other two were looking curiously at him.

"I think it was trying to talk to me," he said.

Hektogarn did not look surprised. "I suppose that's natural," he said. "That's their function, but we didn't expect this level of sophistication for many centuries yet. Could you understand anything?"

Markel shook his head. "Just noise. But I suppose we have no basis for communication at all if this is the first real contact."

"I think that's right," his father said. "It could take another thousand years for them to develop and read other minds of other species before they get any ability to understand each other. But I think this had better be the last visit. It's hard enough even for a Pfafth to withstand these telepathic fields, so I'm certain any other species would be killed by them this close. When we leave in a couple of days, I'll destroy the refuge. Nobody must come to this planet again."

Later that night, Markel awoke in his room in the shelter used by the Pfafth for previous visits. A voice seemed to be speaking to him.

"Markel," it said.

He sat up. "Yes," he spoke out loud. "I am Markel."

He got nothing but a repeat of his name. But it was enough for him to understand what was happening. One of the telepathic creatures was speaking to him, probably the first time one of them had made contact with another species. He laughed out loud in sheer joy. "Give it time," he said. "I look forward to talking to you again in the future."

Chapter 12. Ruling the Universe

"You have been assigned to Sector Alpha Nine, Markel. I am very proud of you!"

Hektogarn looked smug as he looked a little upward at his son. Markel had grown into everything his childhood and training had promised. He had excelled at every program the schools and the Service Training Academy had thrown at him. Only Kerrala had matched him, just as she had done throughout their short lives together. Now at eighteen, they had requested Colonial postings together and had been granted their wish, as might be expected of students who had written new records at school.

"Have you been there, father?"

"Indeed, I have, my son! It was also my first posting! I didn't tell you until the confirmation came through, but believe me, this is a prestigious sector. You have five major galaxies in the region and over twenty intelligent life forms who know about us and are part of the Pfafth Empire."

"Any developing races?"

"Oh yes, several others are in the stages of being carefully watched and you'll get a chance for some fieldwork visiting them under strict disguise and secrecy. I've always thought that's the best part of the Colonial Section, helping bring up new races to maturity."

"You mean I get to go down and visit a race that doesn't know about star travel, or any races other than themselves?"

"Indeed you do, and horribly smelly, dangerous and exciting it can be."

"What do we do about language, though? I can't speak any primitive tongues."

"It's okay, Markel. Most of these primitives have barely developed language at all, never mind any civilisation like building or agriculture, so communication is largely by gesture. And where language does exist, the computers will handle it through your implanted communications chip. You'll get a training program from the computers before each visit and you always carry weapons, so you can't get hurt."

"But if I use a weapon, won't that affect the culture and memories of the locals?"

Oddly enough, Hektogarn looked a little uncomfortable for a brief moment. "There are procedures for accidentally revealing ourselves," he said. "You'll get a full briefing before each visit. Now, when do you leave?"

"In about an hour, father. Kerrala and I are going to transport together."

"Excellent! You've been fully trained in teleportation? Wouldn't want any accidents and have you ending up on some deserted ice-world!"

Markel had every reason for confidence. He and Kerrala had, as usual, excelled at the new training when they were finally introduced to it three years ago. The process was quite complicated when travelling to a planet never previously visited, and needed the assistance of a telepathic species. But he was quite secure in his ability to jump the five million light years that he was about to cross to reach the planet of Tracomal where the capital of the Regency for the sector was established.

Farewells to his family completed, Markel left his house and took the automated vehicle to the government building from which he would teleport himself. There was no great emotion in the parting, for after all, Markel could transport himself home at any time. Teleporting twice within two or three days was not recommended, because the process was quite exhausting, but regular weekends and vacations were quite in order, so his departure was not exactly traumatic. Anyway, travelling the vast extents of the Pfafth Empire was standard for all Pfafth, so the trip was nothing unusual.

He grinned happily as he saw Kerrala waiting for him at the building doorway.

"Shall we start our astounding careers as Colonial Leaders?" he said as she linked her arm in his to walk up to the transportation room.

"Indeed we shall," she said, her eyes sparkling with excitement. "I've been waiting a long time for this."

The room hardly looked like the point from which two people would travel five million light years. It was merely a comfortable office, large enough for a desk at one end and a coffee table with four armchairs at the other. A young woman was sitting in one of the armchairs and she rose to her feet as Markel and Kerrala entered. Her manner was subdued and respectful. She was not Pfafth, but Markel had known that would be the case. This exercise needed a telepath with transmission capabilities and this young woman had been trained in the specific skill of launching travellers to a new location. Markel looked at her. Highly attractive, he decided, with good features, though skin of a distinct blue tinge, very little nose and eyes of a deep, coal-ember red. He recalled from his briefing that the people of the planet Cassolea had evolved this way. He saw that Kerrala was looking at his study of the alien woman, and he grinned at her. Pfafth did not have social contacts with aliens, they both knew that.

"Would you both please be seated?" the woman said. As they sat down, she did the same, facing them both. "You understand what we will be doing?" she said.

"Of course," Kerrala said in some irritation from the seat on his left. "Let's get on with it."

The woman said nothing, but somehow Markel sensed her resentment at the tone. "We have both had a lot of training," he said pleasantly. "I think we will be fine."

"Thank you, sir," the woman replied. "You realise, I am not able to teleport, so I don't come with you. I merely provide the images you need to make the jump. Now, close your eyes, I will start placing images in your mind. First, our present location on the planet."

Markel sensed images flood into his head. Despite closed eyes, he saw a distinct, detailed picture of the building, the complex in which it was situated, and the parklands around it, as if looking down from a few hundred metres.

"And we will start to draw away," the woman's voice seemed to come from nowhere, everywhere, softly, smoothly. He felt as if he was rushing upward from the buildings, soaring into the stratosphere with an exhilarating rush... and it stopped, his eyes snapped open to see the Cassolean woman staring at him. Her eyes glowed bright red with astonishment.

"What the hell?" Kerrala seemed furious. "What's going on, why have we stopped?

"Excuse me, sir," the woman said. "Please forgive my rudeness, but you *are* Pfafth, are you not?"

"Of course I am! Why do you ask?"

"Because you were transmitting telepathically," she replied.

"But we Pfafth can't do that!" His astonishment made him stand up.

"That is the established wisdom," she replied. "But I assure you, you were transmitting. I read all the exhilaration of the flight outward. It has never happened before."

"Does it stop me from teleporting?" he demanded, suddenly frightened that his career might be over before it had started, but she shook her head.

"No, it does not. It was just the shock of reading you that stopped me. Please, sit down, and we'll start again."

"I should damn well think so," muttered Kerrala from her seat. *Why the hell was she so bad tempered?* he asked himself.

"Because of the attention you are giving me," said the soundless voice in his head. Startled, he looked up to see the Cassolean half-smiling at him.

"You saw that?" he asked, keeping the question in his mind.

"I could hardly miss it. Now, let us resume."

Aloud she repeated the second sentence, and Markel settled down to try teleporting again.

Once more, he saw the building from above and again he thrilled to the upward rush into the stratosphere. The images flooded into his mind from the Cassolean as he seemed to fly into space and the planet retreated at a fantastic speed into nothingness. He sensed himself rotate and face the opposite direction and the view changed sharply as if the camera had switched to a different focus.

"Your home galaxy is below you," said the quiet voice in his head, and he looked down to see the astounding sight of the entire galaxy spread below his feet like a glowing white carpet.

"Now look ahead, and that is your neighbouring galaxy. Look further ahead, and that is the target galaxy to which you are going. As you have been taught, reach out your arms and stretch towards that galaxy."

He knew he had no real body, but somehow he reached out his arms, they stretched into an infinite distance to the distant galaxy that became closer as he seemed to pull himself across space.

"Now look to the northern end, see the one large tentacle of stars reaching far, far out, pull yourself to that....."

Obeying the soft instructions, he seemed to fly at astounding speed toward the massive tentacle that reached out from the body of the galaxy.

"Follow me," she said. "That section there..." In front of him, part of the star-arm seemed to glow even brighter as they neared. "Now that star..." He saw a bright yellow sun racing towards him... "And that planet..." Again he reached out and felt that his mysterious, elongated, tenuous arms were touching the planet.

"Take hold of it, possess it," said the soft voice. "Now pull back again, back into the space outside the galaxy, but keep your focus on the star's location, fix its position in the galaxy.... Good.... Excellent... and now that you have it, you will remember it. Now you can pull yourself back to the planet, come closer with me... see *that* continent... *that* town."

In reverse motion of leaving his home planet, Markel swooped down on the city that appeared in the continent, saw the building she pointed out, mentally entered it, saw a room, entered that and took a seat with a huge sigh of fatigue... and opened his eyes. He was in a similar room to that from which he had left and for a moment he panicked. Had he messed this up? But he felt the small difference in gravity, the slightly different colour of the sun shining through the window. In fact, the room was different, larger, carpeted in different colours... and Kerrala was sitting on his right, not his left as she had been. There was no sign of the Cassolean. Markel felt exhausted.

"Whoooooo-eeeeeee!" laughed Kerrala. "Now *that* was some trip!"

"Now I see why we don't do it for every trip," Markel muttered and got to his feet, sensing great weariness. The door opened and another young woman walked in. She gave a smile of welcome.

"Good evening," she said. "I am Jessandra, the Assistant Commissioner for the sector. May I make you welcome to the planet Tracomal and the sector capital of Alladort. I know just how tired you will be, which is why we timed your arrival to be early evening, local time. We will have you taken immediately to your apartments and I have no doubts you will sleep heavily. You will be picked up again at eight hours in the morning."

Barely able to keep his eyes open, Markel followed an equally wilting Kerrala to the outside where a transport took them a short distance to an apartment building. Somebody helped them inside, showed them their places, and Markel was barely able to strip his clothes off before collapsing onto the bed.

Jumping five million light years in a few seconds was certainly not something to do all that often, he decided as the last shreds of consciousness slipped away.

* * * *

Sometimes, the job was distinctly boring, but he'd been warned by his father that government service was often boring, regardless of the fact that his role was part of the governance of the entire known Universe of forty galaxies. Much of his work consisted of merely reading the huge volumes of data that poured into the computers of the Sector Government buildings in the city of Alladort and trying to get some sense of what was happening. But in fact, little seemed to be happening that might cause concern. Factories produced goods, people bought them, climate changes occurred, weather patterns sometimes caused storms, primitive species slowly developed... Nothing happened that might engage the attentions of a god-like species that had more power than any other known race in the Universe.

He saw little of Kerrala in those first few months. She was busy too, much as he was, simply trying to get her intellect round the enormous scale of operations required to govern five galaxies, several hundred populated planets, twenty intelligent races and another ten races with intelligence but not yet the awareness of alien species of massively advanced development compared to themselves.

The Sillaron conducted much of the work of actual administration, anyway. Markel eventually became accustomed to seeing the strange, insubstantial shapes throughout the city, though he never lost the unease he felt at their presence.

In his fourth month he was assigned to his first field trip. It was not a great distance to the planet that was home to a race newly introduced to the Pfafth Empire. The civilisation was advanced enough to have aviation that crossed between continents, conduct wars and begin experimentation in space flight, with a successful trip to its single moon.

"This is unusual, isn't it?" asked Markel after completing his first teleportation across space since his arrival at Sector headquarters. As before, it had needed the assistance of a telepath to teach him the route, but he had been a little less fatigued after the trip and quite ready for work the following morning. The trip had been a mere five thousand light years to a planet within the same galaxy.

"What is unusual, sir?" asked the Sillaron assigned as his guide and mentor. Markel could not quite shut out the sensation that the Sillaron was somehow mocking his youth and inexperience.

"The fact that a non space-travelling race should have been introduced to the empire. My training was quite clear on the point, that a species is not contacted until space flight is a regular part of their culture."

"The laws that your own people wrote do make allowances, sir," the Sillaron replied. "And Sector

Government decided that the Mianten should be granted the joys and benefits of Pfafth rule."

Markel was certain of it now, the Sillaron was laughing at him. He swallowed his sense of discomfort and looked around him. They were in the middle of the main city of the continent, one of three major continents on the planet. A constant state of warfare between all three had existed for centuries until the last few decades, and the general air of run-down seediness everywhere he saw reflected the impoverished nature of the world. The Mianten were a small people, most barely reaching his chest, and their four arms seemed clumsy and overly large by his perception. But his reading on this civilisation indicated that the natives had highly sophisticated manipulation skills and were excellent engineers with notable abilities to control complex devices.

"So what were the circumstances that made us invite this world into the empire?" asked Markel.

"A mistake," replied the Sillaron. "A group of young Masters like yourself unfortunately teleported here while the planet was still quarantined from open contact. They were remarkably young and foolish and played a number of games with some of the citizens. The only way to calm the world-wide panic that ensued when it became obvious that the pranksters were alien was to send an envoy and introduce the people to the fact of inter-galactic commerce. I should tell you that one of the young Masters responsible was your father."

Markel worked hard to ignore the obvious insult he'd been dealt. He knew he would have to raise the issue of the Sillaron's strange behaviour when he returned to the Capital, but for now he had to learn more. As they walked, he concentrated hard on observing the locals and extending his empathic talents to sense what was going on in their minds. This was a skill he had polished a lot in his later years at school, and for once, he had had not been the class leader. Kerrala had been clearly the top performer, but he was still one of the best pupils the school had produced, able to tune in to another's mind and sense the emotions and viewpoint.

The exercise was not a cheerful one. As he watched himself through a local man's eyes as he and his Sillaron subordinate walked the streets, the main sensation was of fear. The man was afraid, more of the Sillaron than of the Pfafth, but there was fear enough for both. And with fear was resentment. These people, Markel realised, had just pulled themselves out of centuries of warfare, had just begun to take control of their own world and see the benefits of peace and commerce. Life was still mean, but they were in control and the fear and privations caused by global war had at last dissipated. But just as they had made these gains, they had been cast right down to the level of dominion state, ruled by a species so powerful it was beyond their capacity to comprehend.

Markel shuddered. This was not anything like the colonial life he had been taught, the Pfafth view of happy, peaceful colonies ruled with the cheerful acceptance and gratitude by subservient peoples. But it was the powerful fear of the Sillaron that worried him most, for it echoed his own unease with this strange race. He realised that their presence had caused a small crowd to gather. He looked around him and saw that possibly two hundred of the Mianten had now congregated in the streets, blocking off intersections, standing quietly but with an odd sense of hostility in their pose. Markel studied them and examined the emotions being radiated from them. As before, there was fear, curiosity, resentment, but no obvious threat.

He decided to use a gentle form of persuasion to clear the way home. Deliberately raising his heartbeat and internal tensions, he focused on creating a very mild form of the mental thunderbolt that he knew could kill many of these people if he wished. When he had measured enough of the energy built up within him, he released it in a scattergun approach rather than a directed bolt at one specific individual. The effect was as he had planned. The crowd wavered as a spasm of fear rocked them and headaches erupted in all of them. In a few moments they had dissipated and the way back to the Administration Building was again clear.

"Thank you, sir. That was well done." Markel sensed that the Sillaron's tone held mocking amusement. "However, I would have advised killing a few to encourage obedience. It has a more permanent effect."

Astonished, Markel looked at the Sillaron. For a moment, the white face with large, oval eyes flashed at him, displaying a wide-mouthed laugh then it vanished again behind the black-smoked camouflage that usually enveloped these beings.

"We are supposed to be their protectors, not their overlords," Markel said. "Since when has killing been a mode of administration?"

The Sillaron made no reply and Markel strode off rapidly towards his office. The less time he spent with these Sillaron the better, he decided.

Months of relatively boring administration work followed that first field trip, and Markel was beginning to wonder if he had made the correct career decision. Surely he was not going to waste all his marvellous talents and skills sitting at a desk reading mountains of data and statistics and attempting to formulate government policies for others to implement?

"No, it isn't all you'll ever do!" His boss, Jessandra, the Assistant Commissioner who had met him on his arrival at Alladort seemed amused. "But nobody goes straight from the training academy to being a Commissioner! The essential part of your job is to know and understand the races we rule, and that comes only from study, learning the facts about all of them and field trips to get the real feel of who and what they are. Until you have that under control, you can't develop management policies."

"Yes, I see," Markel said, still feeling a little frustrated by his boring duties. He was overwhelmed by the sheer mass of information that poured over his desk each day and had no idea of how he would ever absorb it and be able to make sense of it.

"But you get another break," Jessandra continued. "You and Kerrala will make a visit together. There are two planets I wish you to visit and report back your findings back to us."

Markel's spirits lifted. He'd seen almost nothing of Kerrala since arriving and the chance of spending a few days in her company was just what he needed to improve his life, he felt. Encouraged, he returned to studying piles of statistics.

An hour later, something caught his attention in the papers on his desk and he switched from automatic reading and absorbing of facts to looking harder at what he was reading. The paper had the title of *"Cost Support by Planetary Contribution."* But it was not the title that had triggered his increased attention. It was a line that referred to the amount of minerals, manufactured materials and other items that were shipped back to home world from each of the worlds administered in this sector. The value seemed huge, and Markel began to dig further into the statistics of what those worlds produced. By the next day, he was feeling considerable shock and disturbance. On average, nearly twenty percent of the annual production of each planet was being shipped back to Pfafth home world. Even the world of the Mianten, impoverished, battered and recovering from centuries of war paid heavily to the Pfafth for the privilege of being ruled. Sensing that the topic might cause him some difficulties if he raised it with his boss, he said nothing, hoping he could discuss it with his father the next time he went home for a break. Anyway, he had a field trip to make with Kerrala, and that took all his attention as he prepared for the visit.

* * * *

"Our first visit to a planet of primitives," Kerrala said, her voice reflecting a mix of anxiety and excitement. Markel fully understood, feeling exactly those emotions himself. The planet had been discovered only a century or two before, and the inhabitants were still at a pre-mechanical stage of development, having nothing more advanced that wheeled carts drawn by a large, ox-like creature. The most advanced groups lived on a single continent where the total population was quickly rising to the fifty million mark, villages had expanded into towns and a degree of commerce existed between these centres. The language was quite sophisticated and was capable of dealing with conceptual thought, art and such scientific research as was permissible in an autocratic and strongly religious culture.

"Your mission is merely to observe," Jessandra had instructed them. "Again, you have been selected for this one because of your highly developed empathic skills, so we need you to use them to the utmost and discover how the society is evolving. They understand that their world, which they call Mellissiana revolves around the sun, but the concept of alien life on other planets would be frowned on by the religious authorities. So far, however, we cannot detect that anyone has even had a thought along those lines. You have received your instructions on how to behave, the computers have been programmed with the language as far as we have learned it, and I expect you will pick up further understanding on this trip. Keep your weapons thoroughly concealed and only use them as a last resort. Use the mind bolts at whatever degree of intensity you need if trouble arises. And good luck."

They travelled as brother and sister, which permitted them to walk together as equals and dine together in the restaurants and cafes in the small town of Hallias. When asked, they told the locals that they were in town to look at business opportunities for their family in a small town on the coast. The chances of meeting anyone from that town were highly limited, but they took care to eat in a different restaurant every time, and they spent their days tuning in to the minds of the locals and letting their communication systems pick up any new words and phrases to update the language data bases.

After three days, the novelty of seeing a new, primitive civilisation and playing the part of discovery had begun to wear off, falling under the discomfort of harsh clothing material, basic accommodation, food of little variety and the smells and messiness of a non-mechanised civilisation.

"I seriously need a long, hot shower," Kerrala muttered softly as they sat in yet another badly lit, ill-equipped restaurant that served little but the local version of meat, potatoes and beer.

"Another two days," Markel said, equally quietly. "We've seen nothing, I agree, but I suppose our computers have picked up some more words and phrases for the language. Let's finish up this awful meal and get out of here."

Finding the necessary coins in his pocket, he settled the bill and the two walked out, intending a quiet evening in their rooms after comparing notes on the day's work.

It was not to be.

The atmosphere of rage and hatred hit them as they came out into the air. As they appeared, a scream of blind fury cut through the night.

"*Witchcraft!*" bellowed a voice, and it was picked up by the crowd of some hundreds that were gathered in the square.

"Oh my God," whispered Kerrala. "What the hell's happened here?"

"Kill the witches!" screamed the voice again and the crowd began to advance on the young people.

The fear hit Markel like a furious tidal wave. Before he even knew what he was doing, he had slammed a mind bolt out, directed at the leading men of the mob. Several of them collapsed, and Markel knew that they were dead, but it did nothing to reduce the danger. If anything, it made it worse. "Look how they kill by witchcraft!" called another voice. Markel snatched a look in the direction of the voice and for a moment was sure he had seen the dark, unformed shape of a Sillaron flitting between the crowds.

Another three men collapsed dead as Kerrala followed his example and threw a bolt of energy into the advancing mob, but again it did nothing but exacerbate the fury. There was little to do but reach for the weapons hidden under their robes, and Markel frantically pulled the device from the holster at his hip, just as Kerrala did the same.

But the screams of fury changed suddenly to a different note and the advancing mob stopped, beginning to retreat as they had advanced but in increasing speed and confusion. Markel looked to one side and saw a dreadful sight. There were four enormous spiders rearing on their back legs. They must surely have stood twice the height of a man even on all eight legs, but upright like this they stood the height of a small building. His heart froze at the view, and then remembered his parents telling him of the Spiders who could teleport as Pfafth could, and were programmed to save Pfafth when in danger. He and Kerrala shrank back into the doorway and watched the horror. The spiders suddenly jumped at the crowd, landing on top of several people. Dreadful screams rang out as he saw huge jaws open and crush down on the bodies of the terrified people before the appalling creatures pounced on another victim. Within seconds, perhaps thirty or forty bodies littered the village square, some still twitching as the poison seeped through their bodies, and as suddenly as they had appeared, the spiders vanished.

Trembling and weeping from the shock of their experience, Markel and Kerrala crept back to their rooms to prepare themselves for the teleportation back to Alladort and the Sector head office. But even with the terrible scenes he had witnessed, Markel could not forget that he had seen a Sillaron apparently inciting the crowd to a riot intended to kill him and Kerrala. But being uncertain of his memory, he decided not to tell Jessandra when he got back.

*　*　*　*

"They call themselves X'Kasxi, the Kindred." The speaker was Nentahorn, the Planetary Commissioner for the world of X'Katcxo. Despite the youth, good looks and vigour that all Pfafth maintained through their ability to control matter, including the cells of their bodies, he looked tired and worried. "They have developed from a reptilian species that they call the L'Akshi, though such animals are almost gone from their world. They display very high intelligence and we believe they will develop into a powerfully intellectual species. Already, their culture is quite sophisticated, and we believe they have developed some strong spiritual values, but as we are finding increasing difficulty in establishing empathic connection with them, we can't identify what those values are, and that is worrying. However, they pay their contributions and we have experienced no obstructionism or resentment that we can detect."

Kerrala and Markel were sitting in Nentahorn's office.

They had teleported in the previous evening, in standard fashion, and slept off the weariness of the travel before reporting for duty in the morning.

"So what will you want us to do while we are here?" Kerrala asked.

"Your files indicate that you two were the best pupils in the training academy's history," the bureaucrat replied with a smile. "In particular, you were the top graduates ever in empathic communication, as well as the standard skills of teleportation and matter control. But it's your empathic talents I need. We're sensing that the X'Kasxi are pulling away from us and no longer fully tolerant of Pfafth rule, though we have seen no hard evidence. I need you two to travel round the cities and try and read X'Kasxi minds, see if you can detect any sign of possible rebellion."

"Of course, we'll do everything we can," Kerrala replied. "This is the main city, so we'll start here, if that's alright with you?"

"Most certainly," Nentahorn replied with obvious relief, and stood up. Markel and Kerrala did the same and left the office to return to the ones they had been assigned.

"This is very strange," Kerrala said, walking into Markel's office with him and sitting down the other side of his desk.

"What is?" Markel asked as he took his own chair.

"A million years of Pfafth rule throughout the Universe, and suddenly we get the horrible situation on Mellissiana. And now this is the first time I've ever heard of an advanced subject species displaying problems."

"It's not the first."

"Why, what else have you heard of?"

"When I was on the Mianten world, I read lots of resentment, as well as fear when a small crowd gathered, staring at me. I even had to throw a minor bolt to cause enough reaction for the crowd to let me get through."

"*Markel!* You didn't tell me about that!"

"I didn't want to scare you. Anyway, they were more frightened of the Sillaron than of us, but it was still not pleasant."

"But what could they possibly be frightened of? We do nothing but provide safe rule and develop these people faster than they could do it themselves."

"And make them pay through the nose for the privilege," Markel added dryly.

"What?" Kerrala looked astounded.

"Don't you know that every subject world pays about twenty percent of its total production to us?"

Kerrala's open mouth reflected her astonishment and she said nothing.

"And the Sillaron agent with me there suggested we should have killed a few of the crowd to encourage obedience. I wonder if they've done that already without our knowing?"

"I hate those awful creatures!"

"And I wonder if they are really helping us rule the Universe?"

"Markel, what *do* you mean?"

"I don't know. I just don't think we know everything that's going on, and we certainly don't know what the Sillaron really think."

Kerrala looked thoughtful and also worried. "Maybe we should get out and start our work?" she suggested.

Markel nodded and stood up. "Let's go," he said, and the two young Pfafth went out into the streets of the City of Brx'Jashcha, X'Katcxo's main city.

For three days the youngsters wandered the city. It was not a huge place, just about 200,000 people living there, while most X'Kasxi still lived rural lives, but it had all the trappings of a large city, with markets, streets, coffee houses and restaurants. Markel and Kerrala travelled freely with the help of the anti-gravity vehicles that rode them smoothly and silently wherever they wanted, controlled by the communications devices that had been implanted in their shoulders three years ago. Everywhere they went they reached out with their empathic minds to study the thoughts and emotions of the locals and to detect hostility or ideas of rebellion.

But they found nothing.

"Actually, they seem to *like* us!" Kerrala exclaimed as the rode through another street on the way out of town for a planned excursion into the rural areas surrounding the city.

"I'm not sure that 'like' is the appropriate word," Markel said thoughtfully. "There's affection, certainly, but it feels more like the affection an adult has for a child, rather than the liking between friends. I get the impression they feel *superior* to us."

"Hmmm, yes, I think you're right," Kerrala murmured after pondering for a moment. "But how can anyone feel *superior* to the Pfafth? It makes no sense."

Markel said nothing. His general feeling of unease and disquiet over everything he had seen since leaving home was getting worse, and the strangely disconcerting attitude of amused affection he had sensed from so many X'Kasxi in the last two days had done nothing to reduce his worries. He had not found it easy to be around this species, either. They were the only non-mammalian race he had so far encountered, other than the Sillaron, and the reptilian ancestry that showed in the facial structures, leathery skin and distinct odour continued to make him uncomfortable.

The city structures fell away as they entered the countryside, and attractive green fields and enormous trees replaced the concrete and brick. The black roadways ended and became merely pathways, not that this made any difference to their vehicle's ability to move. In minutes, the city had vanished completely and the vehicle accelerated sharply as it headed for the small village that had been programmed into its navigational computer.

"Look! Over there!" Kerrala pointed with excitement as a lumbering, heavy shape moved slowly across a field a kilometre away. "It's a L'Akshi!"

"It sure is!" Mickie was intrigued. He'd been told that this ancient creature, the ancestors of the modern X'Kasxi had all but vanished, and to see one so close to the city was most unexpected. Mentally instructing the vehicle to slow down and move closer to the beast, he stared as they neared it. The L'Akshi briefly raised it head from grazing in the shrubbery then ignored them and resumed feeding. The creature had two large rear legs and smaller front ones that it used to support its body as it grazed. A short but heavy tail gave it balance when it stood upright. Markel could see how the face strongly resembled that of the modern X'Kasxi, though the snout protruded further. The major difference was that the modern X'Kasxi had lost the tails, but also in the huge bone outcropping above the eyes that extended several centimetres forward and seemed to give protection to the eyes from sun and perhaps trees and branches also. In the X'Kasxi, those bones extended just a centimetre or two from the forehead. After circling the animal twice, Markel ordered the vehicle to resume its original course. An hour later, they stopped in the centre of the little village that was their target for the day.

Their reception was completely unlike their expectations. Markel had thought they would be the centre of considerable attention, because few, if any Pfafth would have visited such a tiny location in the ten thousand years or so of Pfafth rule here. But they were largely ignored. People passed them going in all directions on various unknown errands. Most seemed not to notice them at all, but just a few of the inhabitants gave a casual nod in their direction, as if a visit from the ruling power in the Universe was a matter of little or no interest.

Markel extended his empathic senses and looked into the minds of passers-by, just as Kerrala was doing, but after a few minutes, they looked at each other in puzzlement.

"They're just not bothered by us," Kerrala muttered in disbelief.

"The nearest sensation I can get is of an adult seeing a couple of kids in the shopping mall and barely noticing them, other than hoping they'll be safe," Markel added. "This is beyond comprehension. We're supposed to be their rulers."

"But I've not seen a single thought or emotion that says that," Kerrala agreed. "It's as if we're completely unimportant."

"Let's get off this thing and sit down in the village square," Markel suggested. "There are some benches over there, maybe if we sit down, we'll sense more of what's going on."

They alighted from the vehicle and sat down on one of several benches that lined the main square of the little village. They sat without talking as they watched the daily business going on. A small market was in operation and people walked casually between stalls, conducting business at a leisurely rate.

"So what brings the Masters of the Universe to our little village?" The voice was gentle, cultured, and even the amusement in the tones came through the translation devices in the shoulders of Markel and Kerrala. Astonished, the two turned to see who had spoken.

Even to their untutored eyes, the speaker was obviously old. The skin around his eyes was more wrinkled than they had seen before and he stooped a little, leaning lightly on an ornate walking stick. Markel noted with interest that the outcroppings over the man's eyes seemed very small, just a firm line, not much thicker than Markel's own eyebrows. He stood up and Kerrala did the same. The act was automatic, coming from the immediate respect they felt for the man. Behind him stood three younger X'Kasxi and Markel sensed the attitude of awe that they held for the elder. He knew he was facing a leader of this community.

"Good morning," he said courteously. "Won't you please sit down?"

They stood quietly as the old man took his seat in the middle of the bench, and then sat down either side of him, turning sideways a little so that they could look at him. He acknowledged their looks with a small smile, then crossed his hands on his stick and looked into the distance. The three other, younger X'Kasxi took up positions behind their leader.

"I am X'Kaa Gaishaxan," the man said suddenly.

Quickly, Markel used his communication device to direct a mental query to the navigation computer on his transport, which relayed it to the computers at Sector Office in the city. The answer came back immediately.

"The title 'X'Kaa' most accurately translates as 'Guide.' It is believed to be a title earned by spiritual leaders. Beyond that, we know nothing."

"My name is Markel and my colleague is called Kerrala," Markel said. "We are honoured that you chose to greet us."

He sensed the amusement in the old man.

"We must always show respect for the Masters of the Universe," was his reply.

"And yet we detect something other than respect," Kerrala said. "Amusement, perhaps? Possibly superiority and contempt?"

Markel saw the man's eyes sparkle and his awareness of the Guide's amusement increased.

"Presumption of absolute superiority and mastery of the Universe is invariably amusing to us," the Guide answered. "It always precedes a downfall."

"You believe the Pfafth will be destroyed?" Markel felt his breath pulled from his body. He tried to push deeper into the old man's mind but felt a barrier rise against his efforts. Something terrifying was happening, but he could not understand what it was.

"Not destroyed. But your time of mastery of the universe is most certainly coming to an end." The man's voice was soft, but the words hammered into Markel's head like a jackhammer.

"You truly believe that?"

"It is not I who believe it," the X'Kasxi said gently. "But those on a plane of existence above this one, they know it and they tell me."

"A higher plane of existence? What is that?" Kerrala's voice indicated that she too was experiencing some stress at the man's words.

"One of which you know nothing and *can* know nothing," was the baffling reply.

Markel began to realise that this meeting was of major significance and that he had to learn everything he could while he had the chance. "There are people on a higher spiritual plane than this?" he demanded.

The old man glanced sideways at him. "There are *souls* on a higher plane than this," he replied.

"And how does one acquire the title of Guide, X'Kaa Gaishaxan?" Markel asked. Somehow he knew he was asking the right questions, and the man's suddenly sharp, intense stare into his eyes confirmed that.

"We talk to those souls and ask for their advice, and with it, we guide the souls of those newly born to us." The X'Kasxi's gaze returned to the far distance and Markel breathed a little more easily as the ancient eyes left his.

"This meeting was not accidental, was it?" he asked. "You were sent to deliver a message to all of the Pfafth."

"Neither the meeting nor your choice of today's travels," the old man agreed.

"But I chose this village at random," Kerrala protested.

"That is your belief. But you are wrong. Your visit was determined by others."

"But nobody told me which place to choose! I just picked it from several villages within a day's travel."

The man smiled. "I knew of your visit six days ago."

"Six days ago? We were still on Tracomal at Sector Government Headquarters six days ago and we hadn't even been told of our trip to X'Katcxo." Kerrala's face registered massive disbelief.

"So who told you we were coming?" Markel demanded.

"Those higher souls." The Guide smiled gently. "They also guided your choice to visit this little place. My friends, nothing is ever as it seems. Infinite power is not infinite power. Mastery is not mastery. And as you have already seen, young Master Markel, benign rule is not always benign rule."

Markel felt slammed again. How had this old man known of his doubts about the nature of Pfafth rule? He swallowed and fought to regain mastery of his voice.

"And is it the X'Kasxi who will lead the uprising against us?" he asked, still feeling tremors in his throat.

The old Guide rose slowly to his feet as his assistants came round the bench to help him. "The X'Kasxi, Master Markel? How could we possibly lead an uprising against you? You could destroy us in seconds."

"Then who?" Markel felt desperate as his only source of information was about to depart. But the old man walked away without replying, leaving Markel and Kerrala staring at each other in bewilderment and distress.

Chapter 13. The End of The Pfafth Empire

"I wish you had not chosen to visit Sector Alpha Nine, Chairman Markel," the Sector Commissioner said, clearly fighting to keep his voice under control. "The situation here has become very dangerous, far worse than any other sector in the Empire."

"Which is why I'm here," Markel said gently. Since being elected Chairman of the Pfafth Management Committee eight months ago, he had chosen to visit each of the Sector Capitals, certain in his own mind that the reports he was receiving about disturbances were being sanitised for his benefit to try and maintain some sort of calm. Sometimes he had to pinch himself metaphorically to realise that was effectively the most powerful man in the Universe, the leader of the Pfafth species that ruled every known Galaxy in the extensive Pfafth empire.

"So, Commissioner," Markel continued. "Tell me what's been happening."

"The Sillaron have betrayed us," The Commissioner replied. His face was white and his eyes twitched in nervousness. Markel had never seen such physical frailty displayed in a Pfafth before and it dismayed him. *How bad could things have become?*

"How?" he asked.

"They were supposed to keep the Mianten in order. We had realised that there were veins of dissatisfaction with that species, but we relied on the Sillaron to keep it under control."

"I recall that one of my very first reports here as a cadet, thirty years ago, was that the Mianten were displaying resentments. I know that I reported having to throw a low level mind bolt against a crowd in order to get back to the office."

The Commissioner looked embarrassed. "Your report was located just a few weeks ago. It had been filed away with the comment by the then-Commissioner that you were over-reacting to a non-existent danger."

"I see." Markel decided not to pursue the matter. "So what actually happened with the Mianten?"

"A crowd of several thousand suddenly attacked the government building. We expected the Sillaron to put down the attack, but instead, it seemed they had instigated it. There are only a few hundred Pfafth here, and eventually we managed to restore order, but only after we had killed several hundred of the locals with a mixture of mind bolts and weapons. It did nothing to ease the situation and the tensions are still dangerously high."

"And on Mellissiana?"

"That was far worse. Again, we found your report of the event that caused the Spiders to attack, thirty years ago, but it gave no indication that the Sillaron might have caused that incident."

"I deeply regret that mistake," Markel replied. "I was sure I'd seen several Sillaron moving in the mob, but I was too junior and too concerned about my reputation perhaps, to report that. It seemed so far-fetched."

"And at the time, it would have been ignored, I agree," the Commissioner said with a nod. "But we again underestimated how vicious was the rage against us, that we had turned those awful monsters on their people."

"They realised that the Pfafth exist? They comprehend alien life from other worlds?"

"Now they do. It seems the Sillaron have openly revealed themselves, claiming to be a subject race like themselves, and offering liberation. They gave them advanced weapons to defend against the spiders if they reappeared. But that's not the worst part."

"It's not? Commissioner, what could be worse than a primitive people suddenly being armed with advanced weapons and seeing us as their enemy?"

"Chairman Markel, we fear that the Sillaron have developed greater powers. Somehow they must have blocked the abilities of our people on Mellissiana, because when the Mellissians attacked in force again a few days ago, not one of our people was able to throw a mind bolt. Several thousands of locals stormed the grounds and began massive destruction. We had a hundred and eighty people on the planet. When they realised what was happening, they tried to leap back here."

"And?"

"Chairman, only one woman made it back. She was in a state of deep shock, and she reported that while trying to teleport, she had felt something like a huge blanket immobilising her efforts. Finally, she said she had got just a second of clarity, perhaps when the Sillaron arranging this had been diverted, or had loosened control, and she was able to leap. Otherwise, we would not know what had happened. But we must assume that all those who were unable to leap are now dead."

For the first time, Markel sensed real fear. Had the Sillaron finally thrown off any semblance of obedience to Pfafth rule and initiated Galactic rebellion in such force that not even Pfafth superiority was sufficient to withstand it? And had the Sillaron developed their own powers to the point that they could suppress the previously untouchable and god-like powers of the Pfafth?

"But the Mianten are now calm?"

"For now, Chairman. I don't know when we can expect another attack in force, but I believe it will be any time soon."

Any reply Markel may have made was interrupted by the sound of alarm sirens blasting throughout the government buildings. The two men stared at each other, the fear in the Commissioner's face all too obvious.

"Take yourself back to home world, Commissioner, now!" snapped Markel.

"I need to try and get everyone else to do the same first," the man replied, and Markel nodded, recognising the courage being displayed.

"Then go!" he ordered, and walked out of the room, heading for the roof to see what could be observed. But even as he made his way along the corridors and stairways, he heard the sharp snap of blaster weapons, the crunch of falling masonry as sections of the building collapsed and massive roars of unleashed rage as thousands of the diminutive Mianten surged onto the grounds. He reached the roof and moved to the edge, staring in horror at the sight below. Unlike his experience on Mellissiana, the Sillaron were making no effort to hide themselves. The black, mobile shapes were everywhere, moving fluidly through the mob, extorting the Mianten to attack. A shout of triumph bellowed through the crowd as apparently a doorway was breached and the invaders began pouring into the building. Directing his biggest mind bolt, Markel tried to send it searing down on the mob. But nothing happened. Astonished, he prepared another bolt and aimed it, but again, as he flexed the mental muscle that would fire the energy, it failed, like a light failing to come on.

What the hell is going on and where are the Spiders? he asked, remembering the last time he was under attack on Mellissiana and how the enormous and terrifying beasts had arrived with such appalling effect.

He tried once more to slam a bolt into the hordes with the same result as before, and now he heard screams as the mob found the Pfafth unprepared and defenceless. He wondered why they hadn't teleported, and remembered the Commissioner's words about some form of blanketing effect. Could the Sillaron also be blocking the Spiders' ability to sense danger to their masters? It was time to escape, he decided, closed his eyes and attempted to visualise the path home.

And that was when he understood what the blanket effect was. He couldn't see home world and without being able to visualise it, he couldn't initiate the leap. Desperately, he flung his perception round, like an animal trapped under a net, searching for a gap in the blanket that seemed to cover the entire Universe. Then with the frantic sensation of a drowning swimmer suddenly getting a mouthful of air, he glimpsed a small, blue planet. Vaguely he recognised it, he had visited only a few months before. He was part of the study group checking on the progress of the humanoid race they had rescued from a dying planet years ago and replanted on two different worlds. This was one of them and a path there lay open. He stretched out his psychic arms, grasped the planet, flew into the black void of intergalactic space and drove himself as hard as he could for the refuge offered. Somehow, the Pfafth had been able to block off access to Pfafth home world, but had perhaps been careless and left a few gaps in the gates open. Without taking the usual time to select a spot on which to place himself, he merely drove for the centre of what he could see, a large land mass that seemed to stretch almost the whole distance from pole to pole, and dropped himself a little north of the equatorial line.

For a few moments, he fought the usual fatigue that resulted from a teleportation leap across space and then recovered, initially feeling immense relief at having escaped the onslaught of the Mianten mob. That feeling died rapidly. He struggled to come to terms with the fact that he, the leader of the most powerful species in the universe had been forced to flee for his life from a mob of primitive beings who had developed only a basic technological culture. Not only that, but hundreds, perhaps thousands of his fellows had died in such uprisings in recent weeks. The Sillaron were the prime cause of it all, he knew. For the millionth time he wished that the universal telepathic skills being developed in the intelligent plant-like beings had reached the point where he could talk through them with others of his kind and understand what was happening across the Pfafth empire.

He looked around him. He was in open country and he could see for many kilometres across a large plain, spotted at intervals with groups of trees and shrubbery. The temperature and the humidity were both high, far higher than on home world but all Pfafth knew how to adjust their body controls to handle a high degree of variation. He was not in the same area that he had visited on his previous brief stay on the planet. That time he and his party had dropped themselves further north to check on the temperatures that were dropping as the planet entered a new ice age. The scientists had verified that the cold period would last a few thousand years but would not threaten the survival of the humanoid race they had rescued from far worse freezing on their original dying planet. They had seen almost no life on that visit of just two days, just long enough to recover from the fatigue of trans-galactic teleportation. A few large mammals had wondered by, all showing the developmental course of cold-temperature ecologies, but none of the humanoid species had appeared.

Markel shook off his fear and depression, realising that the previous trip had saved his life. Without it, he could not have visualised the blue, watery planet and made his leap from under the smothering blanket the Sillaron had thrown over his teleportation powers. Movement to one side caught his attention and he turned, drawing in his breath sharply as he realised what he was seeing.

Four humanoids were studying him. Markel looked back in fascination. These were truly primitive. They stood no more than chest height to him, their bodies covered with thick black coats of hair, looking more like the primates from which the Pfafth had themselves evolved several millions of years ago. They looked exactly like the creatures he had seen leave the spaceship after being taken from their freezing world forty years ago when he had visited with his father and Kerrala. But Markel knew that these beings represented intelligent life on this planet and would one day evolve into technologically aware creatures with language, art and advanced societies. Physically and emotionally at least, these creatures were the same species as the Pfafth themselves, perhaps would even develop the same skills and powers of the Pfafth and one day rule the Universe. The scientists who had overseen the transportation of these humanoids to this planet from their doomed ice-world three hundred light-years away, and the same transportation of the others to a similar planet had calculated that it would take perhaps a million years for them to develop civilisation and cultures capable of technology.

For several minutes, they studied each other, the four humanoids representing the very beginning of human life, the lone man perhaps representing the end of a culture that ruled the Universe. Deciding that his duty demanded that he cut short the contact as much as possible, Markel directed a very low-power mind bolt at the group, enough to cause them fear and distress and make them retreat. Without surprise, he recognised that he had regained that power. In a few minutes they had walked far enough away that he could relax and start to think about what he should do next.

Leaping to home world was out of the question for at least a day. The physical demands of teleportation were immense and even a man of his power and experience could not leap twice in a day. He would have to find shelter for tonight and gather his strength for the next day. But at least he could check and see if the Sillaron smothering blanket was in effect. He concentrated on visualising home world and to his immense relief, had no difficulty. Suppressing his yearning to be home, knowing that if he tried to leap now, catastrophe could result, ending up in unknown space in an environment that not even a Pfafth could handle.

The group of primitives was about a kilometre away and Markel decided to follow them, assuming that they were heading to somewhere where shelter was available. They seemed to walking towards a small forest another two or three kilometres away, not before time, for he realised that the sun was low on the horizon. Here, close to the equator, night would fall quickly.

But tragedy struck the group ahead. Markel noticed the small waves in the long grass ahead just as an enormous animal leaped out and pounced on one of the four, closely followed by a second attack. Two of the humanoids were dead almost immediately, it seemed and the other two set off at an astonishingly fast pace for the shelter of the trees. But the two carnivores ignored them, concentrating on their prey. Markel shuddered at this display of raw nature, studying the two animals, knowing that his mental powers could protect him against a similar attack. Each of the beasts was at least three metres long and quite beautiful in its grace and powerful lines. Classical predators, he decided. Their most outstanding features were the two, enormous, curved fangs that stood out from their upper jaws, well structured to rip open tough hides of any prey. They were not needed for this feast, for the humanoids were far too fragile. Both animals were feasting on the bloody corpses, emitting a deep growling sound like an enormous engine idling under minimum power. But after tearing away and consuming a few chunks of meat, the two each took hold of one of the bodies and carried them off to wherever they had their lairs, possibly to feed their young, Markel decided. Once they had gone, he continued his own trip into the woods, eventually settling under a dense shrub. Setting the mind bolt capability to a constant, broad transmission that would deter any living creature from approaching him, he lay down and tried to sleep, struggling to forget the horror of what had driven him here.

He woke before dawn, realising that the mental deterrent had not been effective against insects. Several painful bites and stings were spread around his legs, arms and face, but the same cellular control that kept all Pfafth youthful, attractive and healthy quickly healed the problem areas. Strolling around the area, he was successful in finding some fruit to ease the hunger pangs and he made his way back out into the open country. It was time to teleport home.

He experienced no difficulty. He had to assume that the Sillaron had not noticed his escape from their barrier and were ignorant of where he might be. Quickly, he located home world, visualised its location in the Galaxy, related that Galaxy to the one in which he now stood, reached out with his psychic arms across some twelve million light years and a few moments later was gratefully breathing the familiar air within his own house, the same home in which he had lived as a child.

"Mindor," he called, addressing the house computer. "Establish contact with the Management Committee, conference call."

"At once, Chairman," came the immediate response.

"And can you locate my wife?"

"Kerrala is still in conference with one of the sub-councils, Chairman, but her schedule is for her to return within the hour."

"Advise me the moment she returns, Mindor."

Fighting the fatigue of a long teleportation and the worries about Kerrala's safety, Markel sat in the conference room, the same room in which he had watched his father hold such meetings, waiting for the holographic images of the Committee members to appear. Rapidly the twelve other Managers flickered into existence, automatically placed by the computer in two rows in front of him.

"I think I speak for all of us, Chairman, we're relieved to see you." The speaker was Allaran, a man about Markel's own age and a friend for some years. The others signified their agreement with small nods and a few similar words.

"Thank you, my friends," Markel said. "The situation has clearly become appalling. Let me describe what I experienced in the last two days." Quickly, he related the frightening story, and then sat back. Worried, he saw no surprise on any of the faces before him. "I gather this is not unexpected," he said.

"Tragically, that is so," replied Carminandra, the youngest of the Committee. Her face registered great sadness. "Similar reports are coming in from refugees from all over the empire. A few have managed to escape the Sillaron onslaughts, and the story is the same. They seem to have developed some form of blocking capability for our powers. But that is not the worst part of all this."

"Not the worst? Carminandra, what could be worse?"

She shivered. "It is the way so many of our people have died. Those that have been killed by the weapons of the subject races who have risen up, they were the lucky ones."

Markel felt a cold shaft of fear run through him. Something in her expression told of deep horror. "What is it? How did they die?"

"There seems to be something leading the Sillaron. I saw it on Mellissiana as I tried to leap. It looks like one of them, but much larger, somehow more... *evil*. And it killed so many of our people by enveloping them in itself as it expanded. When they appeared again, everything seemed to have sucked from them. Not just their innards, but somehow... their *souls*."

"This is no entity that we have ever encountered before," said Allaran. "Are you sure of the description?"

"There have been several such reports," agreed another of the group. "I thought it was just imagination from such fear, but perhaps not. But even without that thing, millions of our people have been killed and the Sillaron continue to generate massive violence among the local races to attack us."

"Millions?" Markel felt ice around his heart. The entire Pfafth population was only twenty-two million.

"At least eight million, as far as we can calculate," added Jossinert, a young man with whom Markel had never felt at ease, but whose intellectual strengths were formidable. "This is well over the level at which we agreed the final point had come for our survival."

Markel knew he had only one option. Like all good management teams, they had developed any number of scenarios of both calamity and good fortune, for which immediate action plans had to be implemented when required. The plans of this Management Committee were the biggest ever, because they involved the future survival of their race, but the details had been worked out many years ago.

"I invoke Chairman's Authority," he said formally and saw all the other twelve Managers sit back, expressions of resignation on their faces. They had all known this moment had come, but to hear the words initiating the astonishing series of actions that would now follow was still a dreadfully shocking moment.

"Each of you has your role," Markel continued. "Arrange for the Cassolean telepaths to provide the images and location of the world in the refuge galaxy to all surviving Pfafth everywhere they can be located. Every single one of us must leap as soon as they possibly can. This Committee will meet again in twenty-four hours at the location we have all been given to arrange the final stage. Are there any last questions or suggestions?"

Nobody spoke. But on two of the faces he suddenly saw shock and fear. Jossinert and another woman both looked sharply to one side, as something seemed to explode in their immediate locations. Jossinert looked back at Markel and smiled sadly.

"I believe my colleague Kaydrina and I will not be joining you tomorrow, Markel. The Sillaron are already here, and I think..."

A red flame in each position replaced the two images, then they vanished.

"Go, now, all of you," Markel snapped and broke the connection.

"Chairman, your wife is here," the computer said. Breathing a huge sigh of relief, Markel strode out of the room and saw Kerrala standing in the corridor outside. Folding his arms around her, he held her as a dying man holds the hand of a friend.

"I was so worried," he whispered.

"Me too," she replied into the curve of his shoulder and neck. "I only just got away before the mobs appeared, and I knew you were among the Mianten."

"I'll tell you the whole story when we are safe in the refuge," he said, released his arms and looked down on her. He placed his hand on her cheek and she turned her face to kiss it. "It's time to go," he said. "I don't know how much longer we have, but I've just invoked the Chairman's Authority. All survivors will leap as soon as they've got the images of the refuge world. We will go right now."

Tears came to her eyes. "I've always loved this house," she said. "I can't bear to think we'll never see it again."

"I know. We have to make a new home. If you're with me, we'll be just as happy. I've just leaped here, Kerrala. I'm going to need all my strength and all yours for me to leap again so soon."

She smiled, took hold of the hand on her cheek and held it while they walked back to the conference room. They sat down together on a couch, wrapped their arms round each other so that their combined strengths would carry them together, closed their eyes and concentrated on the images and location of the world that had been selected years ago as a possible refuge should any major calamity strike the Pfafth.

In a few seconds, they were over a hundred and eighty million light years from home world and over the next hours they were joined by the surviving eight million Pfafth who had escaped the slaughter by the Sillaron-led mobs.

* * * *

As agreed, the remaining eleven members of the Management Committee met, twenty-four hours after the last awful meeting that had closed with the murders of two of them. This time, they met in person, as all had leaped to within a short distance of each other as previously arranged. Kerrala had joined them because they knew they would need the extra power that she possessed.

There was a single city on this world. The galaxy that held the planet had been carefully selected for this purpose. It was massively distant from any part of the Pfafth-ruled Empire and no intelligent life had been located in any solar system. Over two centuries, small groups of Pfafth had secretly visited, their work known only to the Management Committee. All of the parties had been formed of the most skilled people, those who could use their matter-transmuting and gravity-defeating talents at the very highest level. They had built a city, equipped it with roads, power conduits, water-management systems, everything a civilised people needed. Around the city, they had built smaller towns and villages. It was a far cry from the magnificent splendours of the Pfafth home world, but the Managers who had planned this city knew that should it ever be required, the Pfafth who came here would no longer rule the Universe.

The current Management Committee met in a conference room in the building designated as the seat of power. They had one more astonishing act to complete before they were safe and it would need the last ounce of energy of all of them combined. That they could even do this thing had only been developed in the last hundred years and remained a close secret, only a few people outside the Committee having been taught how to do it, never mind that it could be done at all. And while membership of the ruling Committee of all the Pfafth was by a vote of all adults, nobody but those initiated knew that anyone appointed also had to have the mental powers to be trained in this new, awesome Pfafth capability.

No words were needed. They knew why they were here. A lifetime of training was about to be put to work. All of them closed their eyes. Markel carefully edged his consciousness out and felt the same energy radiating from his colleagues. Despite the normal Pfafth inability to communicate telepathically, a few of them had developed such skills, and each of them in this room was one of that tiny handful. The twelve minds finally merged and while Markel retained a small sense of his own identity, he was now a part of a new individual, a massively enhanced mind that was the total of all of them. Streams of images flew through his tiny, reduced awareness of himself, they were the combined memories of each of the twelve individuals, opened to all of them in an intimacy that could not be imagined by a normal person.

With a soundless shock, all individual minds vanished. Now it was a truly single entity, this new person formed of twelve minds, the most powerful minds in the most powerful species in the Universe. The entity began to expand its consciousness. Within seconds it had enveloped the entire planet, moved on outward to take in the two moons, the next world in toward the sun and the one outward from it. Within just more seconds the mind had taken hold of the entire solar system of eleven planets and the sun and expanded even further, the rate of expansion increasing until it had taken in the nearest neighbour solar system, past that to the edge of the galaxy nearest to the new home planet. With that border reached, the new mind began to take in the bigger chunk of the remainder of the galaxy, raced on further outward, faster and faster until at some moment the entire galaxy of so many billions of stars was held within the mind of this impossibly powerful entity. It then paused and gathered itself for one last expenditure of stupendous energy. It had no real idea of just what it did, but somehow it held the galaxy, went into each and every atom of each and every star, planet, gas cloud, meteorite, every loose piece of matter everywhere within its borders and.... *moved* it. Not physically, for there was no power in all of creation that could move a galaxy away from its path, but.... it *moved*.

Slowly, it might have been seconds, or hours, or days, the new entity had no idea of how long it took for it to return to the room, break itself up, separate itself back into twelve different consciousnesses and for those individuals to recover from the momentous thing they had done.

Markel came to awareness the way a patient awakes from deep anaesthesia. For a few moments he could only sense his own body, the appalling fatigue that prevented him from even holding his head up. His arms felt like they were being held down by a massive gravitational force, every cell in his body screamed for rest. But he directed energy to the muscles and blood flows of his body and gradually became aware of the room, his colleagues, what had happened and what needed to be done.

Sensing the movements in the room, the building computer initiated action. The door opened and two women came in carrying trays of drinks and food. Dimly, Markel recognised his house servants. When she got to him, he took a deep draught of the life-giving liquid and managed to speak.

"How long?" he croaked.

"You were in here for over fourteen hours," she replied, taking his hands and rubbing them between her own to restore circulation.

"That long?" he sighed. "We had no idea of how long it would take."

"But you succeeded." She made a statement rather than asked a question.

"Yes, we succeeded," he replied. "This entire galaxy is now one second ahead in time from the rest of the Universe. Nobody can cross that barrier except us. We are safe now."

Chapter 14. Exile

Markel realised he had reached that age when even a Pfafth could no longer control the cells in his body and fend off aging. He was tired. It was not the almost pleasant fatigue of crossing the light years between galaxies in a few seconds, for only a handful of Pfafth did that anymore. In fact, very few people even visited other planets within the same galaxy they now occupied, and it seemed to him that his species had lost all urge to explore since being exiled behind the barrier of the one second of time that separated their galaxy from the rest of the Universe.

No, this was the fatigue of old age, and he knew his time was approaching an end. He felt that he would welcome death, for it was a horrible burden to know that he had been the leader of the most powerful species in the Universe when their rule had been smashed by their servants and they had been sent to flee for their lives to a spot far remote from the galaxies they once owned. Even Kerrala, his wife of nearly seventy years was showing the same fatigue, and now her hair was white and the first signs of tiny wrinkles had appeared at her neck and around her eyes.

Sometimes, the fatigue could be hidden behind other walls as he engaged in hobbies that he had taken up as he wound down the duties of Chairman of the Management Committee that ruled the single galaxy of the Pfafth when once it had ruled forty. Painting was his love, and music was his relaxation as he listened to the music of hundreds of worlds and many different species, but the weariness was thrust back on him by hearing yet again the argument that had been raging since they arrived here almost forty years ago.

"There is only one goal for us and that is to restore the Pfafth to their position as rulers!" Once, Markel had liked Allaran, the speaker of those furious words, but as the man's rage and frustration at losing the Universe had grown to consume him, Markel had lost most of his liking and even tolerance for him.

"I agree!" shouted Pindramon. "Not only that, but we must make damned sure those treacherous Sillaron are killed, every last one of them."

Markel looked at the last speaker. He was large, impressive in build, but the anger and violence in him had made his otherwise handsome face mean and cold. Markel could not remember when Pindramon had been elected to the Management Committee, but he wished the electors had chosen someone else.

"Let us perhaps consider valid actions, rather than revenge," Markel said. His voice no longer had the power of command it once had, but he had been the Chairman for over forty years and obedience to his authority was still strong in the other twelve Managers. "When was the last time our agents went outside the galaxy and looked at the situation?"

"Two years ago, Chairman," replied a woman at the end of the table. Her name was Zelira and Markel had appointed her as Manager of External Research, a title that in other cultures and other times might have meant head of the spying agency. "And that was the first time we have done it. We only have twenty-two people who have been able to learn the technique for passing through the time barrier, so they spent their time trying to cover as many of the inhabited planets as they could. Their information is rather sparse, I'm afraid."

"And they are back now?"

"They returned just two weeks ago. I've been debriefing them solidly the whole time."

"And what did you find?"

"No trace of any Pfafth survivors for a start," she replied. A small sigh ran round the table.

"The Sillaron are most certainly in charge," she continued. "And a miserable existence it seems to be for all species under their control. They run a most repressive regime, with all music banned and very little self-rule on any of their planets. I believe just about everyone except for the Sillaron would welcome the return of Pfafth rule."

"That's what I keep saying," bellowed Allaran. "We should get out there and kill them all! All the races would welcome us."

Markel tried to hide his irritation. "Maybe you could advise the Committee just what weapons we have that would destroy the Sillaron?" he said gently. "Do we have any evidence that they have lost their ability to suppress all our powers? Zelira?"

She shook her head. "No, we don't. But I am quite sure that the Sillaron have sown the seeds of their own destruction."

A stunned silence sat over the room.

"Please explain," Markel said after a few seconds.

"They cannot teleport," Zelira said. "And there are no spaceships with inter-galactic capabilities. We had a few for transporting equipment, but I found that the Cassoleans organised a complete seizure of all of them within hours of our escape here and they have all returned to their home planet, apart from the few thousand that came here with us."

"Of course," Markel murmured. "They are the greatest telepaths, so they must have known what we would do. And they've taken all the ships?"

"All of them," Zelira said with a small smile. "The Sillaron cannot move between planets at all. They are marooned, effectively. And while we know almost nothing about their breeding habits or capabilities, I suspect the numbers on any world are too small for viable population growth."

"Then we can get out there and destroy them!" Bolartor was another Manager of whom Markel knew almost nothing, but what he did know he didn't like. Like so many of the Pfafth, he was consumed with rage and hatred of the Sillaron and could think of nothing but destroying them. In fact, almost the entire Management Committee was like this, Markel thought. There seemed little interest in building the new home world into a prosperous, comfortable planet. Kerrala had told him that just about everyone on the whole planet was the same. Anger and despair at being made to run and hide by their previous servants was the dominant emotion. *There's too much hate on this planet,* Markel thought.

"Chairman?" Zelira was looking at him with concern and Markel felt embarrassed that he had fallen into a quiet reverie. *Just like any old man,* he thought with a private smile.

"Yes, Zelira," he said.

"There seems to be a problem with the Cassoleans, as well."

"What sort of problem?"

"Their numbers are declining, and their population is breaking up into smaller tribal units."

"Do you have any idea what is causing it?"

"Not really. Our scientists think it may be because they believe their role is over with our disappearance. It is certainly true that they do not wish to serve the Sillaron."

"This is unimportant!" Pindramon had taken up the fight again. "If the Sillaron are marooned, we're the only species that can teleport. We should send out armies to one planet at a time and kill them all."

"You're facts are incorrect, as is your comprehension of reality," spoke up another woman. Markel knew her name was Carminandra. "There is one other race that can teleport at least as effectively as we can. You forget that the Spiders have developed that ability. But you have also forgotten that we have only been able to train twenty-two of our people to cross the time barrier to Outside. How do you propose sending out armies?"

"And we have absolutely no idea whether the Spiders are our friend or enemy now," Zelira added in agreement. "We could find we have two enemies, and any destruction might well be our own."

Silence fell around the table as each of them absorbed the possible implications of her statement. Markel looked in sad amusement at the frustrated and embarrassed anger in Pindramon's face.

"Maybe we should simply abandon all ideas of returning to power," Markel finally said. Astonished faces turned to him. He smiled sadly. "We ruled this Universe for over a million years. Surely that is enough for anyone? Maybe we should simply accept that in the eternal scheme of things, our time is over. Why cannot we just be satisfied with a whole galaxy to ourselves? Isn't that enough for any species?"

"But we used to rule *forty* galaxies!" shouted Allaran. "Why should we be satisfied with just one? Are you becoming a weakling in your dotage, Markel?"

The shock in the room was palpable and for a moment, Markel felt a surge of rage that began to set up the mind bolt ready for execution. Recognising his own anger, Markel calmed down, seeing the wave of fear that had run over Allaran's face as he saw the danger he had just generated for himself.

"Maybe I'm just becoming realistic," Markel said gently. "As we have all discussed, we don't know just how many of our enemies there are, we cannot be sure the Spiders still support us and we have no idea what their weapons are and if ours can combat them. Nor have we any idea at all of what is that...*Thing* that leads the Sillaron. We have no estimate, not the first idea of what it is or what its powers are. And our armies? Even with a massive training program, it seems unlikely that we could train more than a few hundred of our people to cross the time barrier. No military strategist in all of history would recommend an attack under these circumstances. Perhaps it is simply time for us to exit the Universe ruling business. I can think of no realistic reason why we would want to restore our position."

He saw the looks of contempt that passed over several faces of the Management Committee and knew that he had lost the argument. With that realisation, he decided that this was his last Committee meeting. Whatever time was left to him, he decided it was to be spent with Kerrala, his painting and his music. If the Management Committee, the group that was supposed to be the wisest, the most far-sighted and knowledgeable group of all the Pfafth could not accept their position, there was nothing any more he could do. He sat back and simply listened. He would say no more.

"I believe the Chairman is wrong," Allaran said with more confidence, sensing Markel's retreat. "But perhaps he is right that we cannot do anything effective just yet. So let us turn our minds to the future and set a long-range plan in effect for our return to power."

There was a stir of interest round the table, and despite himself, Markel was also intrigued. Allaran had always had an impressive intellect.

"We must plan very far into the future," Allaran continued, confident now that he had their attention. "So far that the Sillaron will also have been defeated by some other race. So far ahead, that the Universe will be a quite different place, when the Pfafth will have been forgotten, when the species whose development we have accelerated are mature and when there is more stability because of their maturity. After all, we anticipate that the Kaloti will eventually develop inter-galactic space travel even more advanced than ours, and the telepathic plants in sector Beta Five will be able to provide instantaneous telepathic communications across the Universe. We have always known that we Pfafth needed these facilities for more effective rule, so perhaps we should wait for them to develop."

"Allaran, you're talking about possibly a million years!" Zelira looked astonished and yet excited.

"Quite possibly," Allaran replied. "In fact, that's what I do estimate."

"And what is it that you plan to set up for that far distant time?" Zelira asked.

"Our leader," Allaran said. "I believe we should plan to breed a Pfafth, actually two Pfafth who will have all the greatest powers we have now, but developed to even greater intensity. And when we feel the time is right, those children should be placed Outside, with one of the species that physically resemble us closely. We will leave them messages that eventually they will find them and from them, they will learn what their destiny is, to locate us and lead us back to our rightful place."

Ignoring the expressions of utter astonishment around the table, he turned to Markel.

"Chairman," he said with deference. "It is no secret that you and I have not been in agreement for some years now. But all of us know that you and Kerrala have always possessed Pfafth powers in greater intensity than any of us. I believe that we should take some of your cell structure and use it as the basis to continue to breed for the most powerful Pfafth we can imagine. When in some future time, our successors believe the Universe is ready for the

Pfafth return, we will arrange for the infants to be placed with suitable races."

"There is really only one suitable race," interjected Pindramon. "Some eighty years ago, we rescued a species from a dying planet. They are identical to us, though without the mental powers. It was your father, Markel, who had them relocated on two separate planets, one of them being the planet to which you escaped from the Sillaron attack."

Markel nodded. "I even met a small group of them in the few hours I had. They were barely into intelligence levels then, and our scientists estimated a million years of development for them to develop space-going technology."

"Then a million years into the future it is," Allaran said. "That's an eye blink in the cosmic scheme of things and the Pfafth must not die."

Markel stood up. "I announce my resignation as Chairman of the Management Committee. I think it is long overdue and now you must pick a replacement. So let me leave with this one statement. I think this plan is insane. I think all of you at this table who approve it are insane. We have been given a chance to restart our species without the burdens of Universal rule and instead to develop a whole Galaxy with the sort of powers that no other species has in total. You are forgetting a constant rule that history has always shown to be true. *You cannot go home again.* We had power and we have lost it. It is the turn of someone else and any attempt to gain back what we have lost is doomed to failure. But I know I cannot persuade you of that. I am curious enough to wonder how this plan will work out, so I will give you some of my cells, and you must ask Kerrala if she will do the same. I think it is time for me to go home."

Ignoring the white faces round the table and the tears in the eyes of some, he walked out of the Committee chamber. Some final time with his love of many decades was all he wanted now.

Those remaining years passed as he wanted them. Secure that the Committee could attempt nothing as mad as an attack on a Sillaron-ruled planet, Markel devoted his time to the painting and the music, but most of all to what he and Kerrala had been able to experience for too little of their lives, their own company.

And then one morning, Kerrala didn't wake up. He sat by the bed for the entire morning studying the beauty of her face, replaying the memories of the astounding lives they had led, how they had always known they were partners, even from the first days at school. Then he lay down on the bed beside her and decided not to go on living.

*   *   *   *

"Mickie! *Mickie!!!!* Please wake up! Mickie, what's wrong with you?"

Slowly, Mickie returned to consciousness, aware of a constant slapping on his face. He opened his eyes, staring in bewilderment at the faces around him. He fought for comprehension, struggling to understand who he was, what had happened. He had just died beside the body of his wife of more than seventy years......

The life of Markel faded behind the rush of comprehension.

"My God!" he whispered. "I'm Mickie Dalton again."

"Of course you're Mickie Dalton! And what's this 'again' stuff, kid?" The voice was Grant's coming from behind him.

"How... how long have I been unconscious?" Mickie stammered, realising that Allie and Grant were holding him upright from where he had been lying on the floor of his cabin. He was leaning against Grant's chest and Allie was on his right side. He could feel the trembles of shock vibrating his body as he tried to come to terms with being a thirteen-year-old boy again after having lived the life of the leader of the greatest power in the Universe.

"About twenty minutes," Allie replied, tears running down her cheeks. "What happened?"

He twisted his head and looked at the Maragos sculpture. There was no yellow light. It looked just like it had looked before, an inert, oddly shaped block of stone. "That sculpture," he said. "It began to glow and I just fainted. Then I lived a hundred years as a Pfafth. I woke up when I died." He saw the shock in Allie's face. "I was on a planet in that galaxy. It's what we thought. The Pfafth are there, hiding."

Still shaking, he realised his throat was parched. "Is there any way I can get a drink? Is the computer working?"

"The captain ordered the ship to turn away from the galaxy just a few minutes ago," Grant said, leaving Mickie in Allie's arms and rising to go to the food dispenser. "As soon as he gave the order, the computers returned to normal. I'll get you a *Sle'Ach*."

A moment later he handed the yellow, sparkling liquid to Mickie who downed it in one gulp and immediately felt better, sensing his memories of his real life returning as fast as the memories of Markel receded.

"Let's get you more comfortable," Grant said and lifted Mickie off the floor, placing him in the armchair, which immediately adapted itself to his body and supported every aching muscle. His father pulled up two more chairs and he and Allie sat down facing Mickie.

"I've called for the doctor to come and examine you. Now, what's this about living as a Pfafth for a hundred years?"

Chapter 15. Normal Service Resumes

For a whole month, Mickie felt unable to talk to anyone about his dream life as Markel.   Inside his head a monstrous battle raged. Part of him was a thirteen-year-old boy with unpleasant memories of a childhood on Earth in the company of ugly, abusive people who were supposed to be his family. Next to those memories lived the delight of his liberation as the galactic-travelling son of beautiful, warm and loving parents and the powerful, deep friendships that had been forged with Fencris, Drellion and Melkana. But there was a hugely powerful additional set of memories.   For despite the fact that he had only been unconscious for less than half an hour, he had in that time lived a century as Markel, a Pfafth who had become the leader of the dominant species in the Universe when it had been defeated and forced into hiding by its one-time servants.

In that month he stayed silent and withdrawn, struggling to control the awful battle within his mind. Several times he burst into tears of overwhelming grief as he recalled Kerrala and the life they had lived together, realising even as he wept that this was not a memory any teenager should have.

For the first time he missed a planetary visit. The ship took orbit around Wissandra, a world not inhabited by any intelligent species and which was farmed as an agriculturally luxuriant place that produced exotic spices and fruits, the most famous of which was the yellow citrus known as *Sle'Ach* from which the wonderful drink was produced. While his friends went down with the teams to gather the harvest and play in the tropical sun and spice-filled atmosphere, Mickie sat alone in his cabin and let the forces in his head do combat.

He was able to tell Allie and Grant enough of his experience as Markel for them to understand and explain it to his friends, so at least he didn't alienate everyone, but he was not able to join in the conversations, the games of Loopies and the wildly imaginative game that had grown up around the bizarre poetry of Albert, the Ship's computer. Once the Ship had returned to normal, the whole school population of over seventy children adopted a new craze as they attempted to outdo each other with poems as weird and silly as Albert had spouted while the Ship was affected by the Pfafth barrier to the blocked Galaxy. Eventually, a council of teachers awarded a prize for the silliest poem to a Cassolean girl, and the craze died out.

"I think I'm okay now," he said suddenly one evening as he sat in his parent's cabin over a quiet dinner. Five weeks had elapsed since the Ship had turned away from the blocked Galaxy.

For a few seconds his parents looked at him and Mickie sensed the relief pass through them as weeks of serious worry fell away.

"I think I speak for both of us that we're very happy to have our son back," Grant said and Allie just nodded, bright tears in her eyes.

"The Pfafth," Mickie said. "They're in that Galaxy, hiding."

"Hiding from what?" Grant asked.

"The Sillaron."

"You'd better explain. You said something about the Pfafth in that Galaxy when you woke up, but that's all we got."

And for the next hour, Mickie talked without a break except to drink large quantities of *Sle'Ach* when his throat dried up. He told them about the rule over forty galaxies that the Pfafth had exercised, how the Sillaron had been their regents in so many areas of the Universe and then led the uprisings that slaughtered over two-thirds of the most powerful species of all time.

"And how have they blocked the Galaxy from any approach, even telepathic?" Allie asked, and Mickie explained how he, as Markel, and the rest of the Pfafth leaders and moved the Galaxy forward in time by one second, thus creating a barrier that almost nobody could pass through.

"Do you think *you* could do that?" Grant asked. "Do you remember how that mind-boggling feat was achieved?"

Mickie thought for several seconds, searching through his memories. "No," he finally said. "It looks like not all of Markel's memories have come through with the dream."

"But that gives me another idea," Allie said, a note of excitement in her voice. "Could you read the script on the Cliffs of Kamotar? If that was standard Pfafth language, you probably have the memories within you."

"You know what, I think I could," Mickie replied, the same excitement blazing in him as he thought about it. "Albert, project the Cliffs of Kamotar."

Immediately, the image appeared in three dimensions of the smooth, blue surface of the enormous cliffs and the large symbols in fresh white somehow engraved on it. Mickie studied the lines and realised he could read them with ease.

"It's the history!" he exclaimed. "Really, it's what I lived through. It tells how the Pfafth used to rule the forty galaxies of the known Universe and how they used the Sillaron as their regents. It talks about how they deliberately set out to breed the Speakers because the Pfafth had no telepathic skills, though a few like me... like Markel began to develop them. But they needed the Speakers to be able to communicate across the Universe. And they bred the Zlan as guardians for the kids who didn't develop the mind bolt until later years, but somehow the Zlan got out of control, despite still having the conditioning to protect all Pfafth in danger. That's why they recognised me and protected me! But then they left the messages about the Sillaron becoming the danger and it's a warning to everyone in the whole Universe. They wrote those before the main uprising began, so there's no word there about where they went until those last lines appeared."

"And did our linguist get it correct?" Allie asked. Her excitement was obvious, and her eyes shone as a whole new school of knowledge was revealed.

"Pretty well," Mickie said. "One of their agents must have come out through the time barrier recently and carved those last words using molecular control. I'll write out the word-for-word translation later for the linguists. The last lines say; *We the Pfafth will soon return and take our rightful place as your rulers. We send greetings to our child who will lead this new war. Greetings also to the other Pfafth Child who will support the leader and between them, they will start the new Pfafth Empire. They are now within the Universe and they will soon open the door to us.*"

Mickie's face was cold. "I know that what Markel told the Management Committee was right. Nobody ever goes home and finds it exactly as it was. The Pfafth are deluding themselves if they think they can just come out of their hiding place and take over the whole Universe again. And if they think I'm going to help them, they have a lot to learn."

"What if they *do* leave the Galaxy and come out?" Grant asked, his tone subdued. "There are still some millions of them, maybe an awful lot more if they've been expanding in the last million years."

"I don't think they can," Mickie replied. "When Markel died, there were only twenty or so of them who could cross the time barrier. I doubt they can raise the numbers for a full-scale war and I suspect they're waiting for me to get back there and show them how to get out."

"And could you?" Allie asked curiously.

"I don't think so. I've absolutely no idea how it works. So there's certainly no way I could bring the whole Galaxy back in time one second so they could all leave. That ability has probably died out, seeing as nobody has wanted to use it for a million years."

"So what do you want to do?" Allie's voice was still showing anxiety.

"Can I just be Mickie Dalton again? I just want to be your son, travel round all these planets, learn how to be a Kalamosian and grow up with my friends."

"Sounds like a plan," Grant said, an obvious catch in his voice.

"Good," said Mickie, grinning widely. "Albert, connect me to my friends."

"Of course," said the computer. "And welcome back."

"Well, thank you, Albert! Hey, you three! Get your fat little bums down to Hangar Ten! Mickie Dalton is going to whip you senseless at Loopies!"

Yells of delight echoed in the cabin and Mickie stood up. "Can I go?" he asked, remembering the manners of a young boy with his parents.

"Go!" responded the two adults in unison, and Mickie dashed out to resume living like a kid again.

Chapter 16. The Massive Intellects of Korrobodor

"This planet was only identified as holding intelligent life a few weeks ago," Allie said. She was talking to a group of social scientists, linguistics experts, cultural specialists and computer engineers who had gathered for an informal briefing in the coffee lounge where Mickie and his friends often met. "The planet's solar system is in a remote arm of a galaxy well away from the usual trading routes, but the Speakers discovered intelligence during the same period in which we were approaching the blocked Galaxy now known to be inhabited by the Pfafth."

She winked briefly at Mickie who was sitting at the rear of the group, and he grinned, delighted to be recognised by his mother and also to feel that he was back as a functioning member of the ship's crew. Most of the memories of his hallucinated life as Markel had faded rapidly since the discussion with his parents and with them, the pain and horror had retreated into a safe place.

"The Speakers ran their standard tests and surveys and recommended contact, and we achieved that only ten days ago. Again, as part of their standard surveys, the

Speakers recorded large blocks of conceptual communications, fed them to our computer and a workable translation system has been gained. So we will be able to talk normally when we arrive."

"And just how high a level of intelligence can we expect, Allie?" The speaker was a young Cassolean woman whom Mickie had seen several times in meetings with his mother. She was unusually tall and seemed to carry herself with a dancer's grace that entranced Mickie. Something about Cassoleans flickered in his mind... there was a puzzle somewhere that he had yet to solve... it scuttled away and hid like a frightened mouse and Mickie returned his attention to the discussion.

"Apparently very high, Fenandra," Allie replied. "In fact, exceptionally so, if first impressions are correct. We have no pictures yet, but the Speakers report that the inhabitants – who call themselves Korrobi and the planet Korrobodor – have bred themselves for large brains and high intellect at the expense of degraded bodies. It may not be a pretty sight, I suspect."

"And what trading opportunities?" An elderly X'Kasxi spoke this time and Mickie directed a sub-vocal question to the computer.

"He is an unusual case," Albert replied directly to Mickie's hearing centres. *"His name is G'Kazx Z'Lasx and he has already completed a most successful career on his home planet as a professor of geology at the main University. But instead of retiring, he signed on to the crew at the last visit you made and is proving a most energetic and useful member."*

"I have no idea, I'm afraid," Allie replied with a smile at the X'Kasxi professor. "Nothing has been identified that they produce of potential value. This trip is therefore almost certainly nothing but a diplomatic exercise to establish first physical contact."

"What was the.. er... Korrobi reaction to telepathic contact?" asked a Kalamosian man from the back of the room, just a short distance from Mickie.

"Kasling Piltonar," advised Albert. *"A leader in linguistics, specialising in translation tools between alien species. His work was key to the current versions of the device implanted in your shoulder."*

"Oddly enough, quite calm," Allie said in response to the Kalamosian. "Speaker 499 who made the first forays into their minds reported that they almost seemed to be expecting him. When he queried them, they responded that the mathematical probability of such a contact was rising and they had been expecting to hear from a Universal communications species within the next decade. This suggests high intellect and capacity for analytical thought, so we can be hopeful of something useful to come out of the visit, even if only fresh intellects."

A small outbreak of discussions occurred between several of the listeners and Allie took the opportunity to take a mouthful of coffee. Then she stood up, waved for silence and spoke again.

"Okay everyone, planet-fall in three days, I'll post the ship's time for the departure in the computer files a little later. We'll take a crew of twenty down, mostly you lot, but again, the computer will advise specific personnel in a few hours after I've consulted with your department heads. We'll land in the morning, local planetary time, so be fresh and ready for a full day's work."

With that, the meeting broke up, most people leaving for other duties, a few staying and ordering more coffee or possibly stronger drinks.

"So you've got the hots for one of my mob, eh?" The laugh in Fencris' voice was highly obvious as he walked up to Mickie carrying two cups of coffee.

"Er... what?" Mickie was amused but puzzled.

"She is gorgeous, I must say," Fencris said, still grinning widely and placed one cup in front of Mickie. "But I never expected you to fancy tall women with blue faces and twice your age!"

"Fencris, what *are* you babbling about?" But somehow, Mickie knew what was coming. He recalled the puzzlement he felt looking at Fenandra, the tall Cassolean woman when she questioned Allie. *Something about Cassoleans....* His mind started wrestling with it as he took a sip of coffee.

"Fencris, Cassoleans aren't telepaths, are they?"

"Huh? Telepaths? Hardly, Mickie. Whatever gave you that idea? We've got about the same latent abilities that Humans and Kalamosians and quite a lot of others have got, and we have to have that to be able to deal with the Speakers. But we're not full telepaths. I thought you knew that?"

"I thought so, too. And I've never really questioned it, because you all seemed about the same as us. Well, not Pfafth, but you know what I mean."

"Yes, so what's brought this on?" Fencris was studying him curiously.

"Just.... some odd memory.... I think from my dreams of being Markel."

"*Damned* odd, I'd say, little Pfafth! If that hallucination was from a million years ago, we Cassoleans weren't around then! We were still primitives, killing animals with clubs and spears and things. Hell, I don't think we even had a language back then."

"But you *must* have done! I remember…"

"Remember what? Mickie, what's going on? Something you remember from the Markel dream?" The boy's red eyes were burning like live coals as his curiosity was roused by Mickie's comments.

"Yes! Fencris, that's it! In my dream, there were Cassoleans! Lots of them! They were the greatest telepaths in the Universe and they helped people teleport to a new planet by giving them the images and sort of leading them there."

Fencris was silent for a moment. Then he spoke. "Mickie, there are legends, but nobody has ever taken them seriously."

"What legends?"

"Crazy legends. As kids we read comics that told stories of the First Cassoleans who lived millions of years ago and then died out. But as we got older, they just got laughed at, like the stories you told me about Father Christmas on Earth. My dad says they are just the sorts of myths every civilization has about itself. Now and again, someone makes a movie about that stuff, or writes a book, but nobody has ever found any evidence of earlier civilisations."

"We have the same on Earth about Atlantis," Mickie said thoughtfully. "But this is different, Fencris, it has to be! I know I really was Markel, and the first time I teleported on my own, it was a Cassolean girl who helped…" He stopped, a warm glow coming to his mind as he recalled the slight flirtation he'd had with the girl and how Kerrala had been so obviously jealous.

"What are you grinning about, young Mickie? You look like I felt the first time I kissed a girl!"

Mickie laughed loudly at the accuracy of Fencris' comments. "Well, I didn't kiss her, but she sure was a pretty Cassolean! But *dammit,* Fencris, that memory *has* to be real! And we had several teaching sessions with Cassoleans at school when they introduced us to telepathic communication so we'd know what it felt like and how to manage it."

Fencris became serious. "I've just called my parents here," he said. "They're both academics, Mother's a historian, maybe they can clear this up. But it seems to me that either your hallucination was just that, with no basis in fact, or there's something fantastically important going on. And I think your hallucination was real. After all, you woke up able to read the scripts on Kamotar."

Within moments, Fencris' parents walked into the coffee lounge. They greeted the two boys with the same formal affection that seemed to be the cultural standard for Cassoleans. Mickie rose to his feet and gave them the same small bow that he had learned when he first arrived on the ship. He was feeling a little shy, having spent almost no time in their company before, not having seen them since the visit to X'Katcxo many months before. He realised he didn't even know their names.

"Selvana is the mother and Devenar the father," said Albert silently into his audio centre in response to his equally silent, urgent question.

"Our son says you have something extraordinary to ask us," Selvana said softly, her warmth immediately causing Mickie's shyness to evaporate. Quickly, he recounted the recollections that had suddenly come to him that evening.

The two adult Cassoleans sat very still for a moment.

"If this can be verified," Devenar said, "it will be the greatest single discovery in our history. I know that Fencris has already told you that we have many myths and legends about the Lost Cassoleans but we have absolutely no evidence anywhere to support them."

"Mickie, you have within you the capacity to change our understanding of our history," Selvana said. "Is there any way that you can recall anything more about what happened to our species as you reached the end of your life as Markel?"

"I don't know," Mickie replied. "I wonder if the Speakers..." With a huge shock, he saw the solution and jumped to his feet. "I'm not the one with the answers!" he said gleefully. *"You* are!"

He saw the astonishment on the faces of the others and quickly explained. "After you had rescued me on Drudyenko, the Speakers did a scan of some thousands of Drudya brains and discovered all the race memories going back thousands of years. That's how they discovered that the Sillaron manufactured the Drudya as a subject race and how they had captured some thousands of Russians from Earth a long time ago for breeding purposes to strengthen them. I bet they could do a brain scan of Cassoleans and see if there are any memories at all!"

The two adults looked stunned, then excited.

"Speaker 356, will you scan this group and include all of us in the response?" Devenar said.

"Yes, Devenar, how can I help you all?" The cool, educated voice of the Speaker echoed in Mickie's mind and again he marvelled at the reality that the same voice was in the minds of the other three, coming from many millions of light years away and in a language that he himself could never hope to learn.

"Speaker, is it feasible to run a brain scan of several thousand Cassoleans and locate any race memories of our mythical Lost Cassoleans?"

"I know of those legends, of course, Devenar. And I have Mickie's memories of his life as Markel also, and they certainly indicate there is something to be found. What a fascinating project! Such million-year-old memories, if they exist, will be very, very deep, so this may take some days as the consent of each Cassolean will be required."

"Can you start?"

"I already have! I'm certain any number of my colleagues will be eager to join the exercise. I will report back when we have some answers."

Devenar smiled. "After a million years, Speaker, I think we can last a few more days. My thanks to you and your colleagues."

"The Speakers will find the truth," Mickie said confidently.

"Then all of Cassolea will be changed," Selvana said seriously. "Because if we had such abilities a million years ago, we must be able to recover them. And that will be a massive challenge to us to be able to handle such a talent."

"But I believe our species is mature enough to do that," Devenar replied. "However, we must set up some conferences with our world leaders to discuss the implications. Mickie, we will leave you and our son. We have work to do."

With another round of small bows to each other, the adults left.

Fencris stared hard at Mickie, his eyes sparkling. "I must say, young Mickie," he said, the laugh bubbling out of him. "You Pfafth seem to like changing whole worlds! Don't you ever do anything *normal,* like the rest of us?"

"What, you mean like building gravity machines that fit in armchairs, or doing maths that would stump Einstein, like you do three times before lunch? That's *normal?*"

"Well, it is for me and I'm a genius as well as a Cassolean. So what's your excuse?"

In great good spirits, the two friends went to find the others and finish the evening with a few rounds of Loopies.

*   *   *   *

"Touchdown in thirty seconds," said the voice from the pilot's deck above the cabin of the large shuttle in which Mickie had ridden down from the orbiting ship. He was in a large group of passengers, this time. Permission had been asked of the Korrobi to have a school excursion of the entire student population on board, so some seventy children were riding down, their excitement almost palpable.

"We're so lucky," Melkana had said as the four friends stood in the shuttle hangar earlier, watching the students board. "We get to go down almost every time because our parents are part of the management of this ship. But the rest of the school only visits a planet when we know for certain it's safe, and a lot of our ports of call are still not really secure."

"Dad said the Speakers looked everywhere for danger signals and couldn't find anything," Drellion joined in. "But I see there are still a few guards going with us."

And he was right. A small platoon of a dozen armed guards had also joined the landing party and when the shuttle door opened on landing, Mickie noticed that the guards led the way into the open air.

"Somebody's not entirely certain about the safety," he murmured to the others.

"Standard Operating Procedure," replied Fencris. "Doesn't matter how safe we think it is, the kids get first grade protection."

"Okay, you still want to join the grown-ups?" Allie's voice came from behind where the four children were standing by the door watching the raucous crowd of their school's students fanning out and obviously revelling in the fresh, outdoor air.

"Yes, I think so," Melkana answered. "I want to see how you deal with a brand new species and they sound pretty weird anyway."

"Then we're glad to have you," Harrokarn, her father replied. "But remember, kids, you've all had plenty of experience in how things are not what they seem, so stick together, follow our lead, and we'll be fine."

"And if anything goes wrong, we just tell Mickie to blast them with his mind-bolts or call the Spiders," Drellion said with a chortle.

Feeling gratified by the trust displayed, despite the humorous and slightly mocking manner in which it was expressed, Mickie joined the group of his parents and the twenty specialists walking down the incline to the outdoors. The air smelled clean, with that untainted feeling that comes from a total absence of industry for thousands of kilometres. Gravity seemed a little higher than was the standard on board the ship, though still lower than on Earth or Kalamos.

The shuttle had landed in the middle of what seemed to be a small town. The highest building had three storeys and the square in which they were standing was a smooth, concrete-like material in a pleasant dove-grey colour. But the square was empty of anything but the students from the ship, and they were rapidly dispersing to look around the town. In a few more moments, silence had descended.

"Strange," muttered Grant. "No reception committee?"

"That may be it, just coming into the square," Harrokarn said, indicating with a small gesture to the left hand side of the area. A single man was walking towards the shuttle.

"Not exactly a rapturous welcome," Allie said, a note of puzzlement in her voice. "Aren't we supposed to be the first alien species the Korrobi have ever encountered?"

"Maybe they're terrified," Grant said. "In which case, this is one brave man approaching."

"Possibly," Allie agreed. "But I thought these people were supposed to be hugely intellectual with oversized brains? This one looks perfectly normal to me."

"The plot thickens," Grant whispered as the lone man reached the base of the shuttle and bowed slightly to them.

"My masters bid you welcome," the man said. "They apologise for not meeting you here, but they never go outdoors. I ask you to come with me to be greeted in a more fitting manner."

The translator devices produced English words into Mickie's mind, but he carefully listened to the sounds as they came from the speaker. While incomprehensible, they sounded like any other European language from Earth. Mickie could make out distinct words, no alien sounds such as the honks and wheezes of Kamotari speech or the musical humming of the Kaloti.

"Of course we will," Grant said in reply to the man. "My name is Grantorel and this is my wife Alliandra." He introduced the other two adults and the four children. "The rest of the team are specialists in a number of subjects and they will introduce themselves as they commence their studies. May we know the name of our first Korrobi contact?"

The man did not answer but turned away and began walking across the square to the other side from which he had entered. The group exchanged puzzled looks with each other, but out of courtesy said nothing and followed him into one of the buildings that fronted onto the square.

Inside, there was a huge hall that took up the entire space of the building. Coloured windows in stained glass reduced the light to almost a cathedral level of dimness. In the centre of the floor was what looked like the entry to a stairway and their guide walked directly to it. As Mickie reached it, he saw that it was, in fact, an incline without steps. The group walked down at a shallow angle, and after some fifty metres, reached a small landing from which the incline continued at right angles to the first part. Three more such turns occurred and Mickie estimated they had descended perhaps fifty metres below ground level when they reached another large hall. Not a single piece of furniture broke the emptiness. The illumination was more limited than at ground level and Mickie found the atmosphere quite oppressive. But he was unable to think long on the subject as his attention was drawn to the sight in front of them.

A person was sitting on what looked like a floating armchair. It reminded Mickie of the armchair he had seen in Fencris' cabin many months ago, when his Cassolean friend had demonstrated the tiny antigravity unit he had installed in it. It hovered about two metres above the ground and Mickie finally saw that it differed from a conventional armchair by having a very high back and the addition of two flat, round dishes that were attached horizontally to the front feet. Whether the creature was male or female was impossible to tell. The body resembled nothing but a series of spheres, a rotund belly with fat arms supported on arm rests. It was possibly only a metre high if it was standing, though it was reclined on the armchair with voluminous cushions. But what held Mickie's appalled gaze was the sight of the being's head. It was huge, far larger in comparison to the body than that of a human newborn infant. The face under the enormous forehead was tiny and wizened like that of an ancient person, with small eyes peering from the overhang of heavy eyebrows. The cheekbones were narrow, and the cheeks fell outward in a large triangle to a wide base below the mouth. The forehead reached up possibly half a metre above the eyes and then the rest of the head continued up nearly half that distance. To the sides, the skull exceeded the width of the person's shoulders. There was not a single hair to be seen, not even at the eyebrows, and the scalp was rippled with the blue veins of blood vessels. The ears were just holes at the side with no trace of flaps. A broad leather band ran round the being's monstrous forehead and disappeared at the back and appeared to support the entire structure. Without that support, Mickie was sure the tiny person could not possibly hold its head up. He decided it was the ugliest creature he had ever seen.

"I am Lakor, the Chief Intellect of Korrobodor," the creature said. Again, Mickie listed to the sounds being emitted, as well as to the translation inside his head. The language seemed to be the same as spoken by the guide, but whereas the guide's voice had seemed strong and clear, Lakor's voice sounded like a painful croak, as if the speaker was not accustomed to using it.

"We are grateful for the opportunity to meet you and see your world," Grant responded. He introduced the rest of the party and Lakor's eyes seemed to study each of them in turn. As Mickie was introduced, Lakor's eyes seemed to stare with extra intensity, but Mickie was unsure if that was just his imagination or not.

"That is one creepy little *yurkel,"* said the voice of Fencris into his mind, transmitted from the Ship's computer. He had clearly instructed the computer to include all four friends into the silent conversation, because Mickie saw both Drellion and Melkana nod back at the Cassolean, their lips twitching as they fought not to laugh.

"What the hell is a *yurkel?"* Mickie asked, drawing on his control to keep his face still.

"Something remarkably like that *thing* on the gravity chair," Fencris replied.

"A yurkel is a slug-like creature from Cassolea," Albert informed Mickie. *"It grows to about a metre in length, and has a head with markings not unlike a human face. Its bite can be painful and poisonous."*

"In that case, Fencris, you're dead right," Mickie said. "I don't think either of us is going to be falling in love with Korrobi girls."

He saw Fencris' lips twitch sharply, and Melkana moved behind her father and held her hand firmly over her mouth. "Shut up, the pair of you," she said silently. "I can't hold this in much longer!"

Mickie saw warning looks from Allie and Grant and took control of himself.

"We must compliment you on the manner in which you have adjusted to your first encounter with intelligent, alien life," Allie said. "For many species, this can be a major trauma

"We have been anticipating such contacts for the last few years," Lakor said. "So this is no great surprise."

"I'll give the yurkel an "F" for warm welcomes," Melkana's voice said into Mickie's mind. "I think it was a mistake to join our parents in this meeting."

"Well, we can't escape now," replied Mickie. "Let's see what happens. But I think it's draining Allie's reserves of politeness rather fast."

In fact, Mickie could see that all four adults were displaying expressionless faces, a sign he knew meant that they were using all their diplomatic skills. A quick glance at the others in the party showed varying degrees of discomfort.

"Then we commend you for your anticipation," Allie said.

"Not anticipation at all," replied Lakor. "It was for us a simple intellectual exercise of forecasting, given the number of planets within each galaxy, the age of the universe and our own technological advances. Such efforts are child's play to us."

"We are very impressed," Allie replied.

"Impressed?" Fencris sounded amused. "That sort of exercise is what every school kid does when they learn the first principles of statistics! I thought these yurkels were supposed to be intellectual giants?"

"Stay with it," Melkana said. "There's something weird about these things. I'm glad I'm here now, I want to see what happens."

"May we offer you some refreshment?" Lakor asked. Mickie decided that the offer was the first signs of civilised behaviour they had seen on the planet.

"That would be a great pleasure," Grant replied. "Will any more of your colleagues be joining us?"

"Perhaps. It depends on whether they can free themselves of their other duties."

Before any reply could be made, a number of people appeared in the hall. Like the man who had first greeted them, they appeared normal and human-like. They carried in several tables that were laid out end-to-end, and chairs that were placed along one side of the tables, facing Lakor. Large wine glasses were placed before each chair and Lakor waved at the visitors to be seated.

"May I ask a question?" Allie said as she sat down.

"Of course," Lakor replied.

"Our briefing was that the entire population of Korrobodor was based on intellectual development that resulted in growth of the brain. The people serving us seem not of this group. Are they also Korrobi?"

"They are not."

"Then may I ask what they are?"

"They are slaves and not for discussion."

The silence at the table was frozen.

"Make that "F" for warm welcomes into a "G" minus," said Melkana through the communication channel.

The servers appeared again, this time carrying jugs of what looked like red wine. About a dozen of them were placed on the table. One of the servers brought another vessel and placed it by a jug. It looked like a glass sphere with a tube protruding down through a small, circular hole at the top. A servant, or slave as Mickie now realised, twisted the sphere, which neatly split into two halves. Into the bottom half, he poured the contents of a jug, and the liquid ran thick and heavy. The top was replaced and the vessel was placed on the right hand dish of the armchair's base by a slave with his face pointed at the ground and his hand raised high to place the vessel on the gravity chair. Then Mickie saw what the point of the flat surface was. It moved upward to the level of the armrest, at which point Lakor picked it up and began sucking through the tube.

Another pair of slaves then poured the liquid into the wine glasses in front of each of the landing party and moved away.

"You may drink," Lakor said.

"Arrogant little yurkel," said Fencris and picked up his glass, staring at the liquid suspiciously then sniffed at it. Carefully, he put it back down on the table. Curiously, Mickie picked up his own glass and didn't need to smell the contents to realise what the liquid was. Like Fencris, he put his glass down, feeling queasy.

Allie had also realised the nature of the refreshments offered, as had all the others at the table.

"There are three species represented in our group," she said. "I regret that none of us is able to drink fresh blood, not of any animal," she said firmly. "I apologise if this causes offence."

"That seems a waste," Lakor replied, not seeming offended. "It is the best brand we were able to produce, fresh from our own slaves."

"From your slaves? "

"Why not? The development of our intellects and the growth of our brains demand the highest quality of food that is easily ingested. Fresh blood is our primary food."

"And are the slaves related to the Korrobi?"

Lakor seemed to have relaxed with the drink he had gulped down. "Vaguely," he replied. "They are the descendents of those who foolishly refused to follow our mental developments that we began so long ago."

Mickie was developing an even greater admiration for his parents than he already had. How they remained calm and polite in this situation was beyond him, but Allie and Grant as well as Melkana's parents appeared to be having a simple academic discussion.

"Then how did you manage to enforce this slavery on them?" Harrokarn asked. "You must have some force or weapon."

"It was a deliberate development," said Lakor. "Our superior intelligence allowed us to develop a mental weapon that can cause great pain on an inferior species such as these. They obey us because they cannot sustain pain that can lead to death."

An interesting power, thought Mickie. He wondered if it was anything like his own mind bolt capability.

"And their blood provides your food?" Harrokarn continued. Not a trace of the disgust he was feeling showed in his expression.

"Of course. All our strength is in the mind as we deliberately allowed the power of our bodies to decline," Lakor said with apparent satisfaction. "Their blood is the finest source of protein available. Mere animals do not provide such quality, though we can use that source if really necessary."

"I see. Let us then change the subject," Harrokarn continued. Mickie knew that the adults were holding the same private conversation using the computer that he and his friends were having. They must have agreed not to continue the topic but instead try and learn more about this strange race of Korrobi.

"As has been explained to you, this ship and its crew is a mercantile venture. We buy and sell throughout the explored Universe, dealing with many different races. I can list the items we can provide, and we would ask what you may have that could be of value to us?"

"Our intellects, of course," Lakor answered rapidly.

"In what way?" inquired Allie.

"We will take any problem, whether technical, or social, or any other. In time, with several of our superior minds employed, we will provide answers."

"That would certainly be immensely valuable," Grant said. "Could you give us an example of such a problem you have solved, and for whom?"

Lakor was silent for a moment and Mickie decided to risk a small experiment. He reached out with his empathic skills and tried to see into Lakor's mind. For a moment, he struggled with a totally alien mindset, rather like trying to find a path though jungle in a dense fog. He began to sense some emotion, some concepts... it was difficult and quite nauseating, and he pulled back, feeling stained with something noxious.

Three slaves returned to the room and began taking away the jugs of blood and untouched glasses. As they began carrying them out, one slipped and fell, the glass he was carrying falling to the floor and smashing, the blood spilling over the carpet.

"Fool!" snapped Lakor. The slave let out a yelp of pain and writhed on the ground, his arms curled hard against his stomach as if suffering from severe cramps. Mickie switched his attention to the slave's mind, reached in and saw where the pain was. He realised he could stop it with ease, but as he was about to block the agony, it ceased of its own accord. The slave slowly got to his feet and walked out, while three more came in with cleaning utensils and attacked the spilled blood.

"I just had a look at that," Mickie said to his friends. "It would have been easy to block that pain, and I reckon the little yurkel's mind bolt is nowhere near as strong as he believes."

"As strong as yours?" asked Drellion.

"Nothing like," Mickie said. "But I still have to get seriously angry before mine lets loose. I can't focus it or send it as easily as that little horror can."

"Cool!" said Drellion. "I hope you get a chance to blast him. That is one nasty little dude."

Mickie laughed internally at Drellion's adoption of some of Mickie's Earth speech patterns. Then he returned his attention to what the Korrobi was saying.

"You saw there how we control our slaves," Lakor was saying.

"Very impressive," Grant said, no sarcasm evident in his tone. "Now, about some references for problems solved and the customers?"

Lakor was silent and Mickie decided to have another attempt at reading the mind. This time he overcame the nausea and sense of displacement and began to read something. He struggled to overcome the alien concepts, but slowly things came through. He sensed... smugness, satisfaction and a powerful sense of hatred directed against the visitors in the room. And something else... something was being covered up.

Not even bothering to hide his communications, he spoke aloud. "Allie, Grant, there's something wrong. Lakor is hiding something and he really hates us."

"Stand by, Mickie." It was Grant who replied. "Allie is just contacting the guards with the children to order them to return to the shuttle immediately."

Mickie had no need to be told what Allie had discovered. Her face had lost its composure

"I cannot contact the guards with our children," she said. "Nor can I make contact with the ship. Lakor, explain what is going on."

The rest of the team had got to their feet in dismay and were obviously trying to make contact with the ship, or in a few cases, with their children.

"I must admit that we have not been entirely truthful with you," the strange person on the gravity chair said.

"You are not our first alien contact. We have long known about you, the Speakers, the other species in your crew and what your role in life is all about. We even know about the Pfafth."

Mickie felt a terrible chill down his back as the Korrobi stared directly at him as he spoke. Something was terribly wrong. How could have the Speakers have investigated this species, scanned them, read their culture and not know any of this? "Speaker 356, are you there?" he called silently, and received nothing but blankness.

And he finally understood. The same, dreadfully familiar blanket of silence had been thrown over them as had occurred when he was captured on Drudyenko. It could only mean one thing. The Sillaron were here and the Korrobi were allied with them.

Knowing he would fail, he tried one more path. "Zlan, I am in danger and I need your help."

Only silence reverberated in his head like footsteps in an empty room.

"So, Pfafth, you have learned that you are helpless?"

The Korrobi was staring at him and Mickie read all the hate and rage against him and all the others. He couldn't trust his voice and so remained silent.

"The Zlan will not come to your aid this time," the ugly being said, the gloating tones dripping with satisfaction.

Mickie knew the rage in him was building to explosive levels and he welcomed the fury, let it build and fanned it deliberately. It roared like a furnace in his mind and he focused his rage at the massive brain in its restraining harness and let fly a mind bolt with every ounce of power he had, worse than when he killed the Smegandri, worse than when he tried to attack the witch-hunters on Merrison.

And nothing happened.

A wave of despair washed over him. He realised the others were looking at him, hoping that his weapons would work once more, but he could no nothing but shake his head miserably and sensed the matching despair in his friends and family.

"And so we have nearly seventy of your children," gloated the Korrobi. "Their blood will provide a wonderfully tasty addition to our food stocks. There is nothing like a child's blood for flavour and freshness. Perhaps we will have a feast with our main clients as we watch the Pfafth die. His blood will be an even more delectable prize and I will claim it for myself as his captor."

Mickie ignored him. He had remembered an episode in the life of Markel. He was on a planet when the Sillaron had incited the local population to riot and attack the Pfafth residents. They had tried to leap home and the Sillaron had blanketed the region so that all the Pfafth powers were suppressed and they had been unable to escape the slaughter that followed. But Markel had been able to visualise just one tiny, unimportant world that he had visited once, and he was able to teleport himself there. Mickie's own memory told him that world was Earth of a million years ago, but he put the thought away and struggled to find a gap in the curtain that the Sillaron had thrown over everything. If he survived this, he determined to find out how the Sillaron suppressed the Pfafth powers. But he could find no gap this time.

"And now you have the answer to the question you asked earlier," Lakor said. "You wanted to know a problem we solved for a client? The blanket that suppresses all your communications, especially that of the Pfafth and his unique talents, we found out how to do that for our clients, the Sillaron. I initiated it just a few moments ago, once I gave the order to capture all the children."

"So it's a mechanical device?" Grant asked. Mickie understood why he asked. Grant was trying to learn anything he could and suspected that the Korrobi was so arrogant he could not stop himself telling him the answer. And Grant was right.

"Over a million years ago, we developed it," Lakor boasted. "Our clients were delighted and paid us well, for it allowed them to bring defeat on the Pfafth."

A million years? Mickie was stunned. This species had been around so long, and he had never heard of them, either through the Speakers or as Markel, the leader of the most powerful species that ruled forty galaxies? How could that be? He tried to build on the approach Grant had exploited so well, of playing to the conceit of the Korrobi leader.

"Lakor, you have defeated us brilliantly," he said. "But how did you hide yourselves from the Speakers for so long? And how did you hide from them the real history and abilities of your race when they contacted you recently?"

It worked.

"We have been working on this for centuries before the Speakers developed their universal telepathic skills. The Sillaron told us it would be necessary and paid us with many fresh young slaves to develop the screen that would reflect back to the Speakers what we wanted them to hear."

With every word, the boastful arrogance of Lakor was becoming more grotesque and Mickie decided that the Korrobi were surely the most evil of all the species he had yet encountered, far worse even than the Gelkka, for the Gelkka did not seem to enjoy the cruelty and dominance as much as this appalling Korrobi did.

"There is nothing too horrible that could happen to this bunch of sickoes that they wouldn't deserve," he muttered aloud.

The doors to the room crashed open and a large number of the slaves appeared. This time they were carrying weapons. They surrounded Mickie's party and stood motionless.

"You will go with the slaves back to the surface," commanded Lakor. "We will decide how best to feed from you later."

The slaves gestured and the prisoners got to their feet and were escorted back up the inclined ramp to the surface. The pleasant village square had changed. Now it was filled with cages, solid metal bars forming numerous, open cells. Already, they were filled with the children from the ship. They stood in groups, many of them weeping and holding to each other for comfort. They stared as Mickie's group was led out and driven into two other cells, the adults in one, the children in another, but as the doors crashed shut, the wails of despair grew louder.

The slave who locked the gate to Mickie's cell looked at him with sorrow in his eyes.

"I am truly sorry," he said. "But they can kill many of us with their minds, and cause so much pain we cannot stand it. We were praying you would be able to help us."

"Then I am sorry, too," Mickie replied.

Once all the prisoners had been secured, a series of the floating gravity chairs appeared from the surrounding building until there were hundreds of them drifting around the square, each with one of the ugly, misshapen Korrobi aboard. They drifted close to the cells, pointing at the inmates, chattering excitedly. He turned away, as much as was possible in the open-barred cells in which there was no refuge from stares or protection against the weather. He wondered how long they would have to last before being taken away to be drained of blood for a Korrobi feast.

He looked at his friends. Drellion had slumped to the ground and hidden his face in his hands. Fencris had similarly sat down cross-legged in one corner of the cell and seemed to be staring fixedly at a spot between his knees. Melkana was still standing and she looked back at Mickie.

"Looks like this could be the end," she said quietly.

"I'm not giving up yet," Mickie replied.

"No, I suppose not. We've got out of some pretty horrible situations before, but we used your Pfafth talents or the Zlan rescued us. We don't have either, this time."

"You saved me on Drudyenko just with your own abilities," he countered.

She nodded, her face becoming sad and tears starting in her eyes. "I don't even have my flute with me."

Suddenly she took a step towards him and put her arms round his neck. Despite the horror of the situation, the joy of the contact overwhelmed him and he put his own arms round her.

"Dammit, Mickie, things were getting pretty good with us," she whispered.

He closed his eyes and simply experienced holding her. Then she stepped away and sat down against the cell wall.

Mickie walked over to the side where his parents were in the next cell. They tried to smile at him, but the pain in their eyes was intense. They put their arms through the bars and touched him.

"Whatever happens," he said, "it was better than being on Earth with those horrible people. I'll always love you for rescuing me."

Allie broke into a burst of weeping and Grant put his arms round her. Mickie knew he had to leave them to their grief, and he was struggling with his own. He copied his friends and sat down against one wall, tried to lock out the sounds of weeping coming from so many quarters and concentrated on a way out.

"Damn, I'm supposed to be the super-Pfafth," he muttered. "I'm the end product of a million years of breeding by the most powerful species in the Universe. Surely I can find a way out?"

He concentrated on trying to communicate with either the Speakers or the Zlan, but nothing succeeded. While working on that, he tried to identify the nature of the blanket that was over them, and to see if there were any gaps in it. He tested it as one tests a curtain in front of a stage, looking for the strength of it, where the join might be. He gathered all his mental strength, tried to visualise the world of Zlan, his last planet fall and the home of his greatest allies and then drove himself as hard he could against the barrier.

It didn't work. Mickie struggled to consider that the adventure might be over and he would die soon. "Maybe that other Pfafth, wherever the hell he or she is could come and rescue us," he muttered to himself. "Because I think I've run out of options."

The dreadful day wore on. They had arrived in the morning and they endured hour after hour of the horrible twittering of the swarms of Korrobi as they floated around the cells, staring at the captors like butchers examining the cows before they enter the slaughter house.

"All men," said Melkana at one point.

"Huh?" he said.

"We've only seen men," she said thoughtfully. "I've been watching those foul little yurkels for hours now and I've only seen men. Where are the women?"

He wondered how she could think about subjects like that when death was only hours away. "Maybe you have seen them, but they look exactly like the blokes. They're so ugly they could be anything. Maybe they only have one sex."

"Could be," she said, and went silent.

Mickie resumed his struggles to find a way out. If only he could get away and call for the Zlan. He pleasurably visualised a hundred monster spiders arriving in a split second and causing mayhem with the vicious blood drinkers of Korrobodor. He thought back on the early stages of the discussion with Lakor and how Fencris had been so contemptuous of the Korrobi's boast about forecasting an alien contact. He reviewed his empathic link with Lakor. He realised that he had detected hatred, rage and hunger but he hadn't noticed any great sense of a huge intelligence. He had no idea what to do with that thought.

Night fell. It became very cool, but not painfully cold. Nonetheless, he helped Drellion to his feet, and he and Melkana went over to where Fencris was still sitting motionless in the corner of the cage. They all sat down close to each other to keep some warmth alive. Fencris didn't seem to notice. Mickie wandered if he had retreated into some form of mental blackout, perhaps a fugue state where he noticed nothing at all as a refuge from the horrors of what was happening. Trying to hide it from Melkana and hoping she was asleep, Mickie wept for the end of the dreams and the dread of what the next day would bring.

* * * *

Dawn almost exploded on them. It seemed to Mickie that one moment it was black, the next the square was alive with movement and the sun was shining over the low buildings surrounding them. Mickie got slowly to his feet and looked around. Most of the children in the other cages were still huddled together, and here and there, the sounds of weeping broke the silence. In the next cage, Allie and Grant were sitting upright against the cell wall, Allie cradled in Grant's arm, her head on his shoulder. Melkana's parents were in similar positions a metre or so away.

The flights of Korrobi gravity chairs were already circling the cages. Mickie decided they reminded him of clouds of flies around a dead mouse and that he hated them more than anything else he could ever imagine. Black depression settled on him. This could well turn out to be the last day of life for the people in this square. He wondered what the Captain on the ship was thinking and whether any sort of rescue attempts could be made. Then he thought that the Korrobi seemed so confident and arrogant, it meant they knew they had some sort of defence against anything the ship could mount against them. Maybe the Sillaron had already invaded the ship and taken it over.

"That was a very interesting conversation we had the other day," said a familiar voice behind him. Mickie turned to see Fencris standing up and stretching. He seemed quite relaxed, showing none of the fear and misery that haunted every other face Mickie could see.

"Which one?" he asked curiously.

"The one about Cassoleans once being powerful telepaths."

"Fencris, we're here in a prison, probably going to be killed and drained of our blood and you're talking about Cassolean telepaths a million years ago?"

"Like I said, it was an interesting conversation. It made me think."

Mickie decided this was better than contemplating the imminent deaths of everyone nearby. And there was a tone to Fencris' words that intrigued him.

"So what did you think, my blue-faced friend?"

"Well, first of all, I remembered what you'd told me, that the Zlan and the Speakers used different methods to communicate telepathically."

"Yes?"

"And obviously, the Sillaron blanket thing affected both those wavebands, which is why you can't get through."

"And?"

"So I wondered if the old Cassoleans had used yet another waveband and the Sillaron had forgotten all about it over the last million years."

"Quite probably. So what?"

"So I also remembered from your stories, how it seems that nobody could use a talent like teleportation or telepathy if they had no idea that they actually *could*. Look how you finally managed to get off Speaker's Planet, once the Zlan told you they did it without knowing how, but just that they could."

Mickie stayed silent. Fencris was getting to something and the tiny smile on his lips meant that it was critical.

"So I sat there all night," continued Fencris. "And I tried getting really deep into my own mind to see if I could find my own trace of telepathic skills. After all, I'm supposed to be some sort of genius, remember."

"So *that's* what was happening! We thought you'd gone into a coma or something. And what did you find?" Mickie realised he'd been holding his breath.

"I found that I could. And I was right. It's on a different wave length from either the Zlan or the Speakers, but they can hear it, even if they can't broadcast on it." He grinned widely. "And the Sillaron effect doesn't work on it. So help will be along, just about.... now."

The square exploded and turned black as hundreds of Zlan appeared in seconds. Immediately, they leaped and struck the many floating gravity chairs, knocking the occupants out of them and they fell helplessly to the hard ground, smashing their huge skulls into bloody masses. They were the lucky ones. Many of the Korrobi were snatched by monstrous jaws as they fell, injected with venom and then placed on the ground, frozen into immobility but still able to watch the scene unfold. Within seconds, all the gravity chairs had gone, but the Zlan had not finished. They seemed overwhelmed with rage. Mickie saw them smashing down the walls of buildings and as gravity chairs swooped out, catching them and biting the Korrobi. Oddly, the Zlan were ignoring the slaves. He saw hundreds of them fleeing in terror, but not one was attacked and paralysed.

The onslaught seemed to be moving away as the Zlan spread out, determined it seemed to catch every Korrobi they could. But one stayed and moved to the cage inhabited by Mickie. It stopped, towering over the bars.

"This has been a good day for us, young Pfafth," the monster said.

"In what way?"

"You gave many of us a chance to fulfil our destinies by helping you."

"You have my eternal gratitude, friend Zlan, and that of everyone here."

"I will move and join my colleagues on the hunt, if you permit it. We have not had sport like this in centuries and we have a whole planet to search."

The question shook Mickie badly. He was being asked to allow the slaughter of every one of these Korrobi monsters? He felt his insides tremble at the magnitude of the problem. However much he had hated them and even though they had planned to kill all the people from the ship, how could he do this?

"Grant, Allie, I can't handle this," he said, turning to his parents.

"That's okay, Mickie, let us do it." Grant turned to the Zlan and spoke firmly.

"We cannot condone the extinction of a species," he said. "My son does not permit the hunt to expand beyond the borders of this town. Here, it was obvious that all were culpable and would join in the killing of the captives, but while we believe it highly probable that all of the Korrobi on the planet would have done the same, we do not know. The decision is that the hunt is limited to this town."

"Is that your decision, Pfafth?" The Zlan's voice reflected no emotion, neither disappointment nor anger.

"It is," Mickie said with relief. "And I think the others will not come and release us from the cages until you leave."

"One more thing. We want to take those we have caught back to Zlan. It is breeding season and we need food for our young. Those Korrobi who still live will make excellent incubation and food sources. Do we have your permission?"

For a few seconds, Mickie thought about the dreadful fate in store for the living, paralysed Korrobi. They would survive for some weeks, feeling the Zlan eggs inside them becoming tiny spiders who would eat their living flesh. Then he remembered what the Korrobi had planned for the children of his crew and he had no further doubts. He looked at Grant who nodded.

"You have my permission to take all the Korrobi from this town back to Zlan," Mickie said.

The Zlan turned a fraction and stared at Fencris who could not stop himself backing away a short distance.

"Cassolean, you have done a great deed this day," the Zlan said.

Fencris swallowed. "Er... thank you," he said nervously and stood frozen, as the Zlan seemed to stare at him for a few seconds.

But instead of moving away, the Spider stood motionless. "There is something puzzling...." it said.

"What is puzzling?" Mickie was startled. It was the first time any Zlan had spoken with less than complete firmness and incisiveness. He sensed confusion in the beast.

"No matter. I must join the hunt," the Spider said and turned and moved at astonishing speed to vanish behind the buildings as it hunted for more Korrobi.

"It was the right decision," Grant said in reassurance. "The Korrobi over the rest of the planet will soon know of this episode as will all the other inhabitants. Their breeding process and enslavement will stop and they will die out as they are replaced by normal people."

"But what was that last bit about? What was puzzling it?" Fencris asked, breathing easier now that the Zlan had departed.

"I have absolutely no idea," Mickie replied. "Anyway, we need those people to come and get us out of here."

It took a few minutes before the slaves began to creep out from the buildings, but at last the guards appeared and unlocked the cages. Mickie ran to his parents to be folded into their arms, and Melkana and Drellion did the same with theirs. All around the scene, numbers of the children were racing to rejoin the parents who had been part of the landing party. But then the four adults came over to Fencris and hugged him too, tears flowing freely from all of them.

Allie finally stood up straight. "I've established communications with the Captain. He wants all the children back aboard immediately. There are a lot of frenzied parents up there who need to see them alive and well. And after seeing the Zlan and what they did, there are a lot of badly traumatised kids needing specialist attention. Fencris, do you want to get back to your parents immediately?"

Fencris shook his head. "I've just talked to them," he said. "They know I'm safe, so they said it's okay for me to come back later with you."

The order to return must have been transmitted to each child, because they were racing for the shuttle and climbing aboard. Within a minute or two it had lifted off and vanished.

"What happened on board ship while all this was going on?" Hektogarn asked.

"The captain says it was much like when we approached the Pfafth galaxy," Allie said. "The systems froze, they couldn't launch a shuttle, nothing."

"What about the guards?" Melkana looked pale and she had moved to her parents who had their arms round her.

"All dead," Grant replied, the anger and sadness showing in his face. "The kids said that a blaster rifle suddenly killed them all at the same moment. There were several of those gravity chairs floating nearby, so it seems the Korrobi had weapons mounted on them. Then they herded the children back to the square and into the cages. That means families back home who have lost fathers, sons and brothers. Mickie, you were right to let the Zlan take the Korrobi. There is no punishment bad enough for them."

Mickie looked around. The ground was littered with the bodies of the Korrobi who had been killed by the fall from their gravity chairs, and many other bodies of still living but paralysed victims lay immobile. Mickie could see the eyes of some of them, glaring with terror and hatred. He felt no sympathy for them. Then he saw that more of the slaves were coming out of the buildings and standing in the wreckage of the town square, staring at the dreadful scene.

"I think we have work to do," Allie murmured and began to move towards the silent people. The rest followed her. As they got near, Mickie suddenly saw that many of the slaves were women. They were the first he had seen since arriving.

"You are free now," Allie said loudly in the general direction of the crowd. One of the men moved forward and smiled at her.

"You have terrifying friends," he said. Mickie recognised him as the one who had first greeted them on their arrival.

"But very faithful ones," Allie agreed. "They have left none of the Korrobi here in any position to harm you again. The rest of them around the world will not dare try to stay in power. This planet is yours now."

"It's almost impossible to believe," the man replied. "They have ruled for a million years or more, but they needed us normals to serve them and provide our blood as their food."

"I'm curious," Grant joined in. "Were all of those grotesque creatures male?"

"They were," replied the spokesman.

"Then where are the women? Did none of them join the drive to become superior intellects?"

The laughter began with the nearest of them and spread like a flood water till the rest of the freed slaves were almost helpless with mirth. Allie and the rest of the group looked around, baffled by the merriment, but grinning widely at the infectious nature of it.

Finally the young man who seemed to be the leader regained enough control to speak again. "Superior intellects? Let me assure you, there were no superior intellects among those airborne blood drinkers."

"But... who developed the suppression device and the anti-gravity controls? Who was able to hide this civilisation from the Speakers? These things take hugely advanced technologies." Grant was baffled.

"You asked where the women of the Korrobi were. Why don't you let them explain it to you?" He pointed to the side of the square behind Mickie and his group and they turned to see an astonishing sight.

Walking out of one of the buildings was a line of women. They looked perfectly normal, and as they got nearer, Mickie realised with a start that they magnificent. Each of them looked tall, well-shaped and athletic, all seemed to have faces of great character and warmth, with intelligence that radiated so much it could almost be felt. Their smiles would have melted a glacier, Mickie thought, sensing the waves of happiness that came from these stunning women.

They all came closer until the two groups looked at each other.

"What can we possibly say to the people who have liberated us?" one of them said.

Grant chose to answer and laughed as he spoke. "You could tell us where to get some decent food!" he said. "We haven't eaten for over a day!"

*   *   *   *

Tables and chairs had been laid out in another clearing away from the town square that was such an appalling scene of death and fear. Here, the atmosphere was festive. The freed slaves had been delighted to prepare and bring out an enormous spread of food and everybody had sat down in the mild air and feasted to celebrate the new life facing the people of the planet.

"Well over a million years ago, the leaders of the planet decided to breed for intelligence," one of the women began to explain. Her name was Karraleen. "The decision was not fully accepted by everybody and the rebels were sent into exile, many of them imprisoned. The normal people here, they are their descendents. The process was begun and initially seemed highly successful. We developed some remarkable technologies and our art forms were quite astonishing."

"So what happened that led to this situation?" Allie was amused and a little irritated by the reaction of the men in the group to these beautiful women. Both Harrokarn and Grant were clearly enslaved by them and even Mickie and Fencris were completely bedazzled.

"What happened was the women of the Korrobi began to develop far higher levels of intellect than anyone had ever considered possible," Karraleen replied. "The men certainly improved, but something in the female brain structure and chemistry responded far better to the program of drugs and training than with the men. Several other intelligent races in this galaxy began to hear of this after we had developed hyperspace communication devices and began to hire us to develop similar technologies or solve complex problems for them."

"And the men began to get all cranky and jealous, huh?" Allie said with a grin at the adult males in the audience who were clearly hanging onto Karraleen's every word with varying expressions of adoration.

"Another of the problems we found was that the drugs mixed adversely with male chemistry." Karraleen said with a nod. "Instead of increasing intellect as sharply as it did with us, it suppressed the men's hormonal development and retarded their emotional growth. Increasingly, they became jealous, angry and less and less mature. It was frightening, but they couldn't see it. Unfortunately, one aspect of development did work. The men were able to throw the mental projectiles that caused serious pain, possibly death in others and this they began to use to oppress the rest of us. We were never able to find a protection against it and we didn't develop that talent ourselves."

"But how did that physical malformation start?" Allie had forgotten her irritation and was equally fascinated by the story unfolding.

"They decided the only way to catch and surpass the women intellectually was to develop larger brains. So for some thousands of years they worked at that, and the end result is what you see. Unfortunately, it didn't have the desired effect, but they persisted, allowing their physical degradation, hoping it would be compensated by intellectual growth. It never did, but by this time, they'd forgotten all about the intentions and fallen into the trap of believing that the larger the brain, the more advanced they were. Simple head size became the measure of status and they became obsessive on the subject, breeding more and more to that objective."

"And they were able to keep the women in captivity and force them to provide the problem-solving skills that paid so well?"

"That's how it happened. Meanwhile, we developed anti-gravity, the entire planetary shield that kept the Speakers from learning about us, many other inventions. We worked to find a defence against the mental weapon, and we were just about there when the Sillaron came."

"When was that?" Mickie had to ask, it was so much part of his entire life as Markel and represented the greatest threat to him now.

"About a million years ago," Karraleen said with a smile that melted Mickie's insides. He heard Melkana mutter something and ignored it. "They came and told us about the evil race of Pfafth that ruled the universe so oppressively. We had no way of verifying the story as we had no knowledge of which races were involved, and anyway, the Pfafth galaxies were so far away from ours, we couldn't know what the truth was. The men accepted the contract of developing the suppression tool and we designed it and built it. We had no idea what the result was."

"And the mental bolts?" Mickie was curious about a talent that paralleled his in some ways.

"We had just developed a defence, but the Sillaron had learned something in that field from the Pfafth who apparently had great powers. Whatever it was they gave the men, it beat our defences. We've never been able to counter it since."

"Could I ask a question?" Mickie had developed an idea, and it gave him a welcome opportunity to talk to one of these extraordinary women.

"Of course," Karraleen said with a smile that melted his insides.

"That suppression tool – could you design something that could counteract it?"

"I'm sure we could. Can you afford to pay for it? We're a commercial operation now!"

"That isn't a problem." Mickie took the small velvet bag containing the enormous diamonds that had been given to him by the cop on Kamotar. There had been four but he had left one at his adoptive parents' home back on Earth. He had kept the remaining three in the bag strung round his neck in case of emergencies. "Would these cover it?" he asked and poured the massive stones on to the table and they flashed in the sunshine as they rolled to a stop. The women round the table looked in stunned surprise. Karraleen called over more of the women from the adjoining table.

"Our young friend here has asked if these would pay for a counter to the suppression device we once built. What do you think, ladies?"

Muted laughs ran round the group. "Our ancestors anticipated the need when they built the things," one of them said. "Give me ten minutes, I'll go and get the ten or so that were built at the same time. We've got a few of the original suppressors too, you can have them as well. And I think just one of those stones will do!" She left the table and walked back to one of the nearby buildings.

"I think this planet is now in good hands," Allie said, and everybody cheered their approval. "The shuttle has returned and is waiting in the square, so it's time to return to our ship and continue our travels. Of course, we'll continue to visit and now the barriers have gone, you can communicate freely with us through the Speakers. The Universe has need of your talents and I have no doubt you can make this planet the technological and intellectual centre for everybody to use."

The dinner party broke up and began ambling back to the square. As they did, the woman who had left caught up again with the party and handed Mickie a small box, together with the bag and the remaining two diamonds that he had forgotten on the table.

The shuttle was there, but so was a horrible sight. The Zlan had returned for their spoils. Most of the local inhabitants ran back into cover, but the Korrobi women watched in horrified fascination as the massive spiders each picked up the living body of one of the men and vanished with a small "pop" of air collapsing into the vacuum their departure had caused. Many of them also picked up the shattered corpses, presumably as immediate food for themselves and vanished. Within moments, nothing remained but the stains of blood and brain material on the ground.

"I know that those things saved us, but that is truly a horrible thing to see," Karraleen murmured. "I could almost feel sorry for the men, but when I think of what they've done, I feel nothing but relief. At least they'll be dead soon and we have a planet to rebuild. The rest of them on the planet will not last long once they are reduced to a diet of just animal blood and no more of them will be born."

There seemed nothing to say to that but to wave farewell and climb back into the shuttle. Like everyone else, Mickie was relieved to see the back of what had threatened to be his killing ground.

Chapter 17. A Bigger, Stranger Universe

"So tell me what happened? Who did you make contact with?

Mickie and Fencris sat together in a pair of seats at the end of the back row as the shuttle flew to make rendezvous with the ship. Melkana and Drellion were inseparable from their parents, still shattered by the experience on the planet, and though Mickie badly wanted to see Melkana again after the brief but joyous hug while captive, he knew that had to wait. Meanwhile, there was a great deal to learn from the hero of the hour, Fencris. His role in the rescue was not yet widely known and he wanted to keep it that way.

"It was damned weird, Mickie, I tell you!" Fencris was more shaken than he had seemed an hour ago when he and the rest had heard the astonishing truth of the world of Korrobodor from the women of the planet. Then he had been like the others, massively exhilarated by the fact of being alive after death had seemed so close and so certain, but also astounded by the role he had played and the new powers he had discovered in himself. "I sat down in the cage, concentrated hard and within half an hour or so, I was somewhere else. I got so deep into my mind that I had no idea of anything going on. I don't remember night falling, I don't remember you and the others gathering round me to keep warm, I just found myself studying every single brain cell I had. It was the wildest sensation you can imagine!"

"I think I have some idea! So when did you discover the telepathic skill?"

"I don't really know. I had no idea of time. But all of a sudden I seemed to touch something that reverberated. You know how you accidentally hit a guitar string, or a jar that echoes with a musical note? Well, that's how it was. I felt that the note was vibrating way out into the distance. Somehow, I seemed to tag onto it and floated way off the planet, into space, right out of the galaxy."

"And you made contact with the Speakers?"

"No."

"Not the Speakers? You mean you talked to the Zlan? Wow, that must have been scary. I know how I nearly wet my pants the first time I talked with them."

"No, not the Zlan. Not at first, anyway."

"Not the Zlan? Fencris? What the hell's going on? They're the only telepaths we know of. Who did you talk to if not one of those?"

Fencris turned in his seat a little to look Mickie straight in the eye. "I don't know," he said.

Shivers ran down Mickie's back. "You don't... Fencris, what the hell was it?"

"Speaker 356, are you there?" Fencris asked, holding up a hand to stop Mickie saying any more. "Include Mickie in this conversation."

"Yes, Fencris, I'm here. I'm greatly relieved to be able to talk to you again."

"No more than we are, I assure you. Speaker, can you access the memories in my mind of the last few hours?"

"Of course, if you permit it."

"I do. I want you to access the memory of when I went into a trance state during last night, up to the moment when I woke up back in the cage. When you have it, play it back to Mickie."

"I'm curious, Fencris. I know that you did not have a conversation with me. Did you talk to another Speaker?"

"No, I did not." Fencris seemed to be enjoying the massive bombshell he was about to throw at the Speaker

"You surely did not make contact with a Zlan?"

"No, I did not. Not initially."

"Fencris, we are the only two galactic-communications telepathic species. To whom did you speak?"

"I'm hoping you can tell us, Speaker. Record the memories and play them back to Mickie, and then you may be wiser than we are. Mickie, sit back and relax. This is one wild trip."

Blackness. That was all there was. Just blackness. But it was a warm, friendly blackness, familiar and yet unknown, alien territory but part of himself, just somewhere he hadn't been before but known to exist. He was moving, sensing rather than seeing, but he felt no difficulty or limitation in moving that way. This was much like the way he had explored his own mind while sheltering from the cold in the protective shield around the Speaker on his own planet. Without surprise, Mickie realised he was experiencing Fencris' memories while still aware of his own identity. He moved on, examining the texture of the darkness around him.   Sometimes he found familiar things... *so that's what gives me the scientific talents.... and that's where the musical abilities lie.... how beautiful....*

Now it was new territory, still familiar, still part of him, but now places he had never known existed. Without feet he moved through this bizarre land, without hands he touched and without eyes he examined the blackness around him... *whoops, what was that?*

A beautiful musical chord rang out and illuminated the blackness like a vibrant rainbow then seemed to radiate outwards in all directions to unlimited distances. *This is it, I think... I need to ride that wave...*

The sensation was the same as Markel had experienced when he first teleported, a wondrous, exhilarating flight into the blackness of space, standing in emptiness while the silver carpet of the galaxy stretched out in all directions... *now I'm three people,* Mickie mused with an invisible smile. *I am Mickie, remembering being Markel while I live the memories of my dear friend Fencris...* The galaxy flung itself away into the far distance, other galaxies appeared and flew by, *where are we going?....*

"Hello, young man, what are you doing out here?"

The voice came from nowhere, everywhere. It filled his head, soft, yet with the power hidden within it that could have broken a world into small pieces. It was the voice of one's favourite uncle or the voice of the Creator of Everything, it was all the power in the Universe.

"I'm looking for help. We're in dreadful danger, we'll all die in a few hours unless I can contact the Zlan."

"The Zlan? Ah, I see. A Cassolean? So you have rediscovered your old powers. How interesting. And your friend is the Pfafth. We were wondering what had happened to those silly people."

"Who are you? You seem to know everything."

"I'm just somebody who happened to notice you passing by. You're a long way from home, Fencris. I don't think you're supposed to be this far out."

"But can you help us? I must talk to the Zlan."

"Ah, I see now, it's the Korrobi being nasty little yurkels again! Then yes, I'll help you talk to the Zlan. Go ahead."

"What? I can talk to the Zlan now?"

"I just said so."

"Zlan, can you hear me?"

"Who is calling the Zlan?"

The voice was as remembered. To Mickie, it was now a friendly, safe ally, but to Fencris it was the first time he had heard the icy, emotionless tones and the fear ran through him like icicles in the blood.

"I am Fencris, the Cassolean, the friend of the Pfafth you rescued so many times."

"We cannot sense the Pfafth anywhere and there is great fear among the Zlan. You are with him?"

"I am. We are on Korrobodor and we are all about to be killed."

He felt the scream of rage echo silently across the void between them. *"Show us Korrobodor. Our senses are blocked."*

Fencris felt panic. He had no idea how to show them the planet's coordinates. He had not checked up on its location.

"Here is Korrobodor and here is the location of the Pfafth's imprisonment," said the astounding voice.

"Who tells the Zlan this?"

"That is unimportant. Go to rescue your charge. And you, Cassolean, you must return to the world. They will be there in seconds."

Mickie opened his eyes to see Fencris watching him with a mixture of pride and amusement. He let out his breath in one long sigh.

"Who was *that?"* Mickie whispered.

"A good question, eh? We might never know, but he seemed friendly enough."

"He knew *everything!* Even what you called the Korrobi!"

"Speaker, can you identify the identity of that telepath?" Fencris asked.

"No, we cannot." Mickie could hear the awe in the Speaker's voice. "We have absolutely no knowledge of a third Universal telepathic species."

"Can you contact it?"

"We will try."

The sight of the hatch opening to the lights of Hangar Ten curtailed the conversation. Mickie and Fencris walked out with the new knowledge that the Universe was even bigger and stranger than they had thought.

But for now, Mickie wanted to see Melkana and broach the topic of the hug she gave him back on Korrobodor.

* * * *

The party in the main dining hall was wild, frenetic and noisy. Almost everybody was there, even some of the

Kaloti crew had attended, their light-shields fitted to their heads like sunglasses protecting them from the glare, though they stayed only a short while as they became fatigued in the higher gravity outside their own quarters.

"There's nothing like escaping death to cause celebrations," Grant remarked to the group that sat in one corner. He and Allie, the four kids and their parents had developed an extra closeness after the horrors of Korrobodor, and all were a little light-headed from the atmosphere and the excess of the various liquids they had drunk. Mickie found that *Sle'Ach* taken in large quantities had made him a little woozy, and Grant and Allie were happy to admit that they had drunk a little too much scotch. But he was more concerned with realising that he and Melkana had become suddenly shy with each other and they were sitting on opposite sides of the area they occupied.

"Anyway, a toast to the man of the hour," Grant continued, lifting his glass and pointing at Fencris.

A general shout of approval was given by all and Fencris grinned in an embarrassed manner. "It wouldn't have happened if Mickie hadn't told me about his memories of the Old Cassoleans," he said.

"Selvana, what's happening on Cassolea after all this?" Allie asked, seeing Fencris' discomfort and seeking to redirect attention."

"It's the biggest thing ever to hit our planet," Selvana replied. "I'm not sure which is causing more upheaval, the confirmation of the old myths and legends about the Lost Cassoleans, or the rediscovery of our telepathic skills."

"There's still a lot of disbelief," Devenar continued. "Many are saying they can't accept it all on the word of one small boy, regardless of the contact Fencris made with the Zlan. There is still absolutely no physical evidence anywhere of a previous civilisation, and only a few people have been able to find the telepathic skill, though there are massive projects being started to research this."

"It's only been a few days," Grant said. "The next few years will be interesting, however."

"I've no doubt," Selvana said dryly. "But we're getting many requests for Fencris to come home to help out in that research. They want to see Mickie too, to see if he can recall any more details of where the Cassoleans went after the Pfafth retreated."

"It's just one of a lot of loose ends," Mickie said. He was feeling seriously overwhelmed by everything that was happening, especially the distance that seemed to have grown between Melkana and himself.

"What other ones, son?" Grant asked.

"I've been thinking about it and there are so many things that need explaining," Mickie said. "For a start, that whole hallucination of Markel's life. It looks like somebody placed the Maragos sculpture there for my benefit, but who? If that someone intended me to learn about Markel so that I'd want to find the Pfafth and lead them in this horrible war they seem set on, then they screwed up, 'cos it turned me right off the whole idea. So was it someone else who left it, someone who <u>didn't</u> want me to help the Pfafth?"

"An interesting thought," Allie murmured. "So there could be factions within the Pfafth inside that Blocked Galaxy."

"And then there are the Sillaron," Mickie continued. "They're still after my blood, it seems. We don't know where they are, where they come from, or what they can do."

The group had fallen silent and were listening closely.

"And then there's the X'Kasxi," Mickie continued.

That caused a stir.

"What about the X'Kasxi?" Allie asked. "What brought that up?"

Mickie felt confused. "I've only just remembered this," he said. "Literally, just a few moments ago. When I was Markel as a young man, Kerrala and I visited the X'Kasxi planet. An old Guide warned us that the Pfafth Empire would soon collapse and that he'd been told about it by higher souls."

"But that means the X'Kasxi were around at least a million years ago!" Devenar looked astounded. "And they would have been a mature civilisation already, if they had that sort of talent. They've never told us about this!"

"No, I've long suspected the X'Kasxi knew more than they were letting on," Allie agreed. "That visit we paid to X'Katcxo really threw me, I must admit. I think they know lots of stuff and they're not telling anyone. But mainly, it means they've always known about the Pfafth."

Silence sat on the group for a few moments as people tried to absorb these new facts.

"Then there's the biggest issue of all," Fencris said into the emptiness. All eyes turned on him. "That's the question of who was I talking to when I was trying to contact the Zlan."

"And that's the one that's got the Speakers into a thorough tizzy," Mickie agreed. "And from what he said, it sounded like he doesn't think all that highly of the Pfafth."

"Yes, I remember that," Fencris said thoughtfully, "He called the Pfafth 'silly people.' And I think there's another odd thing."

"What's that one?" Mickie said, recognising Fencris' expression as one that preceded major issues.

"When that horrible great big Zlan was talking to us in the cage, just before it left, remember how it said there was something puzzling it?"

With a start, Mickie realised he'd forgotten that.

"What was puzzling it?" Fencris continued. "It seemed to look around, then decided it wanted to get back to killing Korrobi and beetled off, fast."

"Yes, I remember that! Damn, there's just too much we don't know!" Mickie exploded.

"Relax, kid," Grant said. "You've got a whole lifetime to find out the answers. I've got a better suggestion for how to spend the rest of the evening."

Mickie looked suspiciously at the small smile on his father's face.

"The music is playing," Grant said. "I think you and Melkana should be dancing, not sitting here with the oldies."

Mickie forced himself to look across at Melkana. She stared back without expression. Then a broad grin cracked the calm and Mickie got up and walked over to her.

"Miss Melkana, may I have the pleasure of this dance?" he asked formally in the style they had used during the visit to Merrison.

She cackled. "Why certainly, Master Michael," she said, got up and walked onto the floor with him.

Mickie decided the Universe was a really fine place, after all.

www.ingramcontent.com/pod-product-compliance
Lightning Source LLC
Chambersburg PA
CBHW070219260626
47160CB00002B/608